Eavesdropping

Other books by the author

1. Knowledge Management: Paradigms, Challenges and Opportunies. Bangalore, India: Sarada Ranganathan Endowment for Library Science, 2002.
2. Library Automation: Design, Principles and Practice. New Delhi: Allied Publishers, 2004 (Published for Kesavan Institute of Information and Knowledge Management, Secunderabad)
3. (as Editor) Remembering B S Kesavan: the Man and his Mission. Secunderabad: Kesavan Institute of Information and Knowledge Management, 2009.
4. (as Editor) Case Studies for Teaching Library Management/N.G. Satish and Anil Takalkar. Secunderabad: Kesavan Institute of Information and Knowledge Management, 2012.

Eavesdropping

A Collection of Short Stories and Poems

LJ Haravu

PARTRIDGE
A Penguin Random House Company

To order additional copies of this book, contact
Partridge India
000 800 10062 62
orders.india@partridgepublishing.com

www.partridgepublishing.com/india

To
My late mother who gave me more than life; the values she
imbued me with have propelled my life's journey.

Acknowledgements

I am deeply grateful to Sri. V. Siddharthacharrya, scholar/diplomat and a retired officer of the Indian Foreign Service and Indian Ambassador to many countries, with whom my association has been a long one of over 50 years. The title of the book came from his insightful mind. I have figuratively sat at his feet to imbibe much of my inspiration and understanding of the meaning of life and how it is best lived. He has thus subtly influenced my thoughts in these stories. His contribution specifically to the stories and poems in this book in the form of guidance and unobtrusive criticism has been invaluable and I pay my homage to him.

Many of my relatives and friends have been the sounding boards for my stories. I cannot list them individually because there are too many. But I must make special mention of Karuna, my niece and her husband Ravi Ganesan, who have taken exceptional interest in reading my stories and poems and have given me painstakingly considered views on the content, presentation, language and story endings. They have helped quite invaluably in the shaping of this book. I must also thank my wife Sharada and my sister Kusum Nagaraj. Their kind words of appreciation have encouraged me to publish this book.

The stories in this volume have been looked at by Dr. D.R. Mohan Raj, a professional editor and a long-time educator in communication skills, who was my colleague at a research institute many years ago. The care and thoroughness of his work and his suggestions for improvements have made for a smoother flow in the writing as it now appears.

I gratefully acknowledge the contribution of the idea of the image for the cover page to the Editor of the web site, www.lifepositive.com.

I am deeply grateful to Deepak Chandrashekar of SDM-IMD, Mysore who has designed the cover page of the book. My gratitude is also to my professional colleague, Dr. M V Sunil also of SDM-IMD, Mysore for his ready assistance in various ways in making this book possible.

Preface

Stories and poems in 'Eavesdropping' have come from the Mind eavesdropping on the mind, conditioned by experiences, recent and remote; memories that come forward for one reason or another: a book recently read, an emotion, a song heard, a face in the crowd, a news item on TV. None of the pieces arrived as one integral idea; they formed over a few days when thoughts form in mind's peaceful moments and magically, almost compulsively, rise to the surface. The intellect has then played its part in polishing the thoughts and emotions that arise. My morning's meditations, recitations of one or other adhyāyās (cantos) of the Bhagavad Geeta, and listening to discourses of the enlightened have triggered many thoughts leading to the poems. Some stories in this collection have a serious intent. A few poke fun mainly at the relationship between man and wife. All positive references to wives were inspired entirely by my own wife, while any observations on the foibles of wives come from observations of other wives! The foibles of men are entirely my own.

My poems, my stories

These poems, stories for you;
Benign missiles;
From my inner space;
Born in heart;
Crafted in mind;
Polished by intellect;
For you to read.

See if these strike;
Sympathetic chord or soft target;
In mind, heart or intellect;
For you to enjoy;
Perchance reflect.

I know not what's happened to me;
Thoughts that come to me;
Come to me in story and poetry;
No matter what;
With God's eternal blessings for you and me.

L Jayaram Haravu
jharavu@gmail.com
Mysore, 2014

Foreword

I don't really deserve the honour bestowed upon me by my nearly lifelong friend, Jayaram Haravu. I may aver that the friendship began, as does true love in Western Novels, at sight; from the start we had something important in common: we earned our living as teachers. We were both parted early from our families and had no inclination whatever for suicide. We both involuntarily found other jobs, too, shortly thereafter. The tide of times that swept us apart, curiously often brought us together too. And now, in our final stages of life, we are back together, making up for lost time, teaching sometimes, but always in the company of teachers. The environment is provided by a hospitable school. It has given us the opportunity to conceive our respective intellectual offspring. My brood were essays, dressed up fancifully as Vignettes. As I was labouring, Jayaram most helpfully midwived. Having no talent as "acoucheur," I am unable to return his favour. Therefore, I try to pass off as a mere foreworder.

His collection, named **"Eavesdropping"** by me, actually peeps into Indian idiosyncrasies. The reader will find that the characters here are very much like others close to him or her. They hold an un-distorting mirror of today's India. In a way, the stories are humorous rather than witty. They are couched in the actual tongue of the man or woman you meet and fall into conversation with. I particularly recommend **Wayside Railway Station**. Of course, mystic India pops up now and then, and is demystified; lovely truth is laid naked. I was most moved by the author's **Indian Soldier**

and Pakistani Fruit Seller, which I consider a faithful rendering of the atmosphere of horror and reconciliation during the partition of India.

If you want a humanistic *darshana* (view or outlook) of India, give yourself the leisurely treat of reading **"Eavesdropping"**.

V.Siddharthacharrya
of Acharya Vidya Kula

Mysore
6-7-2014

Table of Contents

Poking Fun stories of a husband-wife pair

Poems of the head and heart

Life and Living

Divinity and the Divine

Guru's Wisdom

Meditation

The Mind

The Wayside Railway Station

Rajesh had just passed out with a Bachelor's degree in Journalism. His passion for good writing and reading had stood him in good stead, and he topped his class in the degree examination. He applied for a position in the City Chronicle in the small town of Lakhampur. Rajesh did creditably in his interview with the Editor, who was impressed with Rajesh's knowledge of current events and his willingness to work on sensitive issues.

"Good," said the editor, "I shall first offer you an internship. You will work with me, but before that I give you one week: I want you to bring me an interesting story. You have full freedom to go wherever you wish, and meet anyone you want to. I also promise that if your story is interesting, I will right away give you a Junior Reporter's job."

Rajesh smiled, "Sir, thank you. I accept." Rajesh liked the challenge he was offered. He was to go to his home town, Bareilly, 60 km away, for a family wedding the day after. "That might be a good place to get my story," he told himself.

He took the 55-Up the next day, a passenger train that he had taken many times. His mind wandered, searching for ideas for a story that the Editor wanted; he stared vacantly at the passing scenes from his window seat. He closed his eyes for some time, but he could not still the mind. The more he tried to think of a story and from where it might emerge, the more his tired mind eluded him. "To hell with it," he told himself. "If I can't get a good story, so be it."

The train had stopped at a wayside station and he looked out. He did not see anyone; there was nothing extraordinary in the surroundings. Something clicked in his mind; impulsively, he jumped out of the train.

He then saw a dhoti-clad, middle-aged man, flagging the train on its way to its destination. He looked around the station; like many other stations, it had yellow coloured spiked cement pillars, making up its boundary, and a yellow board that announced the name of the station as Kashipur, written in English and Hindi. It also had the year 1957 and 900 ft above MSL (mean sea level) written on it. Rajesh walked up to the dhoti-clad person. He must be a railway servant, he guessed, a rural station master and points man. The two briefly exchanged the usual pleasantries.

"Babuji," he asked, "Whom have you come to meet here?" Rajesh said that he was a *Patrakar* (journalist) and that he wanted to just go around and write something about the village. "Very well, I wonder what you will see in our small village to write about. Will you be staying here for a few days?"

"No," replied Rajesh. "I plan to go to Bareilly as early as possible; if possible this evening."

"There are only two trains on this route to Bareilly: one the 55-Up, by which you came, and the other 685-Down, which does not stop here. The 56-Down comes tomorrow in the other direction."

Rajesh, by now wondering if he had done the right thing by getting down in this godforsaken railway station, engaged the rural station master in conversation. True to his profession as a journalist, Rajesh, trained to probe in interviews asked, "Bhai sahib, tell me why this station is called Kashipur?"

"Interesting that you ask that question. Some years ago, an MLA wanted a stop here, so that he could visit his village some 10 km away, which was not on the train route. His name was Kashiram; so the station was called Kashipur. Kashiram is no more, but the train still stops here."

"Who are the people who use the train?" asked Rajesh.

"During the fruiting season, some of the farm labour board the train to sell guavas, litchis, and chickoos. They come back by the 56-Down the next day."

Rajesh nodded his head. A moment later, he asked, "Is there no way I could take the 685 today?"

The rural station master smiled, "Yes, there is. I could signal the train to stop for a minute or two. Later, I could signal it to leave. Mind you, I am not doing anything wrong. I am allowed to do this when I see cattle on the tracks. Visitors to our village are rare. I will do it for you, but you must come before the train arrives at 3:47 this afternoon; you must be ready to jump onto the train the minute it stops."

Rajesh promised to do so. He pressed a 10-Rupee note into the hands of the rural station master. The station master smiled and politely refused the offering, smiled again, and walked to his small quarters close to the station. Rajesh made his way to the interior of the village.

Five minutes into the village, he saw a Sadhu sitting on a stool-shaped rock. The Sadhu smiled and beckoned to Rajesh, *"Beta tumhara swagath hai. Accha huva ki tum apne purane janm ke parivar se milne aye ho?* [1]*"*

Rajesh was taken aback. His eyes must have betrayed his surprised disbelief. *"Nahin Maharaj, main ek patrakar hun,"* he said. *"Main is gaon ke bare me kuch likhna chahata hun[2]"*

"Abhi tum rail gadi se bina soche samjhe, achanak utter gaye na? Mujh par tumhe vishwas nahnin hai na. Chowdhary Ramprakashji ke pas chale jao, tumhe vishwas hojaayega. Aaj hi jana, kyunki Chowdharyji bahut shigre hi chale jayenge.[3]"

The Sadhu spoke as if what he said was a matter of fact. Rajesh was even more intrigued that the Sadhu knew about his impulsive act to get down at the station. He bowed to the Sadhu, touched his feet, and reached into his pocket to give the Sadhu some money. The Sadhu shook his head, indicating that he did not seek any reward.

ॐ   ॐ   ॐ

Rajesh, shaken by what he heard, but curious nevertheless, made his way into the village. He saw a small thatch-roofed building with a middle-aged

---

[1]   *"Welcome son, good that you have come to visit your family from your previous birth."*

[2]   *"No, Maharaj, I am a journalist. I want to write something about the village; that's why I am here."*

[3]   *"You just jumped from the train did you not? I know you don't believe what I just said. Go to Chowdhary Ramprakash's house and you will know. Go today, because the Chowdhary will soon be leaving."*

man, probably not more than 50 at the most, with a curly moustache, sitting on a charpoy. This is like a scene from a Bollywood film, thought Rajesh. This must be the Chowdhary, he surmised correctly. The Chowdhary got up to welcome Rajesh and seated him on the charpoy.

"*Rajesh ki amma,*" he called out. "*Athiti ke liye paani lana.*[4]" What a coincidence, thought Rajesh; the Chowdhary's son's name is also Rajesh. The lady of the house, her head covered, brought water for Rajesh.

Predictably, the Chowdhary asked next who the visitor was and what brought him to the village. Rajesh confided that, as a journalist, he visited places in search of stories.

This was a good opening move; Rajesh pursued his mission, "Chowdharyji," he said, "*Mujhe aap ke jeevan ke bare me bataiye. Hum shahar ke log, goan ke jeevan ke bare me bahut kam jankari rakte hain. Ho sake to is ke bare me kuch likhna chahata hun.*[5]"

The Chowdhary smiled.

"*Kya bataun beta. Yeh hamara gaon, sath pushton se hamara jeevan ka hissa hai. Jab main baccha tha to mere dada hamare saath jeevith the. Voh bhi apne dada ke saath rahe hain; ab mera beta hamare saath hai.*[6]"

"*Kya aap ke bhayi, behen bhi hain?*[7]"

"*Mera ek bhai tha. Voh Baghvan ko bahut saal pahle pyara ho gaya. Ek choti behen shadi shuda hai; Barielly me rehti hai. Yeh gaon hi hamara jeevan hai. Baghavan is choti si duniya me hame basaya hai; hum ko yahin par sukhi jeevan bitane ka aadesh hai. Isse aadhik hum logon mein kuch bhi nahin dikhta hain[8]"

As he said those words, his face glowed with a smile. The simple man and his contentment with the world he had inherited was so much in

---

[4] "*Mother of Rajesh; bring a glass of water for the guest.*"

[5] "*Please tell me about your life. We city folk have little knowledge of your lives. If possible, I would like to write about it.*"

[6] "*What shall I tell you son. This village has been our forefather's place for at least 7 generations. I was born when my grandfather was still alive; he told me that he too had seen his grandfather; now my son lives here with us.*"

[7] "*Do you have brothers and sisters?*"

[8] "*I had a brother; now he is no more; a sister is married and lives in Bareilly. The village is our world; we do not have ambitions. God has put us in this corner of the world; he wants us to be happy here. What more can we ask?*"

contrast with urbanites, including him, always looking for more and more, thought Rajesh.

He also recalled the words of a guru whose discourse he had heard in college. The Guru had said:

> *"All human beings seek lasting happiness. But, what we experience is a hankering undercurrent of insecurity and un-fulfillment in our lives. There is a constant drone of '**I want, I want, or I am wanting, I am wanting**' playing in our minds. We delude ourselves that by acquiring new material objects, more wealth, or new relationships, we will achieve that elusive, lasting happiness. Like a peg-board that children use with many holes of different shapes, and blocks that fit these holes, we choose block after block to fill the holes. Each time, the block drops into the box, but the hole still remains."*

A farm labourer, hands and legs calloused by hard farm work, face creased by long hours in the sun, walked in and touched the feet of the Chowdhary. *"Kya bat hai"*, Hariya," he asked. The labourer handed over a just ripe papaya to the Chowdhary with obvious glee and said, *"Yeh hamare naya ped ka pehla phal hi Chowdharyji.[10]* The Chowdhary looked at the fruit with interest, and told Rajesh that his son had tried an experiment to grow papaya in the village. "Hariya," he said, *"Yeh tumhara phal hai Hariya. Apne parivar ko khilao.[11]"* The villager bowed and then went on to ask for pardon that he could not go the farm that afternoon as his son had fallen ill. The labourer's face showed concern. Without a word, the Chowdhary walked into the house and came back to press some money into the labourer's hand and tell him that he should go to the village Vaidya. The farmer left, gratitude dripping from his toothless face.

The Chowdhary came back to his seat on the charpoy. Before Rajesh could speak, the Chowdhary walked up to a calf that was bleating. The mother cow was away grazing. The Chowdhary got up and went to the small cowshed in the yard. He stroked the calf gently; it nestled up to

---

[9]   *"What's the matter, Hariya?"*

[10]   *"This is the first fruit of our new tree."*

[11]   *"This is your fruit Hariya, take it to your family."*

the Chowdhary and rubbed itself on the Chowdhary's body. His face glowed, no doubt, in the love that rose from his heart. Rajesh had never seen scenes of such grace; his mind was magically elevated; he had seen the extraordinary in the ordinary in the scenes before him. He lapsed into silence, to savour the thought that had come to him.

The Chowdhary's simplicity, his lack of any inhibition in front of a total stranger; his unquestioned surrender to the will of a higher power, and compassion for his labour and the little calf stunned Rajesh. His encounter with the rural station master, the Sadhu, and now the Chowdhary was a wonderful lesson in selflessness, contentment and happiness. He saw in their lives an intuitive understanding of the unity of all creation. He recalled the words of Gurudev Rabindranath Tagore who had said:

> *The instruments of our necessity assert that we must have food, shelter, clothes, comforts and convenience. And yet men spend time and resources in contradicting this assertion, to prove they are not a mere catalogue of endless wants; that there is in them an ideal of perfection, a sense of unity, which is a harmony between parts and a harmony with surroundings.*

He realized that here was the story he was seeking; it had just fallen into his lap. But, who in the urban world would believe the story of the people in this village? "No one," he told himself. The story has to be seen and felt live to be appreciated. My telling it to others would not make any impact.

A minute later, Rajesh recomposed himself; his journalist self asserted itself. He asked:

"*Kya aap ka beta Rajesh kheti ke kam kaj me dekhrekh kartahai[12]*? he asked.

"*Nahin beta, Rajesh hamare bade bete ka nam tha. Voh ab is duniya me naihn raha. Jab vo aath saal ka tha to ek din hamere nazoron se gayab ho gaya; Gaon ke bachon ke sath khelne gaya. Paschyad kisi ko patha nahin voh kahan kho gaya.[13]*"

The cloud of grief on the Chowdhary's face came and went in a flash as he said those words.

---

[12]   "*Does Rajesh take care of your farm?*"
[13]   "*No my son; Rajesh was my eldest son's name. He is no more. When he was 8 years old, he went out to play with other boys of the village and never returned.*"

Rajesh was shocked at what he had just heard.

He said, "*Mujhe kshmah ki jiye. Jab aap ne bhabiji ko Rajesh ki amma ke nam se bulaya, tab mujhe patha nahin tha ke aap ke bada beta, Rajesh, ab is duniya mein nahin raha.*[14]" The Chowdhary smiled, "*Rajesh ki paidayishi ke bad, main apne dharm patni ko isi nam se hi bulatha hun, beta.*[15]"

"*Kya aap ne Rajesh ki khoj kiye jab voh bahut der ke bad bhi ghar nahin louta*[16]?"

"*Pure gaon aur aas pas ke gaoon me bhe kayii din us ke khoj me ham lage rahe, parantu hamen na voh mila, na ek bhi sulukh tak nahin mila. Police walon ke pas bhi kumplaint likhwaya. Mera bhai Rajesh ka ek chitr banakar unhen soumpa. Phir tho hamen yakhin ho gaya hai ke hamare Rajesh ke is jeevan ka safar poora ho gaya. Kis se iska karan puchsakte hain hum. Jo bhi hota, kisi karan se hi hota hain, kahte hain mahatma aur gnani log.*[17]"

The Chowdhary's second son then came home, as it was almost lunch time. After some small talk between the three of them, the son got up to wash. Rajesh, too, got up to take leave. The Chowdhary motioned him to sit down. "*Baitho beta, aap hamare mehman hain. Aise athithi hame roz, roz to nahin prapth hote. Hamare sath khana ka kar ke hi jao.*[18]"

The Chowdhary's wife called out that lunch was ready and that plates had been laid. The Chowdhary and Rajesh walked into an inner room, adjoining the kitchen. He saw a simple altar on a small table, with lamps just lighted; the family briefly prayed with closed eyes and sat down to eat. Rajesh's eyes roved across the room. A black and white drawing, showing a young boy with bright eyes and hair covering his forehead, attracted Rajesh. He stared at it intently, prompting the Chowdhary to tell him that the drawn picture was of Rajesh, whom the family had lost. "My God," thought Rajesh; "I have seen that face before."

---

[14]   "*I am sorry. I was confused because you addressed bhabiji as Rajesh ki amma.*"

[15]   "*That's how I have been addressing my wife since the birth of Rajesh.*"

[16]   "*Did you search for him after he disappeared?*"

[17]   "*We searched everywhere in the village and outside for many days. We reported his disappearance to the police. My brother drew a picture of him to give to the police. We now believe that his life in that birth of his was somehow fulfilled. Who are we to question His will? Everything happens, they say, for a reason.*"

[18]   "*Please sit, my son. You must share our meal; we cannot ask a rare guest like you to go without eating.*"

After lunch, before taking leave of the Chowdhary, Rajesh bent down and touched the elder's feet. He got up; their eyes met; there was a spontaneous embrace. A fleeting moment of eternity was shared by two souls in harmony with each other. The moment passed; the intensity of that moment would be recalled even after many years.

"Mujhe tum se milkar bahut prassanata huvi. Mujhe mere khoye huve Rajesh se mile jaisa mahsoos huva tum se milkar. Tum par Baghavan ki daya sada rahe. Voh hi sada tumhe jeevan ka marg dikhlaye[19]"

ॐ ॐ ॐ

There was still some time for the 685-Down to arrive. Rajesh roamed the village and took in the peaceful, carefree sights of the cattle grazing in the fields; the branches of trees dancing in the breeze; the leaves, it seemed, in sync with the branches, nodding their heads in blissful peace. He sat down under a tree. Enjoying a unique camaraderie and harmony with unhurried nature in its different forms, he was reminded of William Wordsworth's lines:

> *The world is too much with us; late and soon,*
> *Getting and spending, we lay waste our powers.*
> *Little we see in Nature that is ours.*

The thoughts that crossed his mind and the gentle breeze lulled him to sleep.

He heard the Sadhu, who seemed to have materialized from nowhere. *"Uttho beta; tumhari gadi ab pandhra minute may chuthne wali hai."* Rajesh prostrated to the Sadhu who said, *"Shighra hi punah milenge.[20]"*

Rajesh collected himself and hurried to the station.

On his onward journey and on his return to Lakhampur, Rajesh relived the few hours that he had experienced in the village. His mind recalled the small details of all that had happened. He decided that he would relate his experience in as graphical a manner as possible to the Editor, in the shape

---

[19] *"I feel so happy that you came. It is like I met my long lost son. May God preserve and guide you, my son."*

[20] *"Get up son; you train will leave in 15 minutes. I will see you soon."*

of his story. The simplicity, spontaneity, honesty, generosity, and humility of the people he had met must be told, he decided. It did not matter if it did not impress the Editor.

After reaching home, he took out the family album. As he flipped through the pages, the photo of a boy stared at him. There was an uncanny resemblance to the black and white picture that he saw at the Chowdhary's place. He ran to his mother.

"Whose picture is this, he asked?"

"This is you, beta. I had so much trouble getting you to pose. That's why we don't have many photos of your childhood. I can never forget that photo."

Rajesh was stunned. Could the Sadhu Maharaj have known the truth of his past life, or was it just his conditioned imagination?

Rajesh returned to the album. His mother was right. There were few photos of the boy whose picture he had just seen. Some pages into the album, another black and white photo attracted his attention; this was a group photograph of a few children after they had played *holi*. In the middle was a boy that resembled the boy in the earlier photo. Once again he went to his mother. Pointing to the boy in the picture, he asked, "Is this also me?"

"Of course it is, the other boys are from the neighbourhood. Why do you ask?"

Not satisfied, he asked: "Are you sure you are my mother?" The mother stared at him, red-faced and irate. She said. "What's the matter with you that you ask your mother such an impudent question? I don't like these jokes of yours." She went away in a huff.

Rajesh realized that his curiosity had indeed overstretched itself. He apologized to his mother and made his peace with her with an affectionate hug.

The following day, he walked into the Editor's chambers with a smile on his face. "So, what have you been doing the last few days?" the Editor asked. "Sir, I have my story," Rajesh replied.

The next 30 minutes were spent with the Editor. Rajesh was animated like never before, totally engrossed, emoting his feelings as a consummate artist would in his tale about the people: the Sadhu, the rural station master;

the happenings at Kashipur, and finally about the resemblance of the pictures in the Chowdhary's house of the Rajesh lost to the world to his own pictures in the family album.

The Editor listened to Rajesh with rapt attention. When Rajesh finished his story, the Editor said, "You and I are going to that village tomorrow. I want to meet the Sadhu Maharaj and the Chowdhary." Rajesh was lost for words.

The two went to Kashipur the next day. The rural station master welcomed them with a broad smile, and said that he never expected Rajesh to come back so soon. Rajesh introduced the Editor as his senior officer and told the Station Master that they wanted to meet the Sadhu Maharaj. They began walking into the village. The Sadhu was, as before, seated on the rock. As the two approached him, he beckoned to them. He looked at Rajesh *"Dubara tumhara swagath hai beta.[21]"*

He looked at the Editor. *"Mujhe khed hai. Chowdharyji se aap ka milan nahin ho satka. Kal hi unka dehant ho gaya.[22]*

He looked at Rajesh. *"Maine bathaya tha na ke Chowdharyji shighra hi yahan se chale jayange. Voh sacche Tyagi the. Maine bas har karm ka sanyas le liya tha.[23]"*

The Sadhu's words made an impression because of the conviction with which he had said it; its portents were not fully understood by the visitors.

Rajesh recalled the words of the Bard in one of their lessons in college,

*"There are more things in heaven and earth, Horatio
Than are dreamt of in your philosophy."*

---

[21]   *"Welcome back again, son."*

[22]   *"I am sorry you will not be able to meet Chowdhary Ramprakash. He passed away yesterday."*

[23]   *"Did I not tell you, that he will be leaving soon. He was a true Sanyasi; he renounced all fruits in action; I only gave up all action."*

The Quest

Balu was waiting at a pedestrian crossing in Chennai. He looked at the chaotic traffic in front of him: a motor cycle over taking a car from the left, another from the right, a cacophony of horns, an auto rickshaw squeezing itself between two motor cycles. The chaos and noise was not new, but in all this diversity of people and machines and noise, the occasional frown, curse and awe at the recklessness of the young, he thought there was a unique sense of tolerance, reflected in the mutually negotiated movement.

He felt someone gently tap his shoulder. He turned around and saw that it was a tall young foreign national. Balu surmised that the tourist was no more than 25.

"*Excusez-moi Monsieur,*[24]" said the foreigner.

"*Oui*[25]," Balu replied.

"*Vous parlez Francais?*[26]"

"*Un peu*[27]," said Balu shaking his head. That was all the French that Balu remembered from his school days.

The foreigner and Balu resigned themselves to converse with each other in their own brand of English.

"My name is Patrice, *et vôtre Monsieur*[28]?" he asked.

---

[24]   *Excuse me Sir*
[25]   Yes?
[26]   *Do you speak French?*
[27]   *A little*
[28]   *And yours, Sir?*

"I am Balasubramaniam." That was a mouthful for Patrice. "Just call me Balu," he said.

"Come with you?"

"Sure."

They crossed the road. Balu told Patrice that he was going for his tiffin at a restaurant a little distance away. "You know *petit déjeuner*[29]? Come, let me treat you to a South Indian breakfast." Patrice smiled.

In the small restaurant, Indira Bhavan, Balu ordered Idli Sambar, "*irandu plate konda pa*[30], " he said in Tamil. "*Appruma irandu kapi konduva pa.*[31]" Before the waiter could get the idlis, Balu asked, "Is this your first visit to India?"

"*Oui.* Première. I just graduated from the University of Lyon. I am on *vacances.*[32]"

"How long is your *vacances?*"

"Ten days."

The idlis arrived. The two bestowed their attention to it, then the coffee.

"Will you be touring India?" asked Balu.

"No, I come to study something and I stay only in Chennai. I am doing some historical *recherche*"

Balu's interest was aroused; this must have shown on his face. Patrice continued, "Would you like to hear what I try to do?" he asked.

"Sure," said Balu.

Patrice told his story, reported below:

> "When I was do my degree, I must consult les Archives nationales (French National Archives). There I find very *intéressant*[33] two sheets of paper written by a French priest who went to Banaras in 1787. Hand-written paper was

---

[29]   *Breakfast*
[30]   *Please get two plates*
[31]   *Thereafter please get two coffees*
[32]   *Vacations*
[33]   *Interesting*

report of a meeting between a Brahmana priest and the Frenchman."

"The French priest was scholar, but not one of those whose mission was to convert. He knew Hindi and Sanskrit, so was able to talk with people in Banaras; he became friendly with elderly Brahmana priest in small temple. The Frenchman became guest of the Brahmana priest. They talked mostly about Vedanta, Bhagavatha, Bhagavad Geeta, Purusha Suktam. In one talk, the Brahmana told the Frenchman about how Muslim invaders destroyed many Hindu temples and in their place had built mosques. This was seen by the priest's grandfather. He had told him about a unique figurine of Krishna installed in the temple in which he performed daily *pujas*; the 6-inch figurine was work of a master craftsman. It was unique as it was made of an alloy rare that *permis*[34] intricate sculpting. The face was pure *effulgence*. The flute and body were truly intricately magnificent. A feather peacock carefully sculpted as piece of the figurine adorned it. The sculptor had also *intégré*[35], cleverly and expertly cut, small diamond pieces, in several places. Even when little light fell on *le* figurine, rays of light reflected from it and a halo of light surrounded it. People who worshipped at that temple thought it was miracle. From any angle you saw the figurine, a ray seemed to pierce the eye of beholders. From distance, the halo surrounding it was *mystique*. It was prized possession of the temple, and occupied pride of place in sanctum sanctorum. The priest knew value of the figurine. Every day after *pujas,* he put it away in a box before locking temple doors. When Muslim invasions became more and more common, Banaras was an important target, *particulièrement* temples. The Brahmana's grandfather had heard of vicious destruction of stone,

---

[34] *permitted*
[35] *As an integral part*

THE QUEST 13

granite and marble idols of temples. Afraid that the beautiful figurine would be stolen by Muslims, he took it home. A few days later, he saw a South Indian priest at the bathing ghat of the Ganga; he was reciting the Bhagavad Geeta and had just finished reciting the very last teaching verse (verse 18:66):

Sarva Dharman parityjya,
Mamekam sharanam vraja
Aham tvam sarvapapebhyo
Mokshayishyami me ma sucha.

Renounce all Dharma's unto Me;
Grieve not, I shall relieve thee of all your sins;
Thou shalt be fulfilled in Me.

The Banaras priest, on an *impulsion inexplicable*[36], waited for the South Indian to finish prayers. He told him about figurine and asked if he would take it away with him to the south for worship in his temple. This would prevent possibility of desecration by Muslims. The two priests took to each other during the South Indian's sojourn in Banaras. With great reverence he solemnly promised that he would care for the figurine, and took it away to his place in Sennakotai, today's Chennai. Now my mission is to find figurine in Chennai temples, *Monsieur* Balu."

𝕯   𝕯   𝕯

Patrice had finished his story. Balu was amazed. Here was a young man who had traveled 7000 miles to research the legendary figurine. His commitment to the task was remarkable, thought Balu. "Why is it," he thought to himself, "that we Indians lack the spirit of enquiry that once had produced the great scriptures? We have such a great past, but we don't seem to have a sense of history. Why is it that we seem to have lost the urge

---

[36]   *Inexplicable impulse*

to research into scientific truths that the west has been so committed to?" He waited for Patrice to continue.

"My mission in ten days here is to find *le* figurine in Chennai's temples. Even if it is not on display, I am sure temple authorities may know about it. I just want to see the figurine. If I find it, I want to write about it. Also how it came to where it is. I can make a name for myself."

It was Balu's turn to speak. "Do you realize the enormity of your task?" he asked. "There must be more than a thousand temples in Chennai. Even to just visit them would require months, if not years."

Patrice was unimpressed. "I know," he said. "The figurine must have come to Chennai more than 200 years ago, so it can only be in temples which are old. So, I plan first to go to these. I will talk to the head priests or oldest priests and request help. I would have started the search process. I will make notes of my conversations and idols I saw. These notes would by themselves provide a valuable thesis on Hindu iconography. It may lead me to new areas of research. Maybe I come back for a second round, who knows!"

Balu was bowled over by the young man. He spontaneously offered, "I will join you in your quest. I can speak Tamil, so that would be a great advantage. Since this is a weekend, I am free today and tomorrow."

Balu's skepticism now came to the fore. "Are you sure the 1787 hand-written paper you speak of is genuine? What you showed me is a scanned copy." he asked.

"*Certes Bien sûr, je suis le document daté[37],*" said Patrice. The French spoken was not clear to Balu. It showed on his face.

"Sure," Patrice said. "I laboratory dated the papier. It is 250 *ans.*"

Balu was satisfied. "Let's go," he said

Patrice was overjoyed, which he expressed it in his native French, "*merveilleux, ce serait d'une grande aide[38].*"

Patrice had already listed temples and their locations.

---

[37]   *I am sure. I had it dated*
[38]   *Marvellous. It would be a great help*

Balu looked at his watch. It was almost 10-40. He said, "All temples close at noon after the morning's prayers and open later for evening prayers. Let's hurry so we can visit some before their close."

They hired a taxi and Balu directed the driver to the nearest old temple.

The visit of a fair, tall foreigner accompanied by a swarthy Indian provided a study in contrasts. When the priest became free after the *puja*, Balu approached him and told him the story of the figurine and about the report of it by a Frenchman in 1787. The story intrigued the priest. He called his brother priests, including the oldest of them, who was probably born in the 1920s. Some old Krishna figurines that were not displayed were brought from the temple's stores. No doubt they were well crafted but did not match the figurine described in 1787. None of the priests had even heard of the described figurine. One of the priests, impressed by the young Frenchman's mission, performed a *puja* for the success of the mission. He told Balu that this was the least he could do, to invoke help. Balu prostrated in front of the deity and the two left for the next temple in their itinerary.

As they continued their tour, Patrice had several questions about the history of each temple, and its unique architectural features. He also had questions about the idols and the symbolism of some. He was allowed to take photos on the promise that these would be used purely for research purposes and not for commercial exploitation. Patrice, ever ready with his tablet computer, took quick notes. Their tour of at least 15 temples that Saturday and about 25 temples on Sunday followed the same pattern, but none produced any information about the figurine. Patrice's eagerness to lap up the information he found had, no doubt, given him a better understanding of South Indian temples. Like a true researcher, Patrice was not easily disappointed; he knew that all quests required patience and perseverance.

One of the side effects of the unique quest that the two had partnered was their discovery of common interests in the paintings and sculptures of their respective cultures. Discussions on these became the focal point of their delightful lunch-time parleys. Patrice was keen to learn more about the sculptures of Tamil kingdoms, some examples of which he had seen at the Louvre Musuem in Paris. Balu was keen to know more about the Impressionist movement and its painters of the mid to late 1800s of which he had heard, examples of which he saw in books on French painting. Balu spoke of the great works of temple architecture of the Chola dynasty and of one of its famous sculptures, the Bronze Nataraja. Patrice spoke of Monet, an early impressionist painter and his famous painting, *Impression, soleil levant* (Impression, Sunrise) and others like Camille Pissaro. These common interests created a bond that would stand the test of time. Patrice promised to come back to India to learn more about Tamil art and architecture.

Balu, a resident of Coimbatore and employed by a Chartered Accountant's firm, had been sent to audit a client's account books in Chennai. He had work to do that week. After seeing Patrice's unflagging interest and commitment, Balu felt that the quest was now his as much as that of Patrice's. Balu began to believe that his fortuitous meeting with Patrice was a call from the deity. "The quest is now as much mine as that of Patrice," he felt.

He telephoned his office and requested leave for a week, with the promise that he would extend his stay to finish the work he was assigned to do. That settled, Balu accompanied Patrice for the next seven days. Balu saw himself silently praying that the Lord should guide them; without His grace success would be elusive. Surprisingly, Patrice did not seem overly concerned for the fruit of his search. To him, it seemed that the search was an adventure to be entered into with heart and soul.

The ten days of Patrice's *vacances* came to an end.

"*Au revoir, mon ami; Je suis profondément reconnaissant à vous[39].*"

They parted with smiles. Email IDs and mailing addresses were exchanged. Balu presented Patrice with a large rosewood figurine of Lord Krishna. Patrice said that figurine would embellish his home and remind him of their search. Intuitively, they seemed to know they would meet again.

Balu returned to his work of auditing his employer's client in Chennai the day after Patrice left, but his mind frequently went back to the search that Patrice and he had immersed themselves in.

He had forgotten to ask Patrice for a copy of the scanned image of the 1787 letter that had triggered the search. He felt that both of them

---

[39] *Farewell, my friend. I am deeply grateful to you*

had probably not examined the letter for other possible clues. He sent an e-mail to Patrice. Two days later, he received a copy of the 1787 letter. He pulled out a magnifying glass and examined the letter. It was signed by the French priest. His name was Francois Petrois, the date was 17 Juillet 1787.

Balu wondered, "Could the French National Archive have other documents—a travelogue of the priest, perhaps— which might have shown where else in India he might have traveled to?" he wondered. He sent an e-mail to Patrice. Patrice replied that he would go again to the National Archive in Paris to check.

Two days later, he received a message that there was one more document from Francois Petrois, listing the names of people whom he had met. These were all in Banaras. Among the names was one that was typically south Indian, Annajaiyengar Krishnaiyengar, from a place called Muthialpet. He asked one of the employees of the company where he was working if they knew where the place called Muthialpet was. It turned out that there were two places by that name: one in the George Town area of Chennai and another in Pondicherry. The George Town area had an ancient Krishna Temple. Balu was excited. He decided that he would go there that evening and see if this lead was of any value.

That evening, he went to the temple in Muthialpet and spoke to a senior priest, to see if there was some way to know if a priest by the name, Annajaiyengar Krishnaiyengar, lived and officiated as the temple's priest 200 or more years ago. The priest shook his head. He said that the name was quite common. Quite often, a grandson is named after his grandfather and so on. There was no way of saying if such a priest by that name was present so long ago. Balu was disappointed that the lead had not resulted in new evidence that could lead to the figurine. He prayed at the temple and once again told himself that his search could only succeed if Lord Krishna himself desired that to happen.

A month later, Balu received a parcel at his Coimbatore address. It was a beautifully framed print of a Monet painting that had figured in one of their lunch-time parleys.

𝔇   𝔇   𝔇

The story doesn't end there.

Balu's ancestors were long-standing devotees of the Acharyas of the Prashanti Peetham. Balu's grandparents, now in their 80s, had been regular visitors to the Peetham's headquarters until recently. They had many fond memories of the great Paramacharya of the Peetham. As a young boy, Balu had accompanied his grandparents to the Peetham. The chartered accounting firm in Coimbatore he worked for were auditors for the Peetham. The yearly audit was always conducted by the head of the firm, himself a devotee. That year, the head asked Balu to undertake the task. The work came to Balu a month after his meeting with Patrice. The excuse of work provided him the opportunity to spend a week at the Peetham, with the chance to listen to discourses.

During his stay there, Balu related the story of the unique figurine to the current Acharya and how the Frenchman and he had scoured many temples in Chennai to find it. The Acharya listened patiently to Balu. He then called one of the student priests to go inside and ask a senior priest to come and see him. The priest made his presence. In great secrecy, he was asked to go and fetch something. To the amazement of Balu, it was the very figurine that Patrice and he had unsuccessfully sought. Balu was speechless with joy and amazement. It was exactly as it was described in the 1787 note that Patrice had talked of.

"Is this not what you were searching for?" asked the Acharya. Balu saw the figurine and was stunned.

"*Parama Pujya Swamigale*[40], I am simply astonished. I cannot express my joy. I never imagined it would be here under your loving care and grace." The Acharya smiled.

Balu had an indefinable catharsis on seeing the figurine. His intuition that the Lord himself had meant for him to seek the figurine was true. He silently thanked the divine and felt a deep sense of love and peace.

"Don't you see a wonderful lesson in your outer experience and that of your friend the Frenchman? When a devotee searches for the Lord and only Him, *ananya,* within and unflinchingly, and at all times, *satatam,*

---

[40]   *Most exalted and worshiped swami*

even when the devotee is busy with his *samsaric* roles, he will surely find Him." The Acharya waited for the import of his message to sink in. He continued, "The figurine's symbolism is very powerful and reveals through its physical form a great truth that our ancient sages long ago revealed. "The formless Lord of the Universe is perfect bliss; He is self effulgent. To the true devotee, He is the Light of all Lights, the bestower of the Light of Self Knowledge, *Atma Jnana*. Surrender to him and He will keep his promise to all his devotees, as beautifully put in the Upanishads and Bhagavad Geeta:"

Sarva Dharman parityjya,
Mamekam sharanam vraja
Aham tvam sarvapapebhyo
Mokshayishyami me ma sucha

Renounce all Dharma's unto Me;
Grieve not, I shall relieve thee of all your sins;
Thou shalt be fulfilled in Me.

Balu could not help noticing that the priest in1787 had recited the very same verse that the Paramacharya had just recited.

"Call your friend to come and be here with us, the Paramacharya said. "I will tell him how this beautiful figurine came into our possession. He can then complete the story begun in 1787. This is carefully recorded in our archives. May God bless you."

The Indian Soldier
and Pakistani Fruit Seller

Abdul Ghani and Ramakant Mathur, children of neighbouring families in Lahore, were classmates in school in the early 1940s. Being of the same age, Abdul and Ramakant became playmates. The proximity of their families and the fact that they attended the same school bonded them as if they were blood related.

They were born in an era when the practice of religion was decreed by birth. Respect for other religions, not condescending tolerance, was the key word. Different forms of prayer and rituals were not looked down upon. Important festival celebrations were enjoyed jointly. Sectarian differences among the Muslims and Hindus did not matter when freedom to practice one's faith was implicit.

Abdul's father, Mohammed Ghani, was a goldsmith; he had a small 6' x 4' shop tucked away in a busy street in Shahdara, just outside the walled city of Lahore; his understudy was a Hindu young man. Krishnakant. Ramakant's father, Sridhar Mathur, was an Ayurvedic Vaidya on the same street. His clinic had an annex, where a Muslim apothecary, Ghulam Ali, mixed potions or mixtures to patients. They were simple people and living quietly and unostentatiously.

The Ghani family was among those devastated by the outbreak of Malaria in the monsoon of 1940. Abdul, then an 8-year old, was the only one who survived. Sridhar Mathur had taken his family to his village (in today's Indian Punjab) before the disease struck, and so unwittingly he had saved his family from the scourge.

Mian Mir, which was close to Lahore with its intricate network of irrigation canals, provided a fertile breeding ground for the vector. Extensive spraying of the canals with larvicides was done by the provincial government, to prevent further breeding of the vectors. The government and municipal authorities gave quinine to the afflicted, and relief to surviving victims. Inadequacy of both medical facilities and trained staff hindered the effectiveness of their efforts. Poignant burials and cremations took place amidst the agony of the few surviving relatives and friends.

Abdul was traumatized; he had lost all his young life's anchors, one by one, within a few days. He tottered, his energy drained by the dreadful disease. But for a philanthropist who provided food, water, and facilities for hygiene and basic care, to several young survivors who, like Abdul, had become orphans, many more would have perished in the aftermath of the outbreak.

The Mathurs returned to Lahore soon after the disease had subsided. They found Abdul only a shadow of his former self, devastated in body and mind by the tragedy. They quickly took him home and nursed him back to health. The Mathur family's example attracted the attention of a well-known rich merchant nearby, Salim Ahmed, who had fruit and vegetable farms and a wholesale business in fruits and vegetables. He called at the Mathur residence and offered his help for Abdul's education and upkeep. He had done likewise for other Muslim and Hindu families. Such acts of charity and compassion brought succor to the many poor who felt that all was not lost. Abdul and Ramakant returned to school when it reopened. They were still in Form 2, equivalent to class 6 in today's educational system.

Meanwhile, many parts of undivided India saw rising discontent with British rule. There was increased awareness of the freedom movement, spearheaded by Mahatma Gandhi, Jawaharlal Nehru, and Mohammed Ali Jinnah. Gandhiji's Satyagraha movement and his call for a non-violent revolution shook the British like no other movement had previously done. Many Indians even gave up their jobs to join the movement and contribute to it. The latent two-nation theory proposed in the 1930s was validated in the 1940 Lahore Declaration of Jinnah. The Quit India movement of 1942 triggered protests and fasts by supporters, and targeted arrests by the British government solely of Congress party leaders, to quell the uprisings. Post-war mutinies in 1946 of the British Indian Army and Navy that had contributed significantly to the Second World War were also symptoms of the disquiet. The sub-continent was caught in a vortex of turmoil. Inevitably, young men and women, and even children, exposed to the happenings, were intensely affected. Communal riots in Calcutta, present-day Uttar Pradesh, and Rawalpindi took place; both Hindus and Muslims who lived in areas where they were a minority lived in fear of outbreaks of communal violence and reprisals. The fact that the Japanese Army had come as close as Burma further demoralized the British Government. America's late involvement in the War and its pressure on Britain expedited the inevitable grant of freedom to India and the creation of Pakistan, the dates for which had not been set yet.

Abdul, never a good student, lost interest in studies; the loss of his entire family was a major factor in his attitude; he saw no purpose in school and studies. His father, though a humble goldsmith, had often talked to Abdul about why learning was important to leading a full life. He had set an example to others in his family by studying for his matriculation on his own, with the help of willing teachers who saw the boy's sincerity. This was before he took up the family vocation as a goldsmith. The father's example seemed irrelevant to Abdul. "Who will I please by being educated?" he argued.

The benign influence of the Mathurs, their affection, and the protection of Ramakant, who was now even closer to Abdul than before, prevented Abdul from becoming a waif without a goal. Their piety, their firm belief in the Oneness of all Creation, their exemplary behaviour, all had a profound impact on both boys. Sridhar's wife Kamala was a living example of simplicity; her daily prayers and musical recitation of the Bhagavad Geeta seemed somehow to charge the home's atmosphere with unseen vibrations of grace and peace. Her face glowed with love and inner calm. Asha, Ramakant's younger sister, was a bundle of pure joy. It was wonderful to see her jumping onto her mother's lap when the mother was in prayer, and closing her eyes in imitation of her mother's calm. The others who witnessed these scenes were lifted to a different plane of consciousness.

Ramakant constantly goaded Abdul and helped him with lessons and school homework. It was with some difficulty that Abdul managed to pass the 4th Form—8th class in today's system—in his 14th year, after failing once. Ramakant was by then in the 10th class in today's system.

When the family found that Abdul was incapable of making further progress in his studies, Mathur went to the Muslim benefactor, Salim Ahmed, who had promised to help Abdul. Salim suggested that Abdul should be prepared to seek self employment and take up responsibility for himself. He then offered to induct Abdul into his wholesale business. He told Mathur that he would give Abdul a 4-wheeled cart to sell fruit in busy market areas, as well as door-to-door. Abdul would receive 15 Rupees worth of fruits at wholesale rates each day, free of cost; he could keep half a day's retail sales to himself and return the unsold fruit. This he could do for a whole year, and then he would need to pay fully for the fruits he thought he could sell. Half of fifteen rupees a day or about 230 rupees a month those days was a handsome sum, even to support a small family. This gesture on the part of the merchant was indeed generous. Obviously, the idea was to encourage thrift and business sense in Abdul. With his savings, widely invested, he could start his own business.

Abdul soon became a roving fruit seller. He enjoyed his new role and, in gratitude, he brought small things for the Mathur household, especially his friend Ramakant and the lovable Asha.

Partition of the sub-continent was now a certainty; the date when this would happen was not yet firmly known. Many Muslim families in UP, Gujarat, Bihar, Bengal, etc., had to decide whether they would remain in India or migrate to a new country, which would be almost totally Muslim. Similarly, Hindu and Sikh Punjabis who lived in predominantly Muslim areas, such as Lahore, Sialkot and Rawalpindi, had to decide if they should migrate to the Indian states of Punjab, what later was to become Haryana and Uttar Pradesh, among others. Population migrations began on a colossal scale within a few weeks of the declaration of independence in India and the decreed creation of Pakistan. These happened in a gory background of hatred and communal antipathy. Hatred and anger fed by rumors and hearsay reports of atrocities fed the violence. Brutal and wanton killing of innocent men, women and children, and unspeakable atrocities on women were committed. Trains and buses were attacked by Hindus, Sikhs and Muslims; they reached their destination only to spill human carcasses and blood. The tragic journey of thousands magnified the fears and anxieties of minorities on either side of the border.

The Mathur family decided that they would move to India after the initial orgy of communal hatred had spent itself. Until then, they lived in mortal fear of attacks in their very home. Abdul was told of their decision to migrate to India. "Are you going to leave me then?" he asked. "You are my family now; I will come with you," he pleaded. "Please do not leave me alone here."

Ramakant's mother added her appeal. "How can we leave the boy here?" she asked her husband. "God has left him to our care. If your nephew had lived with us, would you leave him here?" Mathur's arguments that Abdul should seek his destiny in the land of his birth and that he had already found a niche in his fruit business did not convince either his wife or Ramakant; their attachment to Abdul dominated their feelings. Mathur succumbed. Abdul was told that he would also go with them to India. Abdul went to his benefactor, Salim Ahmed, to return the cart. He told Abdul that his help was always available to him and wished him well.

Mathur decided to sell his house. Negotiations with a Muslim buyer were finalized; an advance was paid. After that, Mathur went to his study to be alone; tears came to his eyes. The house that he was selling had been built by his grandfather, who came to Lahore in the early 1900s to set up his Ayurvedic practice, their ancestral calling, which in turn his son had also followed. They had all earned high respect among the citizens of Lahore. Religious differences had never been a concern; Hindus and Muslims alike were treated with the same empathy and care. He now stood in front of the pictures of his grandfather and father that hung in his study, in silent supplication that his hands were tied and he had no option but to sell the house.

The day they took the train to Amritsar, the Mathurs thought, would be their day of deliverance from fear. This was not to be. Their train was attacked by Muslim mobs, even as Hindu and Sikh mobs attacked trains from India to Pakistan. Mathur, his wife and daughter were killed and thrown out of the train, as were many others. A Muslim attacker tried to kill Ramakant, whose identity as a Hindu was not hard to guess when he cried out on seeing his parents dying. Abdul covered Ramakant completely, and prayed loudly for Allah's protection. When the killer heard the word, 'Allah,' he restrained himself and diverted his attention to others.

The train reached Amritsar with its load of human misery. Abdul and Ramakant, hand in hand, got down with heavy hearts, full of uncertainty about their future. The Indian army, paramilitary forces, and governmental agencies, based on the experience of recent weeks, were deployed to deal with the situation. All survivors were considered to be refugees until they were claimed by a relative or friend. An army officer interviewed those remaining, with their papers, if any. When Abdul's turn came, he was asked his name. That was enough; he was herded into a separate enclosure for Muslims. His protest that he had come with Ramakant and could not leave him was summarily dismissed. Likewise, Ramakant was herded into a separate enclosure for non-Muslims. His request that he should be allowed to talk to Abdul was denied.

It was clear that the military wanted to avoid any confrontation between the two communities. Separate refugee camps had been constructed on opposite sides of the city. Abdul was taken away to the camp for Muslims, Ramakant to the one for Hindus and other non-Muslim communities. The two friends were thus arbitrarily separated; the bond that had been nurtured between them was snapped by religion and politics in newly created circumstances, over which they had no control. Each of them grieved in his camp, until sleep overpowered their tired bodies and minds.

Appeals were made by philanthropic organizations to adopt orphaned children in the two camps. There were few takers, given the precarious economic and political situation in the county as a whole. When these efforts failed, the Government had to step in and do something. The Indian Army sought to recruit able-bodied young men in both camps. Ramakant, then just short of 16, was picked up. His education up to the 10th class and his physique were to his advantage. He would first complete his 11th and 12th at the Army College, and later be sent to the Army Ordinance Corps's training centre in Secunderabad.

Abdul was asked why he came as a refugee, and if he had any relatives in India. He related his story of how the Mathur family had adopted him after the death of his parents and sisters, and how he had begged that he should not be left alone in Lahore. He also told his interviewers about how he became a fruit seller, thanks to Salim Ahmed in Lahore and his separation from Ramakant. When he was told that he could opt to be repatriated to Lahore, he accepted the offer. He decided that it would be better to return to familiar territory and seek Salim Ahmed's help. An application for his repatriation was made; some months later, he returned to Lahore.

Ramakant spent 2 years in the Army College, followed by military training for 3 years at the AOC Centre, followed by 5 years of study, including an internship of one year. He graduated as a mechanical engineer from the Electrical and Military Engineering (EME) College in Bolarum, Secunderabad. At the age of 25 in 1956, he was commissioned as a Lieutenant in the Infantry wing of the Indian Army.

His life was determined entirely by the Army's regimen. Abdul had faded in his memory, recalled occasionally when he saw one of the fruit sellers near his quarters. The years that he had spent in Lahore with his parents, his bubbly sister Asha, and with Abdul were consciously consigned to the past. Military training had made him dispassionate. There was no place for sentimentality; the honour and safety of India, he was taught, was paramount; strong attachment to human beings, other than fellow soldiers, was considered to be a weakness. In any case, there were no blood relatives that Ramakant could look up to, or look forward to. Dispassion came easily to him.

Before the festering wounds that Partition had left could heal, if ever, new causes for conflict arose between the two countries. Kashmir was the chief bone of contention; the dispute over the barren Rann of Kutch was another. Skirmishes involving border police on both sides became a regular feature. General Ayub Khan, the Army Chief of Pakistan in 1965, encouraged the covert infiltration of saboteurs into the disputed territory of Kashmir, in the belief that the Kashmiris were discontented with Indian rule.

In August 1965, some 30,000 Pakistani soldiers, dressed as Kashmiri locals, infiltrated across the Line of Control (LOC) into Kashmir. The

Indian Army, alerted by the local populace, retaliated. There were gains in the Kashmir region for both forces, a notable one for the Indian forces was the capture of the Haji Pir pass, 8 km into the Pakistan Occupied Kashmir. The infiltration, code-named Operation Gibraltar, had thus failed. As the war intensified, the Indian Air Force was used; Pakistan retaliated. To divert the attention of the Pakistani forces from Kashmir and Punjab, the western borders were attacked by Indian forces. One Infantry division made progress up to the village, Pehli Kiran, close to the Lahore airport. The US intervened; a temporary cease fire was called. Ramakant, then a Captain in the Army, was part of the troops in the village.

Ramakant, tempted by the fact that the Army had come so close to the city of his childhood, was seized by a strong desire to risk going incognito into Lahore. He went to the Brigadier, the senior most officer commanding Indian troops in the area. Ramakant pleaded that he be allowed 12 hours to go into Lahore. The Brigadier agreed, because the cease-fire was still in force. He advised Ramakant to go disguised as a Pakistani to the best extent possible.

卐　　卐　　卐

Ramakant now needed a vehicle. He found a motorcycle, fully covered with dust, apparently abandoned by its owner. He went close to it. As he was examining the vehicle, he heard a distinct sound. Alerted, he hid behind the building, next to a closed window. Through a small chink in the window, he saw a picture of Lord Rama on a makeshift altar. Ramakant heaved a sigh of relief. He then saw a middle-aged man hiding under a table. He seemed frightened to death. He had hidden there when he heard sounds of footsteps. Now was Ramakant's chance. *"Hey* Ram," he cried. The hiding man stirred. After a while, he said softly, *"Kaun?*[41]*"*

Ramakant then chose to speak, *"Bhai sahib, kya main aap se bat karsakta hun? Mujhe aap se madad chahiye.*[42]*"*

---

[41]　*Who is it?*

[42]　*Can I speak with you? I need your help.*

The man inside answered, shakily. *"Pehle aap bataiye, aap kaun hain aur mere se kya madad mang rahen hain. Agar mujhe maarna hai, to main tayar hun; bas sach bataiye.[43]"*

Ramakant then revealed that he was a Hindu, and that he was a member of the Indian army. He assured the man that he had nothing to fear from him; in fact, he would be protected. The man opened the front door. His name was Kanshi Ram, a third generation resident, originally from a farming family of Rohtak. At the time of the partition's riots, his family had gone into hiding in their farm house. They decided not to migrate to India in the hope that the situation would soon become normal and they could resume farming.

Ramakant told him about his childhood days in Lahore and his family. When the man heard that his father was Mathur Sahib, he exclaimed, *"Hey Ram, kaisa chamatkar hai ye. Mere pitaji app ke pujya pitaji ko jante the. Main prasanna hun ke aap unke bête ho. Batav main kya madad karsakta hun.[44]"*

Ramakant asked if he could borrow the motorcycle outside. It belonged to his son, the man said.

The motorcycle, an old British-made Triumph, was made available.

The next day, before day break, in casual clothes, a fez cap on his head, he went to Lahore. He reached his former home at about 8 in the morning. The family to whom the house had been sold by his parents was still there. He saw the house from a distance with nostalgia; not much had changed. He saw the neighbour's place, wondering about where Abdul had vanished after they were separated on that fateful day in Amritsar. The house, which was already quite old when his parents had parted with it, was now even more dilapidated. He decided to go Shahdara, to see the street and shop where his father had his clinic. The clinic was still there. The clinic was now called, *'Mathur sahib ki khairati dawakhana[45]'*. Earlier, it was known as *Ayurveda Chikitsalaya[46]*. Whoever was running the clinic was apparently

---

[43] *First tell me who you are. What help do you need from me?*

[44] *Oh, Lord Ram; what a wonder. My father knew your father. I am delighted that you are his son. Tell me what help I can give you*

[45] *Mathur sahib's charitable dispensary.*

[46] *Ayurveda clinic.*

connected with his father. He saw an emaciated and bearded elder sitting on the bench in the clinic's verandah.

"*Valai kum saalam,*[47]" greeted Ramakant.

"*As-Salaam Valai kum,*[48]?" replied the old man and then asked, "*Kaun?*"

Ramakant did not reply. Instead he said, "*Baba, main mere dost, Ghulam Ali se milna chahata hun, kya woh andar hain?*[49]"

The elder called out, "*Ghulam bhai, dekho aap ka dost aap se milna chahata hai.*[50]"

Ghulam Ali, now in his 50s, came out. He saw the visitor, well dressed, fez capped, goatee bearded. He was lost for a moment; then came a flash of recognition. His voice choked, "*Baba tum?*" he cried. Ramakant gestured and put his finger on his lip, telling him that he should not talk loudly. They both went inside. They were closeted for some time. Ramakant described the fate that his parents and his sister had met with. Ghulam Ali, unable to hold back his tears, wept. For the first time in years, the recalled memory of his family broke Ramakant's hardened heart strings. He broke down and cried. The old man sitting outside heard the voices inside, but not the content of what was being said; he heard the universal language of grief. He pushed the clinic's door. Now he knew who the visitor was. Unable to contain himself, he cried, "Ramki, is it you?" That was how Abdul used to call Ramakant in their childhood. The voice was familiar. "Abdul is that you, my friend. I thought I had lost you forever, my friend. I just couldn't recognize you. What have you done to yourself?" The two long-lost friends embraced each other, tears in their eyes, and sat hand-in-hand. It was then that Ramakant saw that Abdul was blind.

Abdul narrated the story of his life after their sudden separation. He had come back to Lahore on being offered repatriation by the Indian authorities in Amritsar. On his return, completely at a loss with himself at what had happened to him, he decided go to a Maulvi sahib in the great mosque for counsel and advice. He repeated his story to the Maulvi, who listened patiently to him. The Maulvi then said, "*Tu apne mazhab ko chod kar*

---

[47]   *May peace be with you.*

[48]   *May peace be with you too.*

[49]   *Baba, I would like to meet my friend, Ghulam Ali. Is he inside?*

[50]   *Brother Ghulam, your friend is here to meet you.*

ek Hindu jat ke khandan ka mehman ban gaya. Un ke sath apne quam ko be chod diya. Yeh teri sab se badi galti hain. Jaanta nahin kya, aise logon ko kafir kehte hain; yeh log Allah ke dushman hain.[51]"

Abdul related his story and this is reported in first person speech below:

I was shocked at the Maulvi's words. I protested. "*Ek insaan, jab dosra insan ke takhleef ko samaj kar hamdardi jatata hai aur uski madad karta hai, to yeh kaise Allah ke khilaf hota hain Maulvi sahib? Kya hamare mazhab mein aisa likha hai?*[52] "

My protest only made the Maulvi furious.

He said, "*Jo hamare mazhab ke log, aise saval karte hain, woh to kafiron se bi bade gunehgar hain. Aise qomain ko sazaa, khuda kya, admi dene se be unhain, nijat miljata hain. Mere ankhon ke samne se chale jao, patha nahin main kya kar baithunga.*[53]"

I was unable to bear the haughty Maulvi, and I retorted, "*Mere khayal me aap ko hamare mazhab ke bare mein pura ilm nahin hain. Aap jo kehrahe hain woh sach hai, to mujhe aise mazhab ke bare me sikhane walon aur aise mazhab se nafrat hai.*[54]"

Little did I realize that I had become a marked man; the others sitting with the Maulvi made a move to hit me, but were prevented by the Maulvi. I walked away as quickly as I could.

I then went to Salim Ahmed, my former benefactor, and told him my story of woe since I went to India with the Mathurs. Salim Ahmed restored his old offer to me to become a fruit seller on the same terms as before. I resumed my role as a fruit seller.

---

[51] *You have deserted your religion and taken shelter with a Hindu family? This is your cardinal mistake. Don't you know that such people are infidels and enemies of Allah.*

[52] *How can a troubled soul who is helped by another who shows compassion be an enemy of Allah? Is this what is written in our religion?*

[53] *Those of our religion who ask such questions are greater sinners than infidels. What to speak of God, even human beings can punish such people and obtain salvation. Get away from my sight; otherwise I don't know how I may harm you.*

[54] *In my opinion, you do not know enough about our religion. If what you say is true, then I hate people who teach and practice such a religion.*

I was able to keep body and soul together, but I was deeply dissatisfied; nothing seemed to give me any joy. I saw so many atrocities by the very people who claimed to be men of god. The more I saw this, the more I realized how hypocritical and vicious these people were and how they were misleading ordinary men and, worse, children.

One day in the market where I was selling fruits, I heard a beggar singing a soulful song. The song spoke poignantly of love and compassion. I just stood there, transfixed and listened to the song. The singer's voice was as much an impassioned plea for love for the divine as it was musically elevating. I asked him to teach me the song. He asked me to go to *Kahna* outside the walled city. Ask for the Sufi; the villagers will tell you where he lives.

I did not know who a Sufi was, but I went. I saw the Sufi, deep in meditation. His face glowed with love and peace. I was mesmerized when I saw him. I waited until he opened his eyes. I told him that my mind was always troubled; I had no peace; I was distressed that I saw so much hatred. He saw through my troubled conscience and said that all this was because men had forgotten to love the Divine; they had become selfish and even hated themselves and their fellowmen. He said, "I will teach you to sing and dance to the Divine; you will forget your troubles." He broke into song. I sat there and listened, yet my mind wandered. I thanked him, gave him a few rupees and left.

Impressed with the Sufi and the little I learned about love for the divine, I was still not satisfied. One day, I was passing by the Temple of Loh, which I came to know later was believed to have been built by Luv, the son of Lord Rama, and that's how Lahore got its name. I stopped in front of the temple. A few Hindus who had decided to remain in Pakistan went in to pray. I heard the temple bells ring and some verses recited, which I did not understand. When the morning prayers finished, an elderly priest came out. I walked up to him, and asked him if I could speak with him. He and I sat down. I told him about the deep restlessness I felt and my experiences, which seemed to be only about hatred, destruction and pain. I also told him about my meeting with the Maulvi and later the Sufi, and how my restlessness had lingered, even festered in my mind. I told him that if I did not do something, I would go mad.

He listened to me patiently and said, "The restlessness you feel is universal; only you have felt it deeply and you want to seek a way out. Life has been harsh with you at a young age. In the Vedantic way of thinking, we believe that the chief cause of all our suffering is our ignorance of who we truly are. We always seek outside for peace and happiness. Like the musk deer, we seek everywhere for the divine fragrance but not within ourselves. We don't need to go elsewhere to seek the Divine; it is within the hearts all of creation. Cultivate the habit of concentrating on that divinity within you, shutting out other thoughts as far as possible; let thoughts come, just witness them. If you do this patiently and regularly, you will slowly come closer to the peace of the divinity within you."

The priest truly saw my despair and my trauma. "I know that what I am advising you to do is not easy, but there is a way out," he continued. "Gradually learn to do whatever you do for the benefit of others. Let service, however small, to your fellow beings—your neighbours, a poor man at your door, your friends, animals near you—be the aim in life. Let your service be without any hankering after fruit; let service be your worship. You'll see over time that a joy rises in your heart when you serve others. Try it for some time and prove to yourself the truth of what I say. Don't believe blindly what you are told, believe your own experience."

I thanked the priest; his words got me thinking. He had told me to practice something different: to live for others; believe your experience, but not the words of others blindly.

One day, while I was selling fruits in the market, I saw a blind Hindu beggar on the street. He was asking for alms in the name of Lord Rama. He did not know that he was close to a mosque. Some men came out of the Mosque nearby and saw the Hindu beggar and his appeal. They were infuriated, they kicked the beggar and beat him. I rushed to his aid. One of the attackers was a man who had heard me scold the Maulvi. He turned his brutal attention to me; you see what they did to me. I have been blind since that fateful day.

I lay on the pavement bruised and blinded. God sent Ghulam Ali there. He lifted me and took me to his home. I have been Ghulam's guest since my blindness; I help Ghulam Ali in small ways. Ghulam was a devotee of your father, Mathur sahib. He had seen your father's selfless service to the poor. Before leaving Lahore, your father had handed over the keys of the clinic to Ghulam Ali and all his books. Ghulam had already learned a lot about Ayurveda from your father; the books added to his knowledge. Your father had also had given him 5000 rupees from the sale of his house. Your father was keen that the legacy of his ancestors should be preserved. Before parting, he had told Ghulam that he was leaving Lahore and his ancestral calling to Ghulam, his faithful student and assistant for many years, and that he was best qualified, both as a Vaidya and as a compassionate human being, to continue serving his countrymen.

Ghulam faithfully followed your father's instructions. But he had a family to feed, so he charged fees. I had saved money from my fruit sales. I gave all my earnings to Ghulam. We decided that the clinic's services will be offered free in honour of your dear father. We renamed the clinic in memory of your father. None was asked to pay. We ran the clinic like that for 2 years. Our resources slowly dwindled.

One day, out of the blue, a *sherwani* clad gentleman came to the clinic. He said, "I want to meet the Vaidya, Mathur Sahib or anyone who is now running this clinic." I told him that Mathur Sahib was no more and that he had been brutally killed. The gentleman asked who I was. I told him that I was once Mathur Sahib's neighbour and that I lived under his roof for a year after I was orphaned. Ghulam who was inside came out and bowed to the gentleman. He recognized Ghulam and said, "I came to give a donation to Mathur Sahib; but for his medication and the diet which he advised me to take, I would have died within a year of my dreadful disease. I owe my life to him. I was told that the clinic is running free of charge. Please accept my donation for the noble work you are doing." He then handed a bag. Before we could thank him, he left as mysteriously as he came. The bag contained twenty five thousand rupees. The clinic does not lack resources; we keep on getting sponsors.

Here I am today. I don't know to which *mazhab* I belong; nor do I care. The man in front of me is my god.

ॐ   ॐ   ॐ

Ramakant was deeply moved by Abdul's poignant story. He embraced Abdul and Ghulam. In a voice, choked with emotion, he said, "The two of you are true men of God; not those who do not practice what they preach; worse still are those who preach that only their religion is the way to salvation; worst of all those who preach that salvation is obtained by killing people of other faiths. I am humbled by your noble thoughts and service. Henceforth, I shall contribute regularly to your cause; that is the least I can do." The three fell silent.

Ramakant got up. He said, "I have my duty to my country. I must leave now, but the two of you will remain forever in my thoughts and prayers."

Before he left them, he remembered something. He asked Ghulam Ali, "*Main jab sath ya aat sal ka tha, tho hamara sara parivar, hamare Punjabi gaon chale gaye the. Mujhe us goan to jana hai lekin, uska nam tak mujhe maloom nahin. Kya app ko is bare mein kuch ilm hai?[55]*"

"*Kyun nahin. Aap ke valid sahib ke chittiyan hain na,[56]*" Ghulam said, and went inside to fetch a bunch of letters. These were letters from Ramakant's *Mama*, his mother's brother, Srikant Malhotra. His address was there. The village was 'Kohli Kuan'. Armed with that piece of information about his mother's family, Ramakant headed back to the Pehli Kiran, but before that, he bought fruits for Kanshi Ram. He thanked him profusely, handed over the motorcycle and the fruits, touched the feet of the elder and went back to his camp.

Two weeks later both armies returned to their respective country bases after the cessation of war. Ayub Khan earned the wrath of his countrymen.

A month later, Ramakant took leave from his posting. He decided that he would go to his *Mama* and *Maami's* (mother's brother and his wife) place in Kohli Kuan. He went by bus to reach within 3 km of the small village. As he was walking the last part, he saw a girl riding a men's bicycle. Ramakant saw the gay abandon with which she rode her bicycle, humming a popular Panjabi song. His mind went back to his sister, Asha. Had she been alive, he imagined, she too would be like the girl on the bicycle. He hailed the girl, "Behenji," he called out. The girl turned and looked, stopped and waited for Ramakant to come closer. Ramakant was dazzled by the stunningly beautiful girl. Not accustomed to the company of young women in the bachelor's quarters where he lived, Ramakant asked her haltingly, "*Behenji, kya aap Malhotraji ka makan janti hain?[57]*"

The girl smiled and replied, "*Kisse milna hai?[58]*"

"*Mere maami se.[59]*"

---

[55]   *When I was 7 or 8 years old, the family went to our village in Punjab. I want to go there, but I don't even know the name of the village. Do you know anything about this?*

[56]   *Sure, I have letters written to your father.*

[57]   *Do you know where Malhotraji lives, sister?*

[58]   *Whom do you want to see there?*

[59]   *My aunt, uncles wife*

"*Aap ka shubh nam?*[60]" she asked.

"Ramakant."

"*Bhaito. Main tumhe le jaaungi.*[61]"

Ramakant hesitated.

"*Behenji, aap ka nam?*[62]" Ramakant asked.

"Asha," she said.

"What a coincidence," he thought, "My sister was also Asha." Surprised at the similarity of his sister's character with that of Asha in front of him, Ramakant's face wore a vacant look.

"*Chal na,*" she commanded. "*Punjabi kudi kabhi dekha nahin kya?*[63]"

The imperiousness of the beautiful girl was compelling. Ramakant jumped onto the back seat while she rode into the village and stopped in front of a small but elegant house. She parked the cycle, went in and called out in Punjabi, "*Mummyji, toda milna vich ek fauji aaya ithe*[64]."

"This is my cousin? My God, what an encounter," he thought.

The *Maami* came out of her room to see who the visitor was. She opened her mouth in surprise. "Ramakanth beta? Tu?" Ramakant bent down and touched her feet. The girl broke into a giggle. "Mummyji, my God, is this the same Ramki who came when I was 3 years old. What fun we had with him and Asha. I used to tell him that I will marry him, not knowing what marriage meant. Do you remember Ramki?" she asked.

"I don't remember; it was so long ago. But you frightened me today," he said, giving rise to laughter.

Malhotra came home a few minutes later. He had seen Ramakant 19 years ago, when he was 8 years old, yet the resemblance to the senior Mathur was so evident; he held Ramakant in a warm embrace. The Malhotras had not heard of the tragedy that had struck Mathur, Kamala and Asha. Moments of shared grief followed. Poignant memories of the departed were shared in silence by all four.

---

[60]   *What's your name?*

[61]   *Sit on my pillion. I'll take you.*

[62]   *Your name, sister?*

[63]   *Come on! Haven't you seen a Punjabi girl before.*

[64]   *Muumyji, a soldier has come to meet you.*

The lunch table provided a change of mood and scene. Ramakant asked Asha what she was doing. She said she was a teacher in a private school. The mother intervened and told Ramakant that Asha had got her Master's degree in Economics in first class and had been offered a research scholarship in the Delhi University. But she insisted that she wanted to be a teacher.

"Wow," said Ramakant. "Why did you choose teaching as a profession? You could have got better jobs. Do you like your job?" he asked.

"I have always loved to teach. I find it so satisfying that I shall never exchange it merely for a more paying job. You know, when parents seek admission to a school, they find out if the school has good teachers, whether it has produced good results in the past and so on, but none of them want their children to become teachers. Isn't that so?"

Ramakant was impressed by this girl, who apparently had more than a tomboy in her.

Before he could say something, Asha spoke again, "Incidentally, there is no such thing as a bad job, good job or better job. I know I could earn thrice my salary in other jobs, but can you really equate satisfaction with money?"

"I never knew that in your innocent face, there was so much spirit and maturity," said Ramakant.

Malhotra and his wife were enjoying their exchanges. The Maami interrupted: *"Beta,"* she said, *"Shadi kab karne ka vichar hai?*[65]*"*

"Maamiji, ab tak yeh khayal nahin kiya.[66]*"*

"Toh ab karlo na,[67]*"* interjected Malhotra.

"Tumko hamari Asha beti kaise lagi?[68]*"*

In a rare moment of frankness, *"Bahut accha,*[69]*"* said Ramakant.

"Asha, tu batha beta, tujhe Raamki Kaisa laga?[70]*"* She looked at Ramakant, smiled and lowered her gaze.

---

[65] *Son, have you thought of marriage.*
[66] *I have not any plans as yet.*
[67] *Why not marry now?*
[68] *How do you find our Asha?*
[69] *Very good.*
[70] *Asha my child, how do you find Ramki?*

"*To phir deri kis bat ki,*[71]" interjected the Maami.

"*Wah!, main sab Army schoolon me padasakti hun, na?*[72]

Ramakant left them in the evening, but with a new glow on his face. He now had something to look forward to, away from the routine and insipid atmosphere of the army, which had made him a robot.

The ebullient Asha and the sedate Ramakant became man and wife a month later.

---

[71] *Then why delay?*

[72] *Wow, I can continue to teach in Army schools isn't it?*

The Trader and the Saint

Ramayya was a trader in the small town of Pritapur, a Taluk headquarters, surrounded by many villages. He was born into a family of traders and money lenders. Their trade was in food grains and other crops produced in the region, as well as in products that the townsfolk and villagers needed, sourced from wholesalers. Ramayya, as a young man of 19, espied Shyamamma, 13 at that time, in a village fair; he looked at her fair face, her demure behavior, her flowing locks, and gave away his heart to her, as romantic poets would say. He found out her parentage and soon his parents, much against the tradition that a girl's parents should seek an alliance for their girl, and not the other way, made their way to her parents. They were bowled over by the girl's good looks and her winning ways, which showed the care with which she was brought up. Again, much against tradition, Ramayya and Shyamamma were married with dowry neither offered nor demanded. That was the condition that Shyamamma's father had shrewdly ensured. As was to be expected in a rich man's house with many servants around, the pretty and gentle Shyamamma became nothing more than a doll in the Ramayya household, whose main role was to be around and satisfy her husband.

Two years later, Krishnayya was born. He inherited the genes that determine colour and looks more from the father than the mother. He was born also with the qualities of his father: the characteristics, mindset, and the rough and tumble qualities of politicians, as time would show. He was well built; he had a strong, plastic countenance that could show abject surrender to someone higher one moment, and just as easily anger the next moment that could put lesser humans in mortal fear for their lives. He had a strong Ego, exhibiting a mentality that said: "I can do no wrong, the world is my fiefdom." Even as an infant, he got his way through violent tantrums. Punishments by the mother were stoically tolerated in the knowledge that she would sooner than later relent and regret her punishment. As a school child, Krishnayya asserted himself authoritatively; his looks and strength were enough to put fear into the minds of classmates. His general outlook was "If other boys are not with me, they are against me." The power that comes with brute force and the arrogance of wealth into which he was born were the ideal conditions that would enable him in later life to pursue his destiny as a politician.

Ramayya's God was money: profits were his motivation and master. He did not have time for the family. As a rich man of a small town, he wielded influence. People sought him out for his patronage. He was immersed in his own world.

When Krishnayya was seven, his brother Rajayya was born. Rajayya was the spitting image of his mother: delicate, baby-faced, soft eyes in which compassion and tolerance were writ large. He became his mother's pet; after all, he was born in her image. Krishnayya bullied his brother as well into meek submission. There seemed to be little in common between the brothers, both genetically and in mental makeup. In fact, their inner natures were diametrically opposed to each other. The age difference between the two boys also added to the lack of attachment.

When the boys were 19 and 12, the surrounding villages suffered a severe drought. Small lakes and wells in the region had dried up; crops failed. Small and marginal farmers were devastated. Their livelihood was jeopardized. Some of them, who had borrowed from money lenders and did not find a way out, committed suicide. These were reported in the papers; the Government could do little because they had limited resources, given the scale of the devastation. The rich farmers and traders had resources, but little or no sympathies for the affected. Instead, they thought, this was an opportunity to make money. Ramayya was no exception. He lent money at exorbitant rates, after deducting the first year's interest and after acquiring the papers for the land mortgaged to him as collateral for the loan given.

There was a buzz of activity in his house those days, with tearful entreaties for Ramayya's help. Ramayya sat like a haughty potentate dispensing his cruel justice, gloating at the steady growth of his net worth.

The scenes affected each of the boys differently: Krishnayya saw with glee, his father's greed; he saw his father's fat face bloating with joy, his wealth multiplying and the power he wielded over the minions. Rajayya saw the plight of farmers. Their tearful entreaties carved a hole in his heart. He ran to his mother and asked, "Why cannot father be kind? Of what use is money if it does not help others in their need? I feel so sad to see the cries of the poor."

"Your father will not listen to me, my son; I too feel deeply, but I cannot do much," the mother said. "I can only pray that the Almighty will find a way to relieve the difficulties of the poor. I am worried that your father is setting a bad example to your brother. I'll try and talk to him."

A day later, she called Krishnayya when her husband was not around, and said, "Krishnu, I see you getting excited and happy when your father dispenses his help grudgingly to the poor farmers. Imagine, how you would feel if you were one of the poor farmers. Remember that it is only through sharing and giving to each other that we can bring prosperity to all. If the farmers cannot grow anything this year because their fields are dry, what grains will your father have to trade?"

Krishnayya did not answer. Rajayya was privy to the conversation. He perked up. "Bhaiya," he said, "Let me tell you what happened yesterday. I was eating a banana when the servant's little son followed his mother to the kitchen. He saw the banana I was eating with hungry eyes. I picked up a banana and gave it to him. He smiled and ate it with relish. The servant saw this. She smiled. Mother saw both of us eating bananas; she came and hugged me. I felt so happy."

Mother turned to me and said, "See how one banana could make four people happy." I will never forget this.

The father's greed and his haughtiness distanced Rajayya from his father until the son dreaded the very sight of the father. He dreamt of a freedom where he would get away with his mother to some place where the father could never find them.

Krishnayya, on the other hand, was already inducted into the father's business, which he quickly grasped with a fervour he enjoyed.

Sometime later, a wandering monk of the Giram Order passed through the town. All monks of the Order were ordained to be itinerant Sanyasis for a year every 6 years. The austerity had many purposes: to remove them from the comfort zone of their monasteries, to give them an opportunity to see problems of their fellowmen; to leave their minds free from Monastic duties, so that they could spend more time dwelling on scriptural truths; and the cultivation of dispassion. They were to stay with anyone who offered to host them in their abodes, however humble, and provide them space to spread their small cotton carpet and one frugal vegetarian meal a day. Their day began at 3.00 a.m. on prayer and meditation for 4 hours, followed by advice and counsel to those that sought them, brief rest and reading at noon, then discourses on the scriptures to the interested, and meditation again after dusk. The monk had already reached an exalted state in his spiritual journey. He exuded the glow that came from his inner divinity; his voice, soft and soothing, was like a balm on the woes of the farmers who flocked to hear him. They prayed with him, he prayed for them.

The villagers brought the Sanyasi to Ramayya's home. There, they knew, the Sanyasi would be well taken care of by Shyamamma. She welcomed the Sanyasi, washed his feet, and led him to a small room where he could retire for his austerities and sleep. Rajayya, who had never truly had a father figure to run to as an anchor for his childish woes, was greatly drawn to the Sanyasi. In his innocence and wonder at a face which exuded so much affection, he spontaneously went to the Sanyasi at all times, including when the Sanyasi was meditating. The Sanyasi too was drawn to the boy, inexorably it seemed. When not in his austerities, the boy sat next to him to be told stories. He answered the boy's questions; laughed with him and taught him a few prayer chants. The bond between the two, in the short ordained span of 3 days that the Sanyasi stayed in any one place, became so strong that when the Sanyasi wished to leave, Rajayya would not let him. He would not let go of the Sanyasi's hand and cried his heart out. The Sanyasi was allowed to leave only after he promised to come back. This was, of course, a promise that the Sanyasi could not keep; it would go against the very idea of cultivating dispassion and non-attachment. But the brief visit of the Sanyasi made a profound difference to Rajayya. He saw that there was more meaning to life and being than the humdrum existence that he and his family led. The influence of a saintly person had transformed a mere child into a thinking one, more than all the religious education that Shyamamma had offered. It must have been difficult for the Sanyasi to forget the child as well; there was no way of knowing this, of course.

Rajayya passed out of his 10th class at 15, quite creditably to the happiness of his mother. He was frail like his mother; she did not want the boy to be sent away for college studies. He was tutored at home, and three years later he passed the 12th class as a private candidate. The tutor had introduced him to good reading, in addition to the course subjects. This was a treasure that Rajayya would cherish throughout his life. At the age of 21, he passed his Bachelor's degree also privately. His interest in language and literature flourished, thus expanding his vision of life and living.

Three months later, Shyamamma died. This was a tragedy that Ramayya and Krishnayya quickly recovered from, but not Rajayya. He felt that the only true anchor in his life had left him. His heart cried out, unheard and unseen by others, nevertheless poignant and wrenching in a way that showed on his face. He went into a depression that moved even his father. Ramayya tried his best to soften the shock his son had suffered. He took the son away for some time, leaving his business to Krishnayya, who by then had become quite savvy. Ramayya thought that Rajayya would, with time, come to grips with his depression. He appointed a servant who would be Rajayya's constant companion. There were some signs of regression from his illness. But thoughts of running away from the house that had not given him any joy became more and more persistent.

One night, Rajayya had a dream. The Sanyasi who had visited them some years ago, beckoned to Rajayya. His face suffused with love and compassion, he said, "My Child, your life so far has been full of sorrow, confusion and disappointment; the time has come for you to come to me. Fear not, this has been ordained for you. Your life henceforth will be spent under my tutelage; you shall bring succor to many." Rajayya did not know whether he had really dreamt his dream, or was it a vision that his mind had conjured. The dream recurred time and again, until one day he woke up as if violently shaken in his sleep. He was convinced that this was a sincere call from the Sanyasi, conveyed through his dream. Indeed, he had heard of such stories in the Puranas that his mother had related. That was it. Rajayya remembered the Sanyasi's promise of coming back to their place. He was fulfilling his promise by calling Rajayya to come to him, he thought. He felt new strength rise in himself. A few days later, silently, he packed a few clothes, took some money that his mother had patiently saved from the funds she was given for domestic expenses and walked out into the night, as mysteriously as the dream that had come and left him.

When Rajayya was not found anywhere in the house the next day, his servant companion raised an alarm. Ramayya initially said, "He can't go too far. I am sure he will come back when hunger beckons him." That was not to be. When the son did not return even after two days, Ramayya sent some men to look for him. They took the three main roads that left in different directions from the town. One of them came back and reported that a young man of about 20 was seen hitching a ride with a truck driver. Nobody knew where the boy might have gone. Ramayya sent word to his trading partners and customers about his missing son and that they should let him know if a fair boy of 21 was found in their town or village loitering, and generally seen to be lost. None reported any such instance. Ramayya then gave up all hope and resigned himself to the thought that his son was lost to him forever.

Krishnayya was 28-years old at that time. His inborn business acumen, polished by experience, began to take Ramayya's enterprise beyond what the older man had never dreamt of. Ramayya. had the wisdom to step back and retire. The burdens of his business had already eaten into his life span. Krishnayya had managed to multiply his father's wealth several fold; his influence had expanded to people and areas beyond the small town. Ramayya wanted his son to get married, but the son was so steeped in money that he did not show interest until he was 32.

Ramayya's main occupation now was to find a suitable bride for Krishnayya. Parents of girls from near and far came with attractive propositions. Some propositions were good but not the brides; in some others, brides were good but not the propositions. Finally, Ramayya found one where the proposition and the bride matched each other very well.

The prospective bride was indeed pretty; her father had offered a fabulous dowry and all the accruements that are fancied by the rich and the famous. Krishnayya decided to marry the bride selected by his father. She was Premalata, 27, pretty daughter of a rich politician from the capital city of the State. Her parents were concerned that she had already passed, according to the society they lived in, the marriageable age for girls. The age difference between her and Krishnayya was ideal. She was better educated than Krishnayya, who had long struggled to pass his 10th class and gave up in frustration. Of what use is bookish knowledge, he had argued, when he could spend his time in becoming rich. A formal engagement ceremony was held. The wedding was planned to take place 6 months from that day. There were many comings and goings between the two families; Ramayya was the one doing the rounds from his family's side. The details of the wedding were decided in these visits.

One morning, Ramayya collapsed soon after his breakfast. He was rushed to the hospital. He had apparently suffered a heart attack. When Premalata's father heard of it, he rushed to Pritapur and brought Ramayya for better treatment in a hospital in the Capital city. Unknown to Ramayya, he was an advanced diabetic; his eyes were slowly getting affected. After treatment, he went home. A few weeks later, a massive heart attack saw the end of Ramayya. Krishnayya was deeply affected; he had now become an orphan in more senses than one; both his parents had left him; his brother had left. He was bereft of all blood ties. But for the kindness of his future father-in-law, Krishnayya would not have recovered from his loss as quickly as he did.

Krishnayya's marriage to Premalata was a grand celebration. The high and mighty, the rich and famous, all attended. He brought home his bride with great pomp and celebration, orchestrated by Premalata's parents.

For a while, Krishnayya's life with his new bride was heavenly. The household was abuzz, with many people pandering to the newly married couple. Her parents and relatives flitted and floated like butterflies into the Ramayya household. They changed the furniture; they refurbished the rooms; added new creature comforts of the day; pandered to the son-in-law with expensive gifts that glittered but brought no inner glow. After an extended honeymoon period for the couple, the parents and friends left. Premalata soon began to tire of her husband and the eventless life in a small town. Back in her father's place, she had many classmates and friends; they went to parties; they shopped till they dropped; they gossiped and laughed. Clever girl that she was, she persuaded her husband to spend a week away in her home. Premalata had already planned that she would extend the one-week stay to at least another week. Krishnayya, ignorant of the way that women's minds worked, agreed to go with her to her father's place after calling a trusted servant, Madappa, to take care of the business during his brief stay away. In her father's place, Premalata poured her woes on her father and mother about the lacklustre life she led in her husband's home and how she longed to be back in their home.

Her parents had spoiled her; now her woes spoiled the mother's sleep. She thought, foolishly, like many other mothers have done in the past, to intervene on behalf of her daughter. She went to her husband and said, "Can you not do something about our Prema? She wants to come back here." The man, wiser by experience, said, "Let's not interfere in her life. She has to find her feet in her new environment; you and I should not live her life." The mother, frustrated at the lack of response from her husband, huffed and puffed and left, looking for a new way to approach the husband's intractability. The husband, pilloried day after day by the wife, finally gave in. He promised to do something.

He thought of interesting the son-in-law with a life in politics. As a politician, he had his fingers in many pies; he was chairman of one or other committee; elected member of the Municipal Corporation; patron of many societies including orphanages and old-age homes, and so on. He had also had a stint as a member of the State's Legislative Assembly. The party to which he belonged had lost the last election. The party was biding its time, with a good chance of reelection. All manner of people came to him for help and intervention in their affairs with the Government. The word 'help' in such circles had a built-in *quid pro quo* element, with the politicians at all levels benefitting from the illegitimate largesse that came from many quarters.

The best way to interest Krishnayya in politics, the father-in-law decided, was to take him along to his society meetings and to introduce him to acquaintances, men and women who appeared on the front pages as well as the third page and gossip columns of newspapers. If the son-in-law liked what he saw, then getting him into the political whorl would not be difficult. Krishnayya began accompanying his father-in-law to various forums. He was quite taken in by the importance that was shown to his father-in-law. His meetings with other folk, including junior and senior politicians, their wives, daughters, and the drinks and food served whetted his appetite. He looked back at his lackluster life as a trader, where he met only grain merchants and money lenders with their glum faces, and how he had to haggle for small changes in the prices of what he bought and sold. The father-in-law was delighted that Krishnayya was beginning to see the possibilities of a new life-style. Premalata joined her husband on a few such forays. She was delighted that her husband had seen a different life-style that he found attractive. The one week away from his home had already extended to 3 weeks.

One day, the father-in-law found Krishnayya in a happy mood and seized the opportunity. He said, "Son, why don't you leave your business to be taken care of by a trusted lieutenant. You can then join me. I am sure you and I could together do many interesting things. Join our party. You will learn a lot; you really don't need to worry about money. Your business and my earnings would be more than adequate for all of us. You could go once or twice a month and ensure that your business is doing well." Krishnayya pondered over the suggestion. He said, "I will need to go home for a few weeks and see how things are going. I had planned only a one-week stay away."

So he went back alone to Pritapur. He spent two weeks looking at the books of his trade and the cash in his tiller. Quite satisfied with what his trusted servant, Madappa, had done during his absence, he raised his salary and commission. He had started missing Premalata: two weeks away without her in his bed was not a happy experience. One day, he called Madappa home because he wanted to talk to him in private. He told Madappa about the possibility that he would join his father-in-law in his political career, but make visits every few weeks to ensure that the business was well in hand. Madappa reassured his master that he was quite capable of handling the business, thanks to his long-standing experience under

Ramayya. That settled, Krishnayya went back to his father-in-law's place to a warm welcome.

Thus began a new career for Krishnayya, passionate and greedy to make a new name and gain fame, wealth and fortune. History and legend have time and time again shown that burning desire and insatiable greed are elements that infallibly lead man to his doom. The intellect and its powers of discrimination are dulled, even destroyed, leading to ugliest thoughts, resulting in disastrous actions, which pave the way to inevitable doom and destruction of men.

Krishnayya first became a member of a political party that his father-in-law belonged to. He began as a party worker. The fact that he was rich and thus able to contribute funds to the party marked him out from the other workers. In good time, he was given responsibilities to head committees, to meet with legislators, organize protests and even sleep overnight in police lockups when arrested for acts such as throwing stones at detractors. Such men are assured of bail; they come out of the overnight lockups as heroes, even martyrs. Apparently, in the given political climate, these were necessary and sufficient qualifications to rise up the ladder. His visibility to the public went up. He began to appear in the pages of newspapers and briefly on the news channels. More than the importance that others gave him, his Ego, fattened by conviction of his invincibility, was like a cancer that would inevitably eat into the vitals of his being. This is what happened to Krishnayya.

Five years into his career in politics, he had learned the ropes of the dirty game. His father-in-law passed away. Krishnayaa became his political successor. The legislative seat vacated by the father-in-law became his in a by-election. A year later, he became a member of a Committee which included architects, hospital administrators, and medical professionals. The Committee was charged with awarding a contract for a multi-specialty hospital in the Capital city, to be funded by the State and Central Governments. Several bidders for the project gave their proposals and costs. As is an open secret, lobbying for the contract for such a multi-crore project took place furtively and in all manner of ways, including the foulest. The members of this Committee were targeted by all the bidders. Experienced members of the Committee had learned the art of benefitting from the largesse of one or more contractors, without any trace of why and how their ill-gotten spoils were obtained. The contract was awarded to one of the builders. Two years into the construction, one section of a partially constructed building collapsed like a house of cards, killing some workers and raising a stink. An enquiry commission was mandated to go into the disaster; the project was halted. The contractor was imprisoned. The inquiry report nailed Krishayya and a few others for corruption. The court case went on for two years. Krishnayya was sentenced to jail, but the father-in-law's family bailed him out. They filed an appeal on his behalf to the High Court. The case went on for five years, while Krishnayya became a *persona non grata* in political circles. The High Court upheld the conviction. He went to jail again. Premalata had in the meanwhile found new male interests. She had physically and mentally divorced her husband after her mother had passed away. She had made up her mind to file for a divorce after his jail term. Krishnayya was not to be defeated so easily. His appetite for power and wealth had not been fulfilled. He fell into one trap after another. When he came out of jail, he found that his 15 year career had left him friendless, and cashless, even his wife had deserted him. His only hope was to get back to his town, Pritapur; fortunately, his father's house was there for him. He went back, bald and beaten, a faint shadow of the arrogant man he had been.

When he found his way to his old home, he expected it would be in some disrepair, but he was shocked to see that everything of any value was stolen. His trusted servant Madappa had died. His trading business had gone to seed; others had established themselves. Fortunately, Madappa had not belied his master's trust. The money collected in transactions that he had made was deposited in Krishnayya's bank account. A maid servant who had benefitted from his mother Shyamamma's benevolence recognized Krishnayya and cooked for him. The maid, now bent with age, wanted to repay the debt she owed to her former mistress; this she found in service to Krishnayya. Confused and disillusioned, no longer strong, at close to 55 years, Krishnayya resigned to his fate of loneliness and near penury. Thoughts of a higher order that his mother had talked of, which he had brushed aside arrogantly, and guilt that he had not heeded his gentle mother's advice and warnings racked his mind.

Some months later, a monk of the Giram order, Swami Chidananda, came to the town like the one that had come years ago. The monk was well-known in spiritual circles. His writings on practical Vedanta for simple people were couched in language that even that 7th and 8th class school educated elders could follow. He was proficient in Hindi and important regional languages. He had made it his mission to visit the rural folk and bring to them the vision and wisdom of ancient scriptures. He spent 3 months each year visiting different villages and speaking to the rural folk using their idioms and language. In a few days at Pritapur, he had carved a niche in the hearts of people there. He answered many doubts and questions that the rural folk had about their lives. They prayed with him; he prayed for them.

The maid told Krishnayya about the monk. He went to see the visiting monk and waited until he was free from his austerities. The monk came out. He heard the visitor's tale of distress.

"My brother," said the monk, "Blame not your fate or destiny. Each of us is largely responsible for the experiences we have in life. It is true that we come into this world with both good and bad qualities and aptitudes. We also are exposed to good and bad environments. It cannot be otherwise. There can be no good without its shadow, bad. Both good and bad come from the same source. Some are carried away by the bad influences in them, some transcend their bad tendencies through a belief and understanding of a higher order, by whatever name you may call it. Similarly, the environment you are born into can carry you away into doing actions which destroy you as a human being. Those who transcend the bad in their environment attain success and peace. Our scriptures have time and again warned us of three evils: burning desire, uncontrolled anger, and unquenchable greed, which lead to the destruction of man. These truths are timeless, but not all human beings make these a part of their daily lives. You can still make amends for the mistakes you madein life. Make up your mind to be of service, however small, to others; this is the best way to be at peace. Learn to develop a prayerful mind, one that surrenders to a higher consciousness. It is not what you get that matters, it is what you give that matters, because that brings you joy; you would have given back to the world, the debt you owe it; the world gives you back love and peace many times over."

Krishnayya listened to the monk with rapt attention. His mind recalled the banana story that his brother had told him many years ago. He recalled his mother's advice. How simple and true their words were, he now realized. He got up, prostrated to the monk, and was about to take leave.

The monk spoke, "Bhaiya Krishnu, don't you remember me?" Amazed that the monk had addressed him using the name by which he was lovingly called by his mother, he looked intently at the bearded monk. He saw his mother's eyes.

"My God, are you not Rajeshwara?" He asked, using the name by which the mother had lovingly addressed his brother.

"The very same, but now I am called Swami Chidananda after I was ordained as a monk." The brothers embraced.

One and the Same

Atma and Guru were classmates in the Masters Degree programme in Pure Mathematics. Both were brilliant. They had consciously chosen not to take the beaten path; they believed in chasing their dreams. Passionate about the abstractions of pure mathematics, they were indeed a cut above the run-of-the-mill students.

Guru was an ebullient character whose interests went beyond the logic and equations of mathematics. He believed that imagination is more important than knowledge. He was a dreamer, sometimes with open eyes. His capacity for abstractions beyond what Mathematics had taught him was another characteristic which marked him out as an extraordinary young man. He was always engaged in mental pyrotechnics and thought experiments. He read widely beyond his subjects. He was indeed an enigma to himself. Atma, on the other hand was introspective, focused exclusively on whatever he wished to achieve. They were a perfect foil for each other.

One day, an animated Guru, barged into Atma's room. He did not believe in the niceties of etiquette. Atma did not mind; he was used to the ways of Guru.

"Hey, Atma," he said, "You must hear this."

Atma, down to earth as ever, looked up and reminded him that they had a final exam on Group, Lattice and String theories, in 40 minutes, one of the papers in the Master's Degree examination. The theories are pretty abstract and it required all the intelligence and concentration to grasp the different postulates and equations and their expressions in symbols which, to lesser mortals, looked like crazy squiggles using, what mathematicians called differential and integral equations.

Guru brushed aside Atma's concern and said, "I promise this won't take long."

Atma resigned himself to the ebullient Guru; he knew that there was no alternative. He prepared himself to listen.

Guru began to describe his dream:

> I had a fantastic dream last night. Lord Krishna had come down to earth in the 21st Century. I saw him at a cross road. He seemed confused about which road to take. He was dressed in a pair of faded jeans and an unwashed T-shirt. He had a beautiful peacock feather on his head; that's how I knew he was Lord Krishna.
>
> I walked up to him and tapped his shoulders. "May I have a word with you Lord? I asked."
>
> He turned to me and said, "I suppose, I have no choice, but please be quick about it. I am running an errand for Rukmini and Satyabhama. I am glad though, you are not one of those pesky TV reporters."

Atma smiled. "One more of Guru's fanciful dreams," he told himself. Guru's earlier dreams included Einstein, Ramanujam and Hardy, Schrodinger and Heisenberg. His dreams were fanciful and interesting; some even provided insight into one or other principle which had seemed so incomprehensible to Atma until then. That was the reason why Atma humoured and tolerated Guru at any time of day or night.

> Guru continued. I asked the Lord, "Why you have created so much inequity in the world?"
>
> "My God!" replied the Lord. "I have answered that question millions of times. The sages have answered it in song and story; prayer and scripture, yet Man keeps on

asking the same question. Know that I do not act nor do I have any desire to act."

I asked, "You just said, 'My God.' Are you not God then?"

"You're a naughty fellow, but I am beginning to like you," said Baghavan. "I am an Avatar– a special manifestation of the One Paramatman, the ALL, so I look and speak and do things like mortals. I come to fulfill a divine purpose."

I know that, I said. May I call you Baghavan? I asked.

I didn't wait for an answer. Tell me, just now you said you neither act nor are impelled to act, how then is it you're doing chores for your consorts Rukmini and Satyabhama?

Baghavan smiled mischievously. He said: "You won't understand the answer to that question. You must first get married."

Sorry Baghavan, I said, I want to come back to my first question about inequities that we see everywhere?

"Here you go again," said Baghavan. "An intelligent young man like you dealing with incomprehensible abstractions should not be asking that question. You do act like my beloved disciple Arjuna. He was a mightily confused soul. I had to recite seven hundred verses in the Bhagavad Geeta and give him answers, sometimes to the same question, before I could get him to fight the Kurukshetra war. So, let me answer your question."

Thank you, I beseeched and waited for Baghavan to speak.

"First and foremost, there is neither Creator nor Baghavan, nor Creation. Get that truth into your thick skin."

I was completely at a loss. Baghavan must have seen my confusion. "You and I and all human beings and minerals and animals, the stars and planets, the sun and moon are projections or manifestations of the One Paramatman--also called Bramhan, the underlying, undifferentiated reality--as images on a cinema screen from a projector. When the movie gets over, the screen which, metaphorically speaking is Bramhan, persists; neither the characters nor the scenes remain. Just as the characters and scenes withdraw into the film, all projections withdraw into the Paramatman. It is also like something about your dreams. When you dream, you are projecting through your mind, dreamlike things and characters and events. On waking up, the dreamlike characters withdraw into your mind."

Then Baghavan, I asked. Are all the objects and people that we see, unreal like mirages in a desert?

"Indeed, that is the *Maya* of the Paramatman. Since everything is Bramhan, that which is not Bramhan— everything else—that the sense-mind-intellect perceives, is Unreal, designated by the term Maya. Don't get me wrong. I am not saying that what you see or hear or touch or taste does not exist. I am saying that they exist at one Order of Reality, but that Order of Reality is not the only one. This was beautifully put by the Persian mystic and poet, Omar Khyaam, in his Rubaiyāt. He said:

> 'For in out, above, about below,
> T'is nothing but a Magic Shadow-show
> Play'd in a Box whose Candle is the Sun,
> Round which we Phantom Figures come and go.'

It is the Maya of undifferentiated Bramhan that deludes humans and causes suffering, attached as they are to the unreal. They are like caged birds that know not the freedom of the skies, they flap their wings in vain. All suffering is caused by that ignorance. When you know that you and Bramhan are non-separate and when you apply this truth to all experiences, every moment, in your daily life—not merely know intellectually like you know other worldly subject matter—you transcend Maya. By this I mean that you continue to live in the world of Maya but are untouched by it. The knowledge that you are non-separate from Bramhan—the Fullness of your Being—which is unaffected by the phenomenal world, endows you with dispassion or objectivity to the world. You are untouched by Maya— ever changing phenomenon and impermanence you see all around you. Did not the great quantum physicists of the 20th century undermine the whole premise of a mechanistic universe? Overnight it became a participatory universe; we are not just in it, we are part of it and able to influence it by the mere act of looking at it."

I must have looked confused. Baghavan read my mind.

He said, "Let me explain Maya more simply to you. Human beings live in many orders of reality. The phenomenal world is the order of reality that most of us know and reckon with. In other words, we know we are alive; we see the things and people around and we relate to them; we have feelings of good and bad, love and hatred about people and food and things. Let me call this Order of Reality as Physical Reality. This order is gross. Are you following me?"

I nodded my head.

"Good," continued Baghavan. "In addition to the order of reality that the physical world imposes on us, we often intuit a higher, subtler order of reality that transcends the physical order. For instance, you invoke God when a loved one is sick and things and events in your life are beyond your capability to reckon with. Ordinarily, all men are firmly established in their Physical Reality, but briefly intuit another unknown reality that is beyond. Let me call this Higher Order of Reality. When a man is fully established in this order of reality, the Physical Order of Reality falls back and you know is unreal. For instance a coiled rope lying on the ground in a poorly lighted dark alley on which you are walking may look like a snake and fear grips you. When you shine light on the rope, your fear vanishes because you know that it is a harmless rope. The reality of the rope vanquishes the unreality of the snake. You projected the reality of a snake in your mind—you saw or projected a snake in your mind—another way of saying that you experienced a snake. The light of knowledge—the light that you shined on the rope—vanquished your experience of a snake and revealed the reality of the rope. There are two powers of Ignorance: the first, to envelope or cover up the Truth—create ignorance of the underlying truth—and the second, the power to project. In the ignorance caused by darkness you did not see the rope. That very ignorance caused also your projection of a snake—you experienced a snake. Unknowing the truth of himself, man identifies with his false experience and suffers. When You know the Truth and you identify firmly with Bramhan as the underlying reality, you will no longer be deluded to project the false. For instance, let us say that you have a sore throat; you don't know why that condition arose; you are ignorant of the underlying cause of the sore throat. Your ignorance misleads you to project the worst of fears in your mind, such as that you may have throat cancer. If you identify yourself as the sore throat, you suffer. It is simply a fact; deal with it as such. Reaching such a state of being and being established in it while you are in the physical state is what is meant by Self Knowledge. An Order of Reality which is subtle vanquishes a gross Order of Reality. Firm knowledge that You are the Underlying Pure Consciousness and the realization that all experiences, including your concept of 'I-ness' are mind events illumined by consciousness, to be dealt with as such. This is the hallmark of an enlightened soul. He is free even while he lives in body-mind-intellect. He deals with what is normally seen as problems, as facts. He knows that there is an illness in his body, which He is

NOT. In other words, he does not identify himself with his body-illness. He goes to a doctor and deals with his illness dispassionately. The enlightened man's experience is the same as an ordinary man; the difference is he understands the truth of Bramhan and is not overwhelmed by the experience."

His 'I-ness' is a functional one unlike that of other human beings. He feels hunger, he has emotions, he has pains but none of these overwhelm him; he does not identify himself with these."

"I hope you have understood the relationship of ignorance, knowledge and Maya."

I nodded my head to tell Baghavan that the metaphor of the Rope and Snake was easy to relate to. I began wondering if one might develop a mathematical theory of orders of reality.

I was greedy. I had not had enough of this wonderful encounter with Baghavan. I wanted to tease him. Baghavan, I said, Now-a-days, we live in a digital world. Movies are encoded as a stream of 1s and 0s. There is no longer need for huge projectors.

Baghavan was not impressed. He said, "Now you are trying to act smart with me. The Paramatma mapped the idea of binary notation and before that the decimal notation in the minds of the Arabs, Chinese and Bharatvasis who think they invented the zero, numerals and Abacus; so also with Newton, Charles Babbage, John Von Neumann, and all the geniuses that stalked the Earth. Everything you see, hear, touch, taste; all cerebration, ideas, inspirations, all thoughts are only projections. Each of them looks different, so you deduce they are different?"

My God, I thought to myself, "He knows everything. Maybe I should ask him to take my examination."

I was in for a shock. He looked at me and said, "Mischievous fellow. Don't expect me to do your work."

My God, I thought to myself. "He knows what goes on in my mind, so I have to be careful. But then how can I still my mind?

"Baghavan looked at me and smiled a most mischievous smile. With a twinkle in his eyes, he said, "You have understood the crux of your problem, my dear. To know the solution seek a Guru, or if you are a sincere seeker, the Guru will find you. He will open your inner eye, and purify your mind and intellect."

Baghavan, I asked. How come you are able to read my mind?

"Good question. You live in and through me, so I know all your sensations, thoughts, emotions and feelings. All experiences are vibrations in your mind, illumined by reflected consciousness. In fact, life is a cascade of experiences, each feeding on the other. I am the witness. Is that clear? I am the underlying reality behind your mind."

This is mind boggling, I said. You mean you are sitting in me and seeing everything that goes on in my mind?

Baghavan smiled and said, "The truth of you is you are the spirit or consciousness that illumines your external sensory being and hidden internal being. The spirit within you, conditioned by senses, mind, intellect and the Ego is the Experience-er; the spirit within you and all living beings is the Seer or Knower of your experiences. I am not a physical entity to be 'sitting' inside you. It feels as though I am within you because I am conditioned by your body, mind, Ego and intellect—your natural elements. You are a product of your inner nature and Pure Consciousness or Spirit. I am everywhere; therefore the same ever Wakeful Witness in all beings and all inanimate things. The spirit pervading you and all living and non-living beings are sparks of the Pure Consciousness; in a sense you are me, but you delude yourself that you are the body."

I am confused Baghavan, I said.

He said, "Let me explain this with a metaphor. You said that these days many things are digital – a stream of 1s and 0s. The 1 is Bramhan, the Spirit or Pure Consciousness. The 0 is all projections of Bramhan, including humans. The 0 cannot, on its own, experience anything; it is insentient. The 1 endows the 0 with sentience; sensory experiences and emotions are known to all through Me, the Consciousness abiding in you. An insentient rock has no experience, because it is not endowed with senses, mind and intellect as you are. But, I still pervade the rock. I pervade everything. Without Me, there is no rock; no you, no feelings."

I was now thoroughly confused. But I was enjoying my fortuitous encounter with Baghavan. I thought, I would start off on a new thread of thought exchange with Him.

Baghavan, I asked, Have you lately watched CNN or BBC news channels on TV? Incidentally, please don't watch Indian news channels these days. They only show the speeches of power-hungry and depraved politicians. But tell me, why have you put so many conflicts in the world: in India, Pakistan, Bangladesh, Sri Lanka—close to your *Karma Bhoomi*—and also in many countries in the continents of Asia, Africa, Europe, South America. Do you really enjoy these, reclining unconcerned as you do with your consort on Ocean's Bed of Time? Why does Paramatman project these conflicts, if indeed, as you said, everything is a projection? There are so many conflicts in the name of religion? It is disgusting, to say the least that religion has claimed more lives all the wars than put together from time immemorial. Then again, at the individual level, why do you make a wife quarrel with her husband and vice versa, son with father, neighbour with neighbour? I am upset that you have done nothing to stem this rot.

For a moment, Baghavan looked testily at me, but he quickly returned to his loving self. "I like your anger," he said. "It comes from your ignorance. I don't want to confuse you with the exalted philosophy of the sages. I will try to explain the problem as simply as possible."

I nodded my head.

"My dear," he said. "The problems that you talk of are exclusively that of the human species. I have never heard the earth and the trees, the animals and the bees or the leaves complaining. Consider this: human beings are endowed with keen senses, powerful minds, and sharp intellects, superior to all other beings, but these have not been employed for their good; instead they have been misused. Paramatma does not interfere with your inner nature. Man inherits his inner nature—his tendencies, dispositions, desires, world views and attitudes—from many past births and through ancestral environments. Influenced by his inner nature, he performs all actions, good and bad in his life. The fundamental problem is that humans have forgotten their origins and their interconnectedness with the Paramatman and all his Projections. When you hurt another, you hurt yourself; love proffered to others leads to love, peace and harmony. Instead, influenced by your wrong identity – ignorance of your true nature as Pure Consciousness—your life becomes an ever changing experience of good and bad, joy and sorrow, pain and suffering and conflict within and without."

I interrupted Baghavan. Now, I suppose you are talking of the Karma theory. Isn't it an anachronism that we talk of rebirth and reincarnation in the 21st century?

He looked at me with deep compassion. "I anticipated your question. Karma theory is misunderstood because people think there is no scientific basis for it. Let me ask you: was the law of gravity known to man until Newton discovered it? He had the insight to uncover this eternal law. Much later, with new insight, Einstein interpreted the phenomenon of gravity as the result of warped space. He did not negate Newton's laws. Let me give you another example: It is now proven that all things which look solid are nothing but atomic mass in rapid motion. Do human beings see this as such? How about the atom? Years ago it was thought that the atom could not be split; we know now that not only the atom has been split, many sub-atomic particles have been found. Now they are searching for the God Particle. What next, I ask? The subtle, unseen and unfelt intelligence of the Paramatma pervades the entire Cosmos. The law of Karma is one such law, subtler than the gross laws of physics. In Man's limited understanding, he argues that there is nothing beyond what logic and reason tells us, but that is in itself irrational. The sages of yore had the insight to uncover and formulate the law of Karma. Why should you deny them this possibility? A closed mind is an unscientific mind. All personal deeds lead to consequences, desirable or not, depending on the doer and the deed. What is important to each man is that his own Karma (deeds) are consequential. One enjoys or suffers depending upon his deeds in the past, present and future lives. If skepticism still prevails, and if this or any other incomprehensible cosmic law does not satisfy man's objective mind, ask yourself: does this law help me to lead a better life? If indeed it does, then experience the law and convince yourself. It is a mistaken notion that only the Hindu religion subscribes to Karma theory and reincarnation. Omar Khayyam said so insightfully:

> '*The moving finger writes, and having writ;*
> *Moves on: nor all thy piety nor Wit*
> *Shall lure it back cancel half a line,*
> *Nor all thy Tears wash out a Word of it*'

The moving finger is Karma. Another name for the Law of Karma in the world of phenomenon is the Law of Attraction. You attract whatever you put out. If you put out anger, you will attract anger; love attracts love; every action must have a reaction."

"Coming back to religion and how it has caused conflict throughout man's history. This is because the priests – so called men of god—are not really interested in you. They want to make you blind believers; they mislead you with their notions of God and the paths to God. Remember that all mental constructs of Paramatma are inadequate. Something Infinite cannot be conceived with infinitesimal minds and intellects. Tread carefully with those who ask you to believe that **their** religion alone is your savior; worse still those who say their religion is the only way to salvation; worst of all those who preach that the killing people of other faiths leads to freedom. There is no substitute for your own experience. When you search within sincerely you will slowly but surely discover the truth of yourself."

"Coming to the question of human conflicts, let me ask you: does a pea in a pod fight with other peas? Do leaves on a tree quarrel with other leaves? Does a big tree fight with a small one? I am sure you'll say that these beings are insentient; they have no sense of the 'I' or the Ego. Then, isn't the Ego the one that deludes humans to think they are different from others; from their origins; from the Paramatman? The Ego itself is a projection of the mind. Like all other experiences, the Ego is also a mental event. The great Upanishad's speak of the Sages who see the ONE in ALL and ALL in the ONE."

"The Tree of Life is complex; its roots come from beyond time and space, incomprehensible, but eternal. Its extent is infinite; its leaves, infinite branches represent supreme knowledge, human tendencies and actions. The secret to a purposeful life is the realization that you and the Paramatman are One, because THAT is ALL. All actions in your worldly roles perform with your mind and intellect established in the ALL. See all your mind events are revealed because of the all pervading light of consciousness. Sadness or joy or pain is simply a mind event. Deal with it factually; it is not YOU. You will know conflict neither from within nor from without; your life becomes a paean to the Infinite; you become the Infinite by which I mean that, you ascend to a higher plane of consciousness beyond that of your Body, Mind and Intellect, and your 'I' ness. You would have transcended your Ego. When the 'I' no longer holds you in its grip, you awaken in the Supreme Consciousness or Pure Existence which is Paramatman. You are free even within your mortal bodily existence."

I was humbled. Baghavan had given me a lesson in spirituality in 20 minutes without mentioning any religion by name, without naming any forms or names of deities that we worship as God.

Baghavan looked at this terrestrial watch. He said, "See what you have done. You have delayed my errands for Rukmini and Satyabhama. I hope they will not be angry when I return to them."

My God, I thought and laughed. Even Baghavan is afraid of female wrath.

I winced. I had forgotten that he could read my mind.

"Now, now Guru, it is not what you think? My consorts love me intensely; they only think of me; their minds are immersed in me so completely that they don't see anyone else; they are my true devotees. My love for them is as intense. I am their devotee, so where is the conflict?"

Go forth, "he added, "Live your life as a spiritual being with a human experience. You are That; That you are. Good bye."

ॐ ॐ ॐ

Guru had finished describing his fantastic dream. He had a contented smile on his face. He had obviously enjoyed his dream and its description to Atma.

Atma then remembered that both of them had gone to listen to a discourse on Vedanta the previous evening. No wonder, thought Atma. As usual, Guru's imagination had played its part. He had taken in the words of wisdom he had heard; he had internalized the wisdom of the ancients. He said, "That was a great dream my friend, I enjoyed it."

"Thank you," said Guru, "But, wait. After Baghavan left, I was woken up by a voice that shouted loudly in my ears: "Get up, get up. You have an exam today." I woke up with a jerk.

Atma looked at his watch. "Oh! my God," he said. "If we don't reach the examination hall in seven minutes, we will not be allowed inside."

Guru jumped excitedly, "Wait, wait," he said. "I forgot. Just before he wished me good bye, Baghavan also told me that today's question paper is going to be really tough."

He had said, "You and all your classmates will fail. That does not mean you shouldn't attend the exam. The professor who set the paper had a quarrel with his wife. In the anger that seethed within, he took it out in the question paper. He does not know the answer to his questions," he concluded.

Finally, said Guru, "Baghavan waved out to me and said, you see how conflicts at an individual level affect so many."

"Let's go." said Atma. "Sure," said Guru.

Shivu and Pinni

I beckoned to Shivu and Pinni to come close to where I was standing behind the front gate of my house. I did not know their names, but I had seen them on my morning's constitutional with our little Sydney Silky, Benjy. Each of them carried a large plastic bag in which they collected scraps of paper, pieces of cardboard, items of plastics, broken toys, banana peels and the like that were discarded by people in the surroundings and consigned to the area's large cement garbage bin. When they found something edible like a biscuit that had apparently fallen on the floor in one of the houses and was discarded as unfit to be eaten, they grabbed it and ate it with glee on their faces. I was distressed because they were so small and too young to be doing all this; they should have been savouring the wonders of childhood. The two made the rounds of our area to the cacophony of the many dogs at about 6:30 each day, before the municipality's garbage collection van came to empty the colony's overflowing garbage bins. Unfortunately, the stinking garbage collection vans overflowing as they went through the streets became in turn garbage distribution vans.

When I beckoned to the duo that day, they looked at me, wondering what I wanted from them. They came hesitantly and backed off when Benjy, not impressed by their scruffy appearances, barked his head off. I had to carry Benjy to pacify him and tell him that he should stop judging people by their appearances.

I asked them their names. The boy, about 10, said he was Shivu; the girl about 8 was Pinni. They were siblings. Poverty was written all over their skinny bodies. Pinni had limpid pools as her eyes, full of a child's wonder; the world waiting to be discovered. I asked them where they lived. They named a *Basti*[73] called Rapuram which I knew was just behind the railway station's shunting yard. When I heard that name, my mind quickly pictured the area; I had seen the place on several occasions from trains just before they steamed into the Secunderabad railway station coming from the west. Each time I came back from one of my visits by train, the sight of Rapuram hit me as a rude shock. I had often wondered, in passing, how terrible that in the midst of a bustling city, which boasts of so much wealth, we allow human beings to live in such places. Sometimes the train would stop right in front of the *Basti* waiting for the outer signal to allow the train to enter the station. It was then that I saw the narrow streets of Rapuram, shacks that hugged each other, children running around, naked or half dressed, women in salwar kameez or saris or loose-fitting night dresses and some children in school uniforms. I knew that some skilled workers like carpenters, masons and plumbers too resided in the area; our electrician, Anand lived there. This they did so mostly because of proximity to the areas where their services would be in demand. They were the middle class of Rapuram in the otherwise poor *Basti*. These people were also the respected citizens of Rapuram because they often helped the lesser of their brethren in times of difficulty, mainly financial. They were always addressed respectfully as 'Anna' (elder brother). I also knew that the trouble makers, whom we generalize and call *goondas*[74] also came from Rapuram. My knowledge of Rapuram, hitherto based on a cursory look at the place from a railway compartment soon became better, thanks to Shivu and Pinni.

I asked Shivu and Pinni if they lived with their parents. "No *Ayya garu*[75]," Shivu said. "They are in Vadamapalli." He said this with a certain pride as if Vadamapalli was a famous metropolis like Mumbai or Kolkatta; it probably was, in their innocent minds, as compared to Rapuram. I thought there was a tinge of home sickness when they named their village. I

[73] *Euphemism for a slum*
[74] *Trouble makers*
[75] *Ayya garu: Colloquial term in Telugu for 'Sir'*

found out later that Vadamapalli was a nondescript village in the extremely semi-arid areas of Mahbubnagar district. The children had no inhibitions or self-consciousness about their untidy looks or about their poverty. On the other hand, they seemed strangely contented. I saw so much of unspoilt human nature in them. I became curious; I wanted to know more about their lives.

First, I wanted to befriend them, so I opened the gate, and took them into the veranda, in spite of Benjy's loud protests. I asked them to sit on the lounge chairs and I occupied one opposite to theirs. They insisted that they would sit on the floor. I had to persuade them that it was fine with me if they sat on the chairs. They settled down. I went inside to fetch something that they could eat leaving Benjy with them. Since, I had allowed the two children inside, Benjy no longer saw the two as undesirable company. Unlike human beings, Benjy did not have rigid and unshakeable opinions of people; he had made quick adjustments in his mind. He ignored Shivu and went to Pinni with his tail wagging in merry abandon inviting her friendship. She had worn a faded pink polka-dotted frock, frayed at the ends and quite dirty. "Given the choice, dogs preferred females to males, however poorly dressed," I thought, and smiled to myself. Benjy had taught me this lesson when he always ignored my calls to him when he sat at the feet of Sita, my wife. Encouraged, that Benjy meant no harm, Pinni first stroked him gently and then made bold to carry him. They had become friends.

I came out with two paper plates of Idli's with coconut chutney that Sita had made for our breakfast and gave it to them. They were obviously surprised at the treat they saw in front of them. They attacked the idli's and then licked the remnants of chutney on the plate with a relish that I had seldom seen in human beings. I had seen such unabashed abandon only in Benjy when he was fed his favourite cereal; the world simply vanished for him in the few minutes when he was eating it and then he went off to lie down in the fullness of Nirvana experience, in his favourite corner. The sight of Shivu and Pinni relishing the Idli's warmed the cockles of my heart. When they had literally polished their paper plates, I was moved when Shivu looked at Pinni and asked, "Did you eat well?" Pinni smiled and nodded her head in reply. Having Idli's for breakfast had become such an ordinary experience for me, but here I saw how extraordinary the experience was for the two children.

While the children were eating, I asked myself, "What was my motivation to call them in and feed them? Was it pity? Was it idle curiosity or was it to connect with the two children as one human being with another?" The answer to my question was that it was all three, but my first interest was in connecting with them.

They got up to leave, but before they left, Shivu asked me in their native language, Telugu, for a broom stick. I asked him why he wanted it. He said he wanted to sweep the cemented front yard. I could see that he wanted to do this as an expression of gratitude for the food I had given them. I was touched by his sensibility. He had apparently learnt these graces from his parents, probably by example. I told him that it was alright and they could leave, but before they left, I asked them, "When did you come to the *Patnam (city)*?" Shivu replied, "Ayya, about one month ago." My next question was why they had come to the *Patnam* instead of remaining in the village. Shivu spoke for both of them. There was no *Pani* (work) for them in the village, so they were asked to go to the *Patnam* with their neighbour's family in search of work. I was not surprised. In fact, I had expected this answer, but had hoped that there was a different one.

I wondered, how long would it be before these two innocents would get spoiled by the city and the kind of company they would be exposed to in their *Basti*; how little can be done to prevent the migration of villagers to towns and the terrible lives that they led in the false promises of a city.

I asked Shivu, "What work do your parents do?"

"Ayya, both of them work for daily wages in the farms. For about 4 months in the year there is no work for them. We have 3 goats whose milk we sell and earn some money, but we need money to buy their feed in the dry season." The reality of their harsh lives was stated as a matter of fact; there was neither remorse nor judgement.

As they left, I also thought about those others who had come away from their villages, for whatever reason, and had become entrenched in city life. They would probably have come to terms with the reality that village life, in spite of all its difficulties, was not bad at all, but they had burnt their boats and so there was no way out except to bear their burdens. The realization that there are no rainbows except in the mind, must have occurred to them, I imagined. As I was thinking these thoughts, I wished fondly that the two, Shivu and Pinni, would return to their village and find their haven there. Could I do something about such a wish or should I even think of doing something about this was the next thought that crossed my mind. I decided that I would talk to Sita about this wish, but before doing so, I knew that unless she was involved and participated fully, the wish would remain mere wishful thinking. Sita was having an early bath and so she was not around to see the two children whom I had invited in.

The next day I had finished my constitutional a little earlier than usual. As a rule, I sat in the veranda to read the morning paper. That day, I went into an inner room which served me as a small study. When I heard the sudden cacophony of dogs, I knew that Shivu and Pinni were around in the colony and would soon come close to our home. Benjy had apparently smelt the children; his ears had pricked and he went out close to the gate. Pinni found Benjy and his welcoming tail at the gate, she opened it and had carried Benjy in her arms. The clang of the gate alerted Sita and she went to the gate when she realized that I was not sitting in the veranda. She saw Benjy in the arms of a scruffy girl and was alarmed. She jumped to the conclusion that the two had come to steal our Benjy. She shouted at them. Like two frightened pups they dropped Benjy and took to their heels. The neighbour lady came out when she heard Sita's shout.

Sita was still seething under her misconception that the two scruffily dressed children were about to steal Benjy. I came out after hearing Sita's shout and I realized what had happened. She had taken Benjy in her arms and scolded him. "What's the matter with you, have you lost your mind, becoming friends with all and sundry."

Benjy was barking back at Sita as if to tell her, "What's happened to you? They were not going to steal me. Can't you make out the difference between innocent children and a thief?" Angrily, she dropped Benjy to the ground. She and the neighbour lady, both paranoid about security or the lack of it in the area, exchanged words to the effect that things are getting worse day after day.

I waited for Sita to regain her composure. Fear of the loss of her dear Benjy had not yet left her. She asked me, "Where were you? Just now two street children tried to steal Benjy." I swallowed what she said quietly. She did not appreciate my silence mistaking it for indifference. I knew that anything said at that time would not help.

I generally had breakfast much earlier than Sita. That day, I waited for her at the breakfast table. I was seated opposite to her.

"What's the matter today," she asked, "so late for breakfast?" I told her that I wanted to talk to her.

"What about," She asked.

"It is about the two children who you thought wanted to steal Benjy," I said.

I then went on to relate my previous day's meeting with the two children, their simplicity, their innocence, their poverty and my fears about the loss of their innocence if they are allowed to continue to struggle in the harsh and impersonal city.

"This is nothing new, do we not see this all the time? What is it that we can do about these things?"

"You are right. What the government cannot do or has not been able to do, individuals like us can do precious little. At the same time, if all of us well-intentioned people do not take some initiative about children in our midst, of what use is all our education and wealth. Did not Gandhiji speak of villages as the soul of India? Should we turn a blind eye to the migration of villagers to cities? Should we perpetuate the mistaken notion that villagers have about a better life in the cities? Isn't it true that the influx of villagers who come to cities with false hopes are at the receiving end of all the ills of our cities? Haven't we seen how poverty, deprivation and sickness thanks to the city's pollution, have driven these city dwelling villagers to breaking point? We cannot do much for those villagers who have already burnt their boats and have become entrenched in cities. They cannot go back to their villages; they would probably be unwelcome there. But, why should we not think of doing something for two innocents like Shivu and Pinni?"

"Is that their names," she asked.

"Yes."

"So what's it you want to do."

"I want you to think. What's it that we can do, not me alone," I said.

She did not reply. I had hoped that my thoughts about doing something to put back the two in their village would have made her think. The meeting at the breakfast table ended on that note. I decided that I would wait for Shivu and Pinni the next day.

The cacophony of the dogs began at the usual time. Even before I could reach the front gate, Benjy was there. I smiled at the unspoken affection that he had developed for Pinni. The moment he saw Pinni, he barked for her attention. When they came close to our gate, they were wary. They saw me and became less anxious. "Namaste *Ayya*," they said warmly. I returned their warmth with a smile. Then they saw Sita who had just come out. They stepped back. Sita had not seen the two children carefully enough the previous day, blinded as she was that day by the thought that they had come to steal Benjy, but her curiosity was aroused after what I had told her at breakfast the previous day.

Sita looked at them. Open mouthed, she said, "My god, they are so small and thin."

I corrected her, "So undernourished," I said.

Sita had a soft corner for children. She had shown great initiative in helping our maid servant, Lakshmi's daughter, Ramya, to get a decent education. We had sponsored Ramya's education since her nursery days; she was now in the 9th class. Sita had also introduced Lakshmi and her husband to the need for small, but regular savings in a post office. Over the years the regular savings had grown to Rs 30,000. Lakshmi had become increasingly arrogant and demanding; she believed that Sita's gesture of helping her child and her family was somehow a right she enjoyed. One fine day, Lakshmi walked out on her on a flimsy excuse. Our support to the child would continue, we decided.

"Have you eaten anything this morning," Sita asked Shivu and Pinni.

The two shook their heads. "*Amma garu*, our first meal is always at noon," said Shivu.

Sita told me to bring them in. I did so and like the other day I seated them in the veranda. Benjy jumped onto Pinni's lap. Sita went in and brought a sandwich for each of them. Their eyes glowed. Like before they saw a feast; their eyes showed it. They gobbled up the sandwiches as if what they saw in front of them was a mirage and would vanish if they did not consume it quickly. The sight moved Sita. She went inside.

After they had eaten, Shivu called out, "*Amma garu*[76], can you give me a broom stick." Sita heard Shivu. She came out and looked at me. I told her that they had made a similar request the day before and that it was their way of returning the favour they saw in her offer of the food that they had just eaten. I told them that they need not clean the front porch; it would be cleaned later when the maid came.

They left with a warm, "*Dandam*[77] *Amma garu, dandam Ayya garu,*" on their famished lips.

I went back to my morning's newspaper. Like the previous day, I joined Sita at breakfast. She looked at me with an unasked question in her mind. The question, I knew would be about the two children she had met that morning.

I looked at her and said, "You know Sita, when I was reading today's paper, I found so many news items about wants and demands. For instance, a sub-caste wants, in fact, demands, more reservation, the corporation wants more jobs for keeping the city clean, the hospital wants more funds to provide better facilities, rich sugarcane farmers want more for their crop each year; oil companies want more prices; schools want more playgrounds and so on. We seem to be living in a society where 'Get-as-much-as-possible' seems to be the predominant motivation. This mentality seems to have percolated to all sections of society. I am reminded of Acharya Vinoba Bhave's observation when he saw so much greed, selfishness and self-seeking in the country. He had asked, 'Is this the same country which had produced the Bhagavad Geeta?' We see fewer examples of 'Give-as-much-as-you-can' or 'Give-back-something'. Don't you think so?"

In her characteristic, down-to-earth manner, she asked, "What's new about all this? What has this do to with the two children we saw today and what you spoke of yesterday? Don't beat about the bush."

"Okay, okay," I said.

---

[76] *Colloquial for 'Madam'*

[77] *My gratitude*

"My idea is that if we can empower these two children to becoming 'giving' citizens of their village, I believe their life would be better fulfilled and they would be making a contribution to their village. They would be examples that other children can follow."

Sita did not respond immediately. Again, out of her strong sense for the need to be practical and not be bamboozled by high-flying words, she asked, "Do you have any practical examples that we can copy?"

I said, "No, not that I know of."

"So, what do you want to do?" she asked.

"Before I spell out my ideas, I want you see to my ideas as a bold experiment in human development with us—you and me—as its prime movers and with the involvement of others wherever possible."

"Okay, let's hear your ideas," she said.

"I have a whole project plan, if you like, in my mind. The overarching goal of the project, the target being this generation of village children, is to empower them to give back to their village so it becomes a mutually supporting community, less and less dependent on doles; not a mere survival arena for its landed producers and landless dependents. I would like us to be the prime movers and coordinators. We will need the support of many agencies and individuals. Broadly speaking the project will: ensure continued survival earnings for the parents, availability of education for children, but with emphasis on a mix of vocational education and the three R's. The end all of such education should not be the mere passing of exams. It would also place great emphasis on value education that inculcates the spirit of giving back to their village as an important purpose of their lives. The idea is that when the children reach 21 or so, they become fully 'Giving'—contributing members of the village in a useful vocation, giving back to their village and nearby ones and earning enough to meet their needs. In this experiment as I call it, I know there will be many road blocks, pitfalls and detractors. We may fail. We may achieve small successes or none at all. We will never know if we do not try. If we can prove that a village can give back to its people as much or more when they give back to it, we would have demonstrated that the experiment was successful. If the Israeli's can show how their Kibitzes have transformed their lives, I don't see why India cannot do this."

Sita heard me patiently, but there were question marks on her face. She asked, "Aren't all the governmental schemes aimed at what you are talking of?"

"True, there are so many agencies and NGO's. But, what we see is there is little or no coordination, not enough participation of villagers, there is duplication and wastage of funds, corruption and so on. Even after so many years of independence, villages, in general, with rare exceptions, have benefitted only marginally. The more backward the village, the less impact there is from all the schemes. The rare exceptions have come about because of a few dedicated individuals and their ability to coordinate things."

I stopped a while and then added my final word, "Whether the village at large benefits or not, I would consider the mission successful if just Shivu and Pinni return to the village and seek their fulfilment there instead of getting stuck in the city and suffering in it."

Sita did not respond at first. I felt that what I had said did make her think. After a while she said, "I like your ideas, but it requires resources in money, human beings and management that we cannot on our own muster. I suggest that you talk to people whom you can influence; I will talk to my women's group."

"That will be great. I propose to develop our idea. I will speak with many of my friends who can bring to bear influence in this work." I said.

The following day, Shivu and Pinni appeared as usual. They did not have the large plastic bags on their shoulders. Instead, Shivu had a broom stick in his hand. I asked him, "What happened, why aren't you carrying your bags today?"

"Ayya, today the *Maistry* (contractor) who pays us is not there, whether we collect things or not, we will not get paid."

"How much does the Maistry pay you every day," I asked.

"Ayya, that depends on what we bring back. Sometimes we get Rs. 3, sometimes only Rs. 2."

There was no need for them to make their rounds that day, but they came because they had found that Sita and I had shown compassion for them.

"Come inside," I said.

Like the other day, I brought two sandwiches, one for each of them. Shivu's eyes moistened with tears that he fought hard to keep out. I could see that he did not want to speak. Pinni noticed her brother's condition. She nestled up to him. That was the trigger. Both of them started crying pitifully. I allowed them the freedom to let their emotions subside.

"Tell me what happened to make you cry," I asked.

Shivu, in a choked voice, blurted out that they had not eaten since the previous morning. The sight of the sandwiches had overwhelmed Shivu. I waited a moment and said, "You can eat now. You must be very hungry."

Sita had come out by then. She saw the uneaten sandwiches and looked at me. I shook my head. Sita asked, "Have your neighbours eaten since yesterday morning?"

"No *Amma garu.*"

She went inside and brought a loaf of bread, some butter, pickles and jam in a box. She packed these in a plastic bag and asked them to take it back and give it to their neighbours. "You can eat now," she said. The sandwiches were eaten solemnly.

On a sudden impulse, I told them, "I am going to Vadamapalli."

Sita looked at me and realized that I meant what I said. I really wanted to go their village.

The children heard the name of their village; their faces brightened. They could not hide their home sickness.

"When, *Ayya garu*," asked Shivu.

"Tomorrow."

"Is *Amma garu* going with you?"

"Yes, and Benjy" I said and looked at Sita.

Their faces fell. It was clear that their anchors in Rapuram were themselves leading precarious lives. They were struggling with their own battles to fight.

The two rose to leave. *Dandam Amma garu, dandam Ayya garu.*"

Shivu began cleaning the front yard with his broom stick. I allowed him to express his gratitude. Pinni was playing with Benjy.

After Shivu had finished cleaning the front yard, I went out, "Would you both like to come to Vadamapalli with us?" I asked.

Shivu, not quite believing my question, looked at me. Pinni went to Shivu with a plea in her eyes. He spoke only after he had subjected my question to its consequences.

"*Ayya*, my father will be angry if he sees us. Also we can go only when our neighbours from the village who brought us here go back."

"Of course," said Sita, "We will come and meet them."

Sita had taken the words out of my mouth.

"Do you know Anand the electrician who lives in Rapuram?" I asked.

"The man who looks after lights, *Ayya*?"

"Yes."

"Anand *anna* knows the place we stay."

Sita understood my plan.

I went inside and put Rs. 100 in an envelope and sealed it.

"Good. Here take this," I said, and gave Shivu the envelope. "Give this to your neighbour who brought you to the *patnam*. Tell him that we will come there this evening to talk to them."

The children left with some cheer on their faces, the packet in their hands, wondering why we were coming to see their village neighbour.

Sita, practical as ever said, "If nothing we will get to see their village and their parents. This in itself may be interesting and educative."

I called our electrician, Anand, and asked if he would come with us to Rapuram that evening. I parked my car some distance away and we walked to the place shown by Anand. Sure enough, we found an eager Shivu and Pinni waiting. As soon as they saw us, they ran inside and called out, "*Athamma*[78], they have come." The lady came out. After a few minutes the man of the house, Venkatayya, came out coughing violently. It was clear that he was unwell. I told him that we were very sad to see the two children struggling to collect things from the garbage for the small remuneration they earned. I explained to him that they were exposing themselves to disease when they searched garbage bins and even ate what was discarded. Without going into the details, I explained to them our plan to take the two children back to their village and provide for the family and to educate

---

[78]   *Aunty*

them and make them fit for them to earn a living in time to come. There was no need to talk beyond the basics.

The two looked at Anand. "Anna, what do you say?" the man asked. Anand told them about how we had helped our maid's family and daughter in her education and that it was safe and in the interest of the children that we should be allowed to take them to Vadamapalli. That settled, we told the children that they would be travelling with us to their village the next morning. The thought of going to their village, I saw, brought joy to their faces.

I told Sita, "Did you see how much their village means to them?" She just smiled.

I told Shivu and Pinni to pack their things and come to us as usual at 6-30 the next day.

Before returning home, I asked Anand about the work that Venkatayya was doing in the city. He worked as a mason's assistant for daily wages. In the village he was a daily wage earner like Shivu's father. Because he was weak and was not as productive, the mason paid only half the normal payment. He had to spend a considerable portion of his wages on medicines. He had not gone for work the previous two days and hence had not earned his wages. His life was precarious and out of sheer compassion, he had agreed to take along Shivu and Pinni when they came to the *Patnam*. He was given Rs. 200 to take care of expenses for Shivu and Pinni during their stay in the *Patnam*. He had already spent this amount on food and medicines. They expected to be here for 2 months. The site of Venkatayya and his condition was depressing to say the least. The *Maistry* had given Venkatayya and his family a shack in which all of them lived. No wonder, the two children were so keen to get back to their village.

On the way back from Rapuram, I told Sita. "I think we are doing the right thing by taking the children back to their village."

"True," she said, "But, my concern is, are we biting into something that we will find difficult to swallow."

"As long as you are with me and I am with you, the journey will be worth it. Let's enter into this experiment, heart and soul."

When we reached home, our son in the US called as he did every fortnight on his way to work. Sita did most of the talking. When it was my turn, I told him about the experiment we are about to launch. He was concerned, "Is mother with you on this foolhardy venture?" he asked.

"Of course she is, and contrary to your notion, we think about this experiment as exciting. I would not think of taking on such work without your mother's able and willing participation."

I could understand my son's concern. He did not want us to put ourselves out at this stage in our lives.

The matter was not discussed any further. Here was one detractor, concerned though he was for us; how many detractors we would meet, who were neither concerned about us or about the people whom we had hoped would benefit from the mission we wanted to embrace, I wondered.

I Google mapped to locate the direction to Vadamapalli that evening. I had a fairly good idea of the route to take. I didn't think the App on my mobile would recognize the interior roads to the village. The GPS on the mobile would probably not be helpful. I decided to take my digital and video cameras fully charged.

The next day, Sita got ready the food, snacks and water we would need to carry. She had made Idli's and coconut chutney with the children in mind. There was mild excitement in my mind, not knowing what to expect on the trip.

Benjy sensed that there was more activity and excitement in the home than usual. He went from Sita to me and back to her, sizing up the situation, occasionally barking for our attention. He did not want to be left out of the excitement. I did not hear the cacophony of the dogs that day. Shivu and Pinni were expected at 6:30. They did not turn up. Even at 7:30 they had not come. Sita and I gave up. "What an anticlimax to our ideas," I thought, with some sadness. I am sure my feelings were shared by Sita whose silence said more than words.

We did not say anything more about this to each other. We went about as if nothing had happened. In the back of my mind, I was unhappy that the grand experiment that I had conceived had fallen flat like a kite that refused to fly. Was this the same fate that many governmental schemes had suffered?

I called Anand to be told that he was out of station. I left word with his wife that he should call us on his return. Two days later, Anand called. I asked him to find out about Shivu and Pinni and why they had not come to us as arranged. He said he would do so. An hour later, he gave us the news that Venkatayya had fallen very sick the night we had seen him. He passed away peacefully in his sleep. His wife, her child and the duo of Shivu and Pinni had returned to Vadamapalli.

The Idli's remained un-eaten, to be discarded to the dust bin.

ఆ   ఆ   ఆ

A new day dawned. I saw Sita already up and brewing coffee. She looked at me and said, "Get ready quickly, we are going to Vadamapalli. We must write the second chapter of their story."

Ramaswamy, the Watchmaker

Ramaswamy, the watchmaker, sat behind his glass cube, mounted on a 24 inch square table; his eye piece jutting out of his left eye. The table had two drawers: one with an assortment of precision screw drivers, tweezers, screws, button cells, batteries, small gears and so on; the other drawer had wrist watches that customers had left for repair, and an assortment of small pocketbooks. He sat unobtrusively, in the verandah of a small shop selling peppermints, biscuits, ball point pens and cold drinks. I call Ramaswamy a watchmaker, because he did make watches—even the fancy ones— work after the owner had lost hope.

Take my own case. I had one of those first generation solar-powered watches, presented to me by my son some 15 years ago at the Sears Mall in New Jersey, from his first salary after graduate education in the US. I was proud of the watch; in fact, attached to it because of what it meant. One fine day, the watch stopped. I took it to the manufacturer's showroom. They said, "Sorry Sir. This model is outdated. Parts for this are no longer available."

Then I thought I would take it to the street-side watch repairer close to where I lived. Skeptically, I showed him my watch. He opened the back cover of the watch as deftly, I suppose, as a heart surgeon opens a diseased heart. He then pulled out one of the mini pocketbooks and gave it to me. "Sir," he said, "One small part is spoiled. The solar battery has to be changed. Please open the battery page Sir and read what it says Sir." I did as I was told and gave him the information he sought. He scribbled a note in his pocket notebook and told me that if I could wait for two or three days, he would have it working. He told me that I could leave the watch with him if I wanted to. Not willing to trust my watch to him, I said that I would come back after a few days.

It was when he was peering intently at the opened innards of my watch that I saw him closely. He had a blacker than black, kindly face, skin that was slippery smooth, and whiter than white teeth. He was dressed in a white collarless *jubba* and a spotlessly white dhoti. I also noticed on the back of his glass cube, the words scrawled with a felt pen in English, "Ramaswamy Wasch Sop." I smiled at the spellings, but now I knew that his name was Ramaswamy. In the few minutes he took to examine my watch, two customers came for repairs. One of them was telling the other about how Ramaswamy had repaired an old Swiss Tissot watch that his uncle had given him as a legacy before he died.

I went back after 3 days. He smiled and said, "Sir your watch can be repaired." I put the watch in his hand. While I sat on a stool next to his table, he worked on my watch with his deft hands. Soon, he showed it to me. My skepticism about this simple man vanished. My watch had woken up from its coma. I looked up and smiled. I asked him, how much I should pay. He said, "Sir, spare part 80 rupees, new battery 35 rupees, bus 14 rupees, my charge 15 rupees; 6 months guarantee." He said this so spontaneously that I didn't think twice. I willingly parted with the cash, but with a new respect for this simple soul.

One day I was walking down the Main Street close to where I live. I saw Ramaswamy leading a beggar by his hand. The beggar was disgustingly unkempt; he was either drunk or mentally challenged; his gait was unsteady and, therefore, he needed to be held by hand. I wondered where Ramaswamy was taking him. I saw them stop in front of the Main Street doctor's clinic; they stood outside. I guessed that Ramaswamy did not want the beggar to sit in the doctor's ante-chamber because the other patients would not like an unkempt chap sitting there. My curiosity was aroused and I decided to wait there to see what would happen next. When their turn in the queue came, he led the beggar into the doctor's chamber and spoke to him in Tamil. I understood enough to learn that a stray dog had bitten the beggar; Ramaswamy had found him fallen on the pavement in a drunken stupor. I heard the doctor telling Ramaswamy that the beggar needed anti-rabies injections; he wrote a prescription and asked Ramaswamy to come back with 6 vials of the injection. My curiosity further aroused, I waited for them to come back; they returned 10 minutes later with the injections. Ramaswamy obviously had paid for them. He led the beggar once again to the doctor's chambers. The doctor injected the beggar, dressed his wound, and asked him to come back the next day at the same time. Ramaswamy must have attempted to pay the doctor; I heard the doctor tell him that he could not accept money from Ramaswamy. This further increased my curiosity about Ramaswamy. I went away and decided that I would come back and talk to the doctor when he was free.

Two days later, I saw no one sitting in the doctor's ante-chamber. I walked into the doctor's chamber, wished him, and asked his permission to talk about Ramaswamy. "You mean our watch repairer?" He asked.

"Yes," I said. "The other day I heard you telling him that you could not accept any money from him for treating the drunken beggar, I was curious and I wanted to know why you refused your fee from Ramaswamy."

"Before I answer that question," the doctor said, "Let me ask you a question. Tell me what goes on in your mind when you see a beggar?"

I did not answer immediately. A few seconds later, I tentatively said, "I would feel pity, I suppose" I said.

"What about disgust or anger?" asked the doctor. I remembered my own feeling of repulsion when I saw the unkempt, drunken, dog-bitten beggar the other day. "True, sometimes, I have felt disgust," I replied.

"Well," continued the doctor. "If you feel pity, you might drop a coin or two in the beggar's bowl. If you feel disgust, you will probably walk away as fast as possible. If you dropped a coin in his bowl, the memory of the beggar lasts for a few hours at most; soon the beggar becomes a faceless, nameless being in your memory. Not so with Ramaswamy. He feels neither pity nor disgust; he truly empathizes with them. He feels their emotional and physical pains. He knows the background of the beggars and why they were forced into beggary. He never helps beggars without knowing their background. Many are the beggars whom he has rehabilitated patiently." The doctor paused. My face must have shown complete amazement or total disbelief.

The doctor continued, "Let me tell you how this most unlikely human being has brought a change in my attitude. I had a man servant named Venkata three years ago. He was a good fellow, sincere, honest and hard working. I paid him well. One day, I saw him pocketing my wife's wallet while he was cleaning the house. I caught him red-handed and called the police. Venkata's entreaties and his efforts to tell me about his problems fell on my deaf ears. I was full of myself. "Why should I care for this man whom I paid well," I thought. The Police took him into custody and after that I couldn't care less what happened to him. Apparently, the police battered him black and blue and put him in custody for some time without any trial. When they threw him out of the lockup, he was emotionally and physically shattered, unfit for any work; he had lost faith in himself; he lost all meaning to his life. He found his way to the territory familiar to him near our house. It was Ramaswamy who recognized him and saw his pitiable condition. Ramaswamy took him to his place, fed him, and brought him some fresh clothes to wear. In his own intuitive ways, Ramaswamy made Venkata feel that he was not alone in the world. A few days later, when Venkata had recovered his composure, Ramaswamy asked him what had driven him to steal. Venkata was apparently stressed because his sister's husband, a drunkard, had stolen all the money that Venkata had earned and run away. The sister had apparently exaggerated her misplaced anxiety that they would have nothing to eat after one or two days. Venkata's sister was pregnant. In his concern for his sister, in sheer desperation that her nutrition was vital, he stole the wallet. His salary would not be available until two weeks later. He had already taken an advance on his salary and he felt delicate to ask for help again."

"My wife and I had implicit faith in him," the Doctor continued "He had never stolen trinkets, gold ornaments, cash, or handbags that we left carelessly around. If I had some sense in me, I would not have reacted so impulsively. I would have sat him down to find out why an apparently honest man tried to steal. Once I knew, I could probably have helped him. But, no. Most of us better off people are unthinking. Venkata slowly drew strength under the care of Ramaswamy, who got him a job in another locality. But that is not the end of my story."

"One day, Ramaswamy came to my house accompanied by Venkata. I was surprised. I asked Ramaswamy irately, "Why did you bring this rascal here?" Very calmly, Ramaswamy told me the story of what had happened to Venkata after the police took him and how Venkata had fallen into an emotional ditch that denied him any dignity and self-respect. Ramaswamy did not say anything about his own efforts to rehabilitate Venkata. The fact that Venkata was brought by Ramaswamy was enough for me to know that but for his efforts, Venkata might have become another beggar or recluse or thief. After hearing the story, I felt ashamed that I had been the cause of so much agony for Venkata. I had been impulsive. Like an immature child, I reacted to the event; instead, I should have responded like a mature human being. Ramaswamy must have seen my disturbed face."

"He spoke to me, "Sir, you did right by reporting the theft, but our society has no empathy. If you had not reported the theft, Venkata would probably have continued thieving. On the other side, the police show no human feelings; they treat human beings worse than animals. Venkata was in no position to work after his release. Should not the police have done something about this before releasing him?"

"I took some time to answer his question. "Yes," I said without elaborating my confused feelings. Here was an unlettered man, I thought to myself, who has more humanity in him than I exhibited in my educated arrogance. Ramaswamy continued, "If you see the Beggar's Home that the Corporation has built and where beggars are taken fitfully and forcibly to please some politician, you will be shocked. They are ill-treated there. It is understandable that the beggars run away from there."

"I had a feeling that Ramaswamy had come that day with Venkata to subtly, unobtrusively teach me a valuable lesson on human nature, the rights of a human being, however poor, however uneducated." The Doctor stopped to collect his thoughts. He continued, "I should have listened patiently to him before making hasty judgements; some patience and compassion on my part could have brought out my own innate goodness. Instead, my Ego had made me react. Just before they left, Venkata bent down to touch my feet and placed my wife's wallet on it. I wanted to hide my face in shame. The wallet contained about fifteen rupees and a few coins; he had not used the cash in it at all.""

"After Ramaswamy and Venkata had left, I introspected. As a doctor, I asked myself, "How much empathy have I shown with my patients?" I felt ashamed that I was sometimes arrogant and impatient with the poor patients. I looked at their faces and judged them by the clothes they wore. As a doctor, I should have inculcated great patience and understanding. Ramaswamy had shown me how a simple soul like him could feel for the less privileged. I wanted to make up for my past mistakes; I also wanted to help Ramaswamy in whatever way I could in his humble efforts to heal the wounds of the poor. So, whenever he needs me, I am there; I think of him when I see a haggard face, burdened by worries. Just this one thing alone I believe has made me a better person."

The doctor had not finished his story. "There is another little known facet of Ramaswamy, which I came to know only later. One day, when he brought a reasonably able-bodied beggar woman to my clinic, I treated her. I asked Ramaswamy why she had become a beggar instead of seeking suitable employment. Ramaswamy then told me her story. As a woman recently widowed, some men had abused her in the village; the men were not punished. Instead she was thrown out of the village. She begged her way to the city. When she joined a group of beggars at a temple, they directed her to meet Ramaswamy. The trauma of what she had experienced had devastated her. She had lost the will to live. Ramaswamy took charge of her. He then told me that with the kind help of an elderly seamstress, he was teaching her simple tailoring work. Later, I found out that she is a seamstress in a tailor's shop on Market Street. You will be surprised to know that the simple, less-educated folk whom you and I take for granted are Ramasawmy's greatest allies; not educated, arrogant people like you and me. The empathy that the poor have for their brethren is what sustains many of them from falling into dire straits. Government schemes for rehabilitating beggars unfortunately do not have the empathy required; they are cold and impersonal.

The doctor continued, "The poor are the true heroes of modern India, not the CEOs of companies who draw fat salaries, nor the secretaries and babus who lord it over the poor. Neither you nor I do anything for the poor. If each one of us could do a little more than just paying our maid servants and drivers, we would be doing them so much good. But tell me, do we give any thoughts to this?"

The doctor's story moved me; a few days later I went to Ramaswamy. He greeted me warmly and asked if my watch was fine. I told him that I had come just to talk to him. "Ramaswamy," I told him, "I have heard so much about your silent work for the beggars and the poor, allow me to help you. Whenever you need anything, please ask me."

Ramaswamy was touched, "Sir," he said, "your words come from God. I am blessed that we have so many good souls here. I shall seek your help when needed, Sir."

My curiosity about this simple man and what had prompted him to take interest in beggars provoked me to ask, "Ramaswamy, why have you chosen to help beggars?" He replied, "Sir, I came from a family of beggars. One day, a watch repairer like me, saw me standing beside my elderly grandfather, begging close to his shop. I was about 12 years old and quite able bodied. He called me to his side and said, "Would you like to learn how to repair watches like these?" and held up a watch for me to see. I had seen so many school children with wrist watches and my dream was to get one for myself. I eagerly shook my head, showing my interest. He called my grandfather and asked him, "How much do you and this boy earn each day as beggars?" My grandfather replied that what they earned varied from 15 to 25 rupees a day from 9 in the morning till 6 in the evening. He asked him to leave the boy with him to learn the watch repair business and do odd jobs like fetching things and minding his shop when he had to go away for parts. He said, he would pay me 8 rupees per day. My grandfather agreed and that's how I learnt watch repair work. I can never thank the man–his name was Ramaswamy–enough for his kindness. He is no more now. That's why I have named my shop after his name. Now people call me by that name. I thought I should do something for the very same beggars whose plight I had seen as a boy."

I was moved by Ramaswamy's story. Here again, I thought, was another example of Ramaswamy's self-effacing nature. I recalled the doctor's words. He had said, "People like Ramaswamy are true, unsung heroes. What he had done for beggars was immeasurably more than what all of us have done by the mere tossing of a few coins into their begging bowls."

I suddenly remembered the unkempt, dog-bitten beggar whom Ramaswamy had taken to the doctor for treatment. I asked him, "What happened to the beggar who was bitten by a dog. I saw you take him to the doctor. Where is he now?"

Ramaswamy got up from his work.

"Please come with me Sir," he said, and led me to a shop where a young man was operating a copier. "This is the man Sir," he said, pointing to him from a distance. I admired Ramaswamy's humility and his keen sensitivities; he did not want to embarrass the young man. There was no mention of how the young man was rehabilitated; there was no need to. I became a visitor to his "Wasch Sop" whenever I could. It was like a pilgrimage to see him. He asked me for help from time to time. I gave as much as I could to the small causes he espoused, in both time and money.

Once he was hauled to the police station. The police suspected a beggar of a crime. At the police station, the beggar repeatedly denied any role in the crime, in spite of being battered. One of the constables suggested that Ramaswamy, the watchmaker, should be called to the police station. He was a mentor to many beggars; he could persuade the suspected beggar to tell the truth. Ramaswamy knew the beggar and his antecedents, and vouched for the innocence of the beggar. He also knew that the beggar had cancer and would die in 3 months. The police refused to believe him; they suspected Ramaswamy of abetting the beggar. They resorted to merciless beating till Ramaswamy passed out. When he regained consciousness, he asked a policeman to call me for his assistance. I went as quickly as I could. I was shocked to see Ramaswamy's condition. As a lawyer, I had earlier occasions to deal with the police station. I threatened the inspector with dire consequences and took Ramaswamy home. The Main Street doctor came home and treated Ramaswamy's wounds. My wife and I convinced Ramaswamy to stay with us for a few days, so that he could recoup. A few days later, he looked better. He was keen to get back to his work; he said: "Sir, my customers will be waiting for the repairs I promised. I should get back." We allowed him to leave; his eyes filled with tears of gratitude for the small favour that we had done him.

Some months later, our house maid came home weeping. When my wife asked her what the matter was, she cried out loudly, "Anna died half-an-hour ago. I want to go to his funeral." My wife did not understand.

"Where was Anna," she asked.

"Madam, I am talking about Ramaswamy the watch repairer. He died in his shop," she said.

I rushed out into the street where Anna had his shop. The news of his passing away spread rapidly in our locality. A crowd of beggars, shopkeepers in the Main Street, and former customers had already gathered; the doctor was there. This was the first time I saw so many people weeping for someone who was in no way related to them. Ramaswamy had touched their hearts at some time or the other. One of them had brought a white bed sheet, in which they had wrapped his mortal remains. A priest from a nearby temple came over and recited prayers for peace of the departed soul. A spontaneous drive was launched to contribute money to pay for his last journey. The funeral procession was long; it was silent; it was somber. I felt I had lost a little of myself with the final departure of Ramaswamy.

A few days later, Venkata came to my place. He said, "Sir, a month ago, Anna gave me a key to his house and wanted me to take you and the doctor to his house after his death. I cried at the thought that he would die one day. I never expected that this would happen so soon. He told me that he was leaving a few things and that both of you would know what to do." The doctor and I went to his house, a humble shed with an asbestos roof. There were two pairs of Jubbas, three Dhotis; a sealed envelope with a letter in it. I opened the envelope, pulled out the letter and gave it to the doctor. It was clear that he had asked someone to write it in Tamil for him.

The doctor's eyes filled with tears as he read the letter. In a choked voice, he told Venkata, "There is a gunny bag under his bed. Pull out the bag. Ramaswamy has left something there." What came out of the bag was a large envelope with notes of various denominations, payments for the repairs he had done.

There was a request in the letter that the money should be used for the medical expenses of beggars.

When you see a watch repairer behind his glass cube, spare a thought for him. He could be a re-incarnation of Ramaswamy, the saint with a heart of gold.

Accident's Child

Rahul was not unfamiliar with accidents; he was accident's child. As an infant, he was found alone, close to the banks of the river Mandakini, crying loudly, not knowing what had happened to the hand that rocked him to sleep and fed him her milk. His cries had alerted rescue workers to the shack devastated by the flash floods. His mother had apparently sacrificed her life to protect the child from the fury of the rushing waters; she had bound her baby to a pillar with a piece of her sari, hoping that the pillar would not collapse. Apparently the mother and presumably the father were both washed away, nobody knows where, given up for dead among the many that perished that day. They were all pilgrims on their way to Badrinath to seek the grace and blessings of the un-manifested when the floods occurred.

The baby was taken to Almora, the headquarters of the religious order of the monks that had rescued Rahul and many others during those floods. There, the baby was handed over to the Children's Home, a sanctuary for uncared children and orphans run by the monks. The monks gave the the child its name, Rahul. He grew up in the austere surroundings of the Children's Home. His school education was begun in the school run by the nuns and monks of the order.

As a 5-year old school boy, he had seen his classmates brought to school and later picked up by mothers or fathers every day, while he waited for one or other orderly from the Children's Home to accompany him back to the Home. He noticed the eagerness with which his classmates waited for a parent to come. The love that he saw on the faces of his classmates and on parents when they met, caressed or kissed their child prompted him one day to ask a monk, "Guruji, where are my father and mother? Why do they not come here to see me? When will I be able to see them?"

These were questions asked by other orphan children at one time or other. The monk did not answer the question directly, as the boy was too young to understand the meaning of death. Instead, he pointed to one of the orphans and said, "See, there are many others whose parents are not here, and so we act as father and mother to all such children."

The answer did not satisfy Rahul. He allowed the un-answered question to remain a dormant shoot in the soil of his mind; it sprouted whenever he felt that he was alone and loveless. It was only when he was 10 years old that he understood from an older boy, who had seen his parents die, that his parents too were probably not alive. The realization of this truth was traumatic, as was the understanding that such a thing happened to some children and not to others.

Children, 12 years and over, were introduced to the universal values of Hindu philosophy till they left the children's home. The Upanashadic mode of teaching was used, which consisted of talking to children, questioning them, expanding on the values through parables, and encouraging them to question their own experience to see if some of the values taught made sense to them. Initially, children were baffled; they often wondered how what they were being taught was relevant to their lives. Gradually, the children became more receptive, and there was evidence that new doors of thought had opened for them. The monks knew that the seeds of thought and ideas they had planted would one day bear fruit.

Only in his teens did he learn that the apparent injustice to him of losing his parents when he was still a child was explained in the Hindu religion as the result of his past life's Karma. He questioned a senior monk about this.

"Guruji," he asked. "How is it that God treats different people differently? Some are born rich, some poor, while some children like me lose their parents at an early age. You have told us that we are all God's children and He treats us alike. I see contradictions in what you have told us and what I actually see."

"My child," said the monk, "I appreciate your thoughts and observations. True, there are many contradictions in the world. Let me explain this as simply and directly as possible. To do so, I must first explain to you the Karma theory, which has been an important part of the Hindu religion and culture. By karma is meant the right and wrong in actions which we all perform. Any intentional action, mental, verbal, or physical is regarded as Karma. All good and bad actions constitute karma. We believe that all of us are born according to our accumulated karmas over several previous lives. These determine the circumstances of our birth and the characteristics of our mind and body. What you sow; so you reap, is what the law of Karma tells us. It does not mean, however, that one does not have the choice of improving one's conditions by good deeds and pure living. Otherwise, a thief will always be a thief and a rich man always rich. In the working of karma, one's attitude of mind is most important. Take, for example, the case of a surgeon. He may, out of the noble intention of curing a patient's illness, cut open his stomach to remove a tumor and this may lead to death in some cases. In this case, no bad karma accrues as the intention was noble. No one can prove or disprove the theory of Karma and rebirth, or that events in the lives of all of us are determined by our past karmas. The theory of Karma is neither final nor fatal. Remember that all our lives are subject to two forces, **one**: the fruits of good or bad karmas, and **two**: our free will to evolve into better human beings. Each of us has free will to do good acts; all such acts, however small, are bound to have good results. Instead of lamenting about our conditions, we should accept what we cannot control and look forward to doing whatever good we are capable of. Remember your tomorrows in this life will be determined by what you do every single day. This is the teaching for all human beings that our great religion offers. You are a bright child. I can see that there is good for you in the future. Believe in yourself."

Rahul was a quiet child; introspective, compassionate of physically challenged children, and helpful to the monks in their chores. As a student he was diligent and neat, and did well in his exams. The monks saw these intrinsic qualities and encouraged him. Rahul, it seemed, was particularly influenced; he made up his mind that he would devote a part of each day in being of service to others. He spontaneously offered his help to the monks when school work was done. The maturity and consideration that he showed beyond his years was a thing of joy for the monks and other workers in the Home. He had set a wonderful example to other children.

The day that Rahul was ready to leave the Children's Home was an emotional one. He was called early that day to the Head Monk's room.

The monk said, "Son, your journey through life, which began here 17 years ago in the Children's Home, is now poised for change. You will go into the world outside and seek your future. We believe that we have given you the strength to face up to the challenges that life will throw at you. Believe that you are the captain of the ship of your life; the dedication that you have shown to act in the best interest of others and yourself will carry you forward. Remember, your actions should uplift you. Before doing something, question yourself about it; seek answers within your mind and intellect; do what it tells you to do fearlessly."

The monk stopped a while as he looked intently at Rahul, who said, "Yes, Guruji. I shall do my best."

The monk smiled. "You will always remain our child, whether you are physically with us or not. Feel free to write to us or visit us whenever you wish. We will always be here to help you."

The monk had not finished. "Son, you have the right to know about your origins and how you came to the Children's Home. The Home gets its inmates in all manner of strange ways. Some children are left at our gates, we don't know by whom; some are left by parents who are not able to take care of their child; some are brought by policemen; some are left to die in the streets, until some passerby notices them and brings them to us. Some children, like you, are found in places devastated by nature. In such cases, if we are the rescuers, we make all effort to trace the parents of the child. We collect as much evidence as we can find at the rescue site to help us trace a child's parents. Sometimes we succeed; many times we fail. In your case, we found a piece of cloth tied to you in a shack, in a village close to the river, Mandakini." The monk stopped and went to a cupboard full of neatly labeled boxes. After a while, he picked out one of these. It had a date and name on it.

"One of our monks found this," he said, and showed Rahul a piece of cloth, which was in all probability part of a sari, going by the pattern of a border on it. "Your mother had bound this cloth around you and to a pillar when you were found. Your mother must have done this in a moment of desperation and in the hope that you would be saved from the flash floods that day by this piece of cloth and by divine grace. We used this evidence to try and locate your mother after the floods had receded, but did not succeed. Your mother, no doubt, had made the supreme sacrifice. If she had instead tried to flee the floods with you in her arms, you too would not have probably lived to see another day. This piece of cloth is really a testament of your mother's love for you. Keep it. Cherish it."

The monk stopped, overwhelmed at what he had said. Rahul, who sat immobile till then, saw the cloth, touched it with reverence, and then tears flooded his eyes. The monk allowed Rahul's emotion to spend itself. "Now, my son, go ahead into the future with faith in yourself."

After his schooling, Rahul was sponsored by the Home to enter a junior college in Nainital, where he did his 11th and 12th classes. Three years later, he earned his law degree, thanks to the benevolence of donors whom the monks encouraged to support him. In the campus interview that took place, a Delhi law firm offered Rahul the position of a junior lawyer. His diligence and his application had earned him a good name. After two years with the law firm, he started practicing on his own.

In Delhi, Rahul found a guest house for unmarried working men, run by an elderly couple. This he now made his home. One day, Rahul switched on his transistor radio, as was his habit, during his morning shave.

"There are no accidents in life; everything that happens, does so for a reason," said the voice on the radio. The words made an impression. The voice continued. "Life is a cascade of experiences. Man accumulates one experience after another from womb to tomb. These take place in both states: waking and dreaming; only in deep dreamless sleep, as in death, there is no experience. All experience is witnessed in the mind. Some experiences make a lasting impression; others just happen and vanish into the dim corridors of memory. What we call accident is an experience of a different kind; only it leaves a deep impression in the mind. Accidents happen for a reason. These are not the acts of a vindictive God; they are meant for all of us to see a higher force in our lives. They are meant to teach us to rise above our little selves. The brave and the bold are those who rise above their circumstances and accomplish great things for the world and themselves."

The radio talk was inspiring. It reminded him of the words of the head monk in the children's home. But, Rahul had work to do. He was to present his arguments before the District Magistrate that morning. He quickly finished his shave, bathed and got ready for the day ahead.

Rahul made his way on his two-wheeler to the Magistrate's court. He pondered over the brief he had prepared for arguments that day, confident that he had all the facts and figures in his head. He was conscious of being on the street and of the blind corner ahead, and he slowed down. Another two-wheeler turned from the other side of the blind corner at some speed and rammed into his two-wheeler head-on. Both the riders fell down. Luckily, both had worn helmets. Rahul quickly recovered from the shock, stood up and lifted his two-wheeler to its upright position. Protected by his lawyer's coat, he did not have any outward injuries.

The other rider was a young woman. She was conscious, but in shock. Her vehicle had taken the brunt of the impact. Passers-by rushed to her aid, as the two-wheeler had fallen on her leg. They saw bruises on her leg. The young woman was clearly at fault; she had turned the blind corner at high speed. Fortunately, the injuries she sustained were not deep.

This was no time for recriminations, thought Rahul. He went to her and offered to take her to a nearby hospital. Still quite dazed, she accepted the offer. It was getting late for his court appointment, so he saw that she was being attended to in the hospital and left, after giving her his phone number.

Once in the court's premises, Rahul forgot about the accident and went about his work normally. The din of the courts helped him to forget the accident. Back in his room that evening, the accident played back in his mind, as did the radio talk that he heard that morning. Well, if this accident was meant to happen, what indeed was the reason why it happened, he pondered; what purpose did it serve, other than giving him a lesson to be even more careful on the roads. Perhaps the reason why the accident took place will reveal itself in time, he thought, and turned his attention to a book he was reading. But his mind brought him back to the accident. The young lady who was involved in the accident had not even bothered to call him and thank him for taking her to the hospital.

The selfless service of monks, which he had seen in the Children's Home where he grew up, had made a lasting impression on Rahul. He wanted to do his bit for the disadvantaged, as the monks had done so selflessly. He decided that every Sunday, he would visit an orphanage or an old-age home and offer his services. He decided that he would go to a different one each week. This became a routine in his life. During these visits, he made friends with men and women who served in these homes. He helped in the kitchen, in washing clothes, sweeping the floors, walking with, and talking to, the elderly. At the end of each Sunday, he felt great peace and a sense of renewal of himself. In one of the Children's Homes, three years after Rahul began to do this service, a young woman came up to him and asked: "Do you remember me?"

Rahul looked at her and said, "I am sorry, I don't think we have met." The woman then reminded him of the two-wheeler accident and how he had taken her to the hospital.

"Oh yes, I remember now," said Rahul. "What are you doing here?" he asked.

"My mother and I come to this place on this day of every year as volunteers," she said. "This was the day my mother lost her son, my elder brother, years ago in a flood. I was not yet born when the tragedy occurred."

Despite his normal tendency not to delve into the lives of others, the word flood triggered Rahul's curiosity.

"Can I see your mother? I lost my mother to a flood many years ago."

The young lady then took him to see her mother, who was helping in the kitchen, and told her that Rahul was also a volunteer in the home. He had lost his mother in a flood when he was an infant.

Tears came to the mother's eyes, "Beta," she said, "Do you know where the flood took place?"

Rahul said, "Maaji, I was still a child. I was rescued by monks. I was later told that the flood happened near the river Mandakini. The only link with my mother is a piece of cloth that my mother had bound me with to a pillar when the floods came. The monks searched for my parents unsuccessfully, using the piece of cloth as evidence. They don't know if my parents survived."

"My God, what you tell me is too much of a coincidence. I too had tied my child to a pillar with a piece of my sari, torn in a hurry before the waters of the river closed-in on us. My husband and I were carried away by the rushing waters; the next thing we both remember is that we were in a hospital surrounded by nurses. I can never forget my fevered cries for my child."

The three fell silent. Both Rahul and the young woman's mother spoke almost simultaneously. Rahul allowed the lady to speak, "Can you show me the piece of cloth that you have?" she asked.

A Hole in the Heart

Many love affairs begin within organizations. A young man and a young woman are attracted to each other, no one knows why; the reasons could be many; we only know it happens. Mohan and Pamela were no exception to the phenomenon of attraction and love. Their relationship, however, had gone beyond the purely physical.

Mohan was the only son of a traditional family, who lived in their ancestral village, far from urban settlements. The village had a strong Khap *Panchayat*, a locally elected/selected governance group. The rules and traditions enforced by the *Panchayat* traced their origins to hundreds or even thousands of years, blindly followed, not necessarily by scriptural sanction, natural justice, or in the interest of the community of the village. Violations were punished ruthlessly. The village's remoteness insulated it from the influences of other villages and towns. The *Panchayat*, controlled by the rich upper caste, was an autocracy of the rich in the garb of democracy.

Mohan's father, a rich upper caste farmer, was a member of the *Panchayat*. As a child, Mohan had shown exceptional intelligence, a curiosity to know about natural phenomena that set him apart from children of his age, and a natural interest and capacity to learn new things. The father had not studied beyond the 6th class; his younger brother, also a farmer, who lived in another village 15 km away, had graduated from the college in the Taluk headquarters. This uncle of Mohan's had savoured the joys of reading good books. He brought many books for Mohan to read and discuss. Mohan's natural instincts and his readings aroused his sensitivities to the many inequities that he saw in the village; he questioned his parents and uncle about these. On one occasion, the *Panchayat* decreed that a young girl of 6 from a lower caste, who had dared to drink water from a well meant for the upper caste, should be kept under lock and key for 24 hours without food as punishment; this was a rule that had been enforced for many years. Mohan was touched by the tearful entreaties of the child's parents. Mohan, 10 years-old at that time, found the punishment inhuman and disproportionate to the alleged wrong. He questioned his father, "If I ate in a lower caste's house, will I also be punished? How is it that a great saint like Swami Vivekananda often stayed and ate in the lower caste shacks?" The answers he received for his many anguished questions were unconvincing, and the blind faith behind actions and attitudes that he saw around him rankled in his sensitive mind. Mohan resolved that he would find, one day, a way to change the attitudes of the village elders to a more humane one.

He was also appalled at the rampant sickness among the poor in the village and their suffering and lack of access to hygiene and medical care. In a rare moment of inner resolve, he told his father that he would like to study medicine and open a hospital in the village. His father, surprised at the intensity of his son's feeling, smiled and promised to do his best to bring about Mohan's wish.

A small primary school in the village and the college in the Taluk were unsuitable for Mohan's native intelligence to flourish. After his sixth year, his father sent him to the best schools and colleges in the capital of the state and then the university. He pursued a degree in medicine, followed by bio-medical research. An American professor, after reading a paper written by Mohan, considered that the work could be better pursued in the US because of better instrumentation and other facilities. Mohan was offered a fellowship that would enable further research and lead to a doctoral degree in the US. All this had kept him away from home and his parents for 17 years, except for brief visits during vacations. It was in the US that he met Pamela, a post-doctoral student in the same department. Right from the first day of their meeting, the inexplicable, magical attraction of the Yin and Yang in them seemed to have taken effect.

Pamela's parents had separated when she was 17 and just in college. The parents had their own windmills to battle; they left Pamela to live her life as she thought fit, knowing well that Pamela, an intelligent girl, mature beyond her years, was quite capable of taking decisions and acting in her best interest. She had kept in touch with her parents as dispassionately as would be the case between friends separated by time and distance; there were no emotional overtones in their relationships. Mohan, on the other hand, had the characteristic emotional attachment to his parents, like most Indians; education or lack of it did not matter.

Mohan and Pamela's relationship had flowered for 7 years in the US. Mohan knew that this relationship would result in a conflict between traditional values and the values of changed times, and would likely be a great disappointment to his mother. Mohan's commitment to Pamela was built on the strong bonds of love and respect for her; his desire to be of service to his countrymen was something that Pamela shared with him. The two committed themselves to making it happen. This was as much a binding force between them as their attraction for each other. The two decided that they would get married in India, with the concurrence of Mohan's parents.

They were now living together under the same roof. Neither Mohan nor Pamela was perturbed that their relationship did not have the social sanction of marriage. Except for the ritual marriage vows, they were as strongly committed to each other as any formally married couple. Mohan's parents were unaware of their relationship. Pamela had written to her parents about Mohan and their live-in relationship. Her parents took this news in their stride, as it was something not unusual in their culture. Her mother had written to her, almost as a gentle warning: "How long would such relationships last and become true commitments to each other is another matter. Your father and I have perhaps set a bad example for you."

Mohan had specialized in pediatric cardiac surgery, a specialization that was rare in India. Pamela had specialized in endocrinology. After they came to India, Mohan and Pamela easily found jobs in a corporate hospital in Delhi. Mohan's village was about 300 kilometers away. New roads to the village had been now laid; Mohan could drive down to the village in 6 hours. Connectivity to the other villages in the neighbourhood had improved. All the external signs of development were seen, but there was not a similar change in attitudes and social relationships.

Within 6 months of their work in India, both Mohan and Pamela had carved a niche for themselves in the hospital. More than their skills, it was the empathy that they brought to their work that marked both of them as skilled specialists and warm human beings. Pamela's understanding of childrens' minds and how they should be handled as patients made an impact among parents, creating a ripple effect; children who came to her for fresh or further treatment saw her more as an angel that cured, not as someone who hurt them.

Mohan waited for an opportune time to tell his parents about Pamela and his intention to marry her. He knew that his mother would have none of it, despite the fact that she would likely not find anyone in the village or close by who would be a suitable bride for her brilliant son. There had been the occasional proposal from parents of girls, far and near, but none that Mohan's mother approved.

Mohan had not forgotten his childhood dream of building a hospital in his village. He got the architect that had built the hospital where he worked to visit the village and suggest the land area needed for a 50-bed hospital. The architect and Mohan worked on a detailed plan for the hospital and estimates of costs of building, equipment, furniture and a training centre for nurses to be drawn from the women of the village.

On a visit to the village after the plans were drawn up, Mohan reminded his father of his long-felt desire to build a hospital in the village and showed him the plans. They then went together to the Sarpanch to discuss the proposal. The politics of the village had changed. The previous Sarpanch was a rich upper caste farmer. After his death, a young educated lower caste small farmer was elected as the Sarpanch, thanks to the increased awareness that better education had brought about, as well as the awareness that the print and electronic media had provided, in addition to the increased support that they had received from politicians eager to expand their vote base.

Mohan was happy to see that the less privileged classes in the village had acquired more voice in matters of governance of the village. The new Sarpanch was enthusiastic about Mohan's proposal to build a hospital. He promised to get vacant government land allotted for the purpose. True to his promise, he went to the Deputy Commissioner in charge of the

District, whose advice was that he should meet the Health Minister. The State's legislative election was due in 6 months; this was the right time to strike, Mohan was told.

The Sarpanch and Mohan met the Health Minister. Mohan's qualifications, the Project Report prepared, the estimates of cost and the fact that Mohan was from the village clinched the issue. Land was allotted to the hospital quickly. The Health Minister then laid the foundation stone in a well orchestrated ceremony; all this was good for votes. The Minister promised to allocate funds for the hospital building. The Sarpanch knew that unless he pursued the matter as an election issue, nothing would come out of it. His frequent trips to the Capital city exposed him to the insincerity of politicians, the blatant sycophancy and the corruption that vitiated elections. The Sarpanch decided that he would also play their game. When he went to the State's capital, he wore the colours of the Minister's party, soon passing off as a dedicated worker. The more he was seen in and around party meetings as a self-important member, he knew that the better his purposes would be served. The Sarpanch became a consummate politician in his own right.

Regular visits to the State's capital by the Sapanch, his increased visibility and the apparent power he wielded over a section of the electorate, coupled with reminders that funds for the hospital should be released, paid off. The Minister announced an initial sum of 20 lakhs for the hospital project from his constituency funds. Here was the Sarpanch's opportunity to make money. The State Govt. appointed the contractor for the hospital; the Sarpanch would supervise the works. He called all the shots with the contractors appointed for the construction; he would get a 10% cut of the contract.

To the world at large, Mohan and Pamela were already man and wife; their closeness to each other was so obvious. They both felt that had they had kept their relationship a secret for longer than necessary. It was decided that the best thing for Mohan to do was to bring his parents to Delhi, so that they could meet Pamela. This way the parents could get to know the intensity of their relationship. He would then let them know that he and Pamela wanted to sanctify their relationship in a formal marriage, according to Indian customs. He knew that it would be an emotionally difficult task to convince his mother.

The parents came to Mohan's place. When they saw Pamela there, they were quite surprised. Mohan introduced her as Pam, his friend of many years since his stay in the US, and his colleague in the hospital. Her pleasant looks and gentle behavior won the parents over. Mohan allowed his parents to see for themselves the closeness of their relationship, mostly through unsaid words, but clearly demonstrated through the way they talked to each other, and looked at each other. Mohan had laid the groundwork.

After lunch, Mohan went on to say, as unequivocally as possible, "Mother, Pam and I have been with each other for many years. We love each other; we share common values. We want to get married in Indian customs with the concurrence and blessings of you and father."

The mother was initially stunned into silence. Then she said, "I knew there was something between the two of you. But you know our customs and traditions. It does not allow inter-caste marriages, much less marriage to a foreigner. Our relatives will shun us; the village *Panchayat* will banish you from the village; our lives will be almost like that of outcastes. Tell me, do you want us to suffer such a fate?"

Mohan allowed his mother to calm down. He then said, "I know that the *Panchayat* will do as you say. I know the traditions which have been followed for many years. I would like to ask if you truly believe that everything the *Panchayat* does is correct. When two human beings like each other and are willing to become partners for life, what right has the *Panchayat* to deny them the right to do so? Is there anything in the scriptures of our great religion which says that this is wrong? On the other hand, our scriptures talk of the oneness of all creation; are we not all the many manifestations of the One? Just because Pam was born in another country, does it make her less of a human being? What, I ask you, is more important: the love between two people and their willingness to seek their destiny together, or an old rule that inter-caste or inter-religious marriage is wrong? Should all of us become blind believers and succumb to these superstitions? Have we all not changed from what our forefathers believed and did?"

It was now clear to his parents that Mohan had made up his mind to marry Pamela. The father spoke, "Son, I can see that your education and your long stay abroad have changed your perspectives; unfortunately, this is not the case with villagers. If we allow free thought, there is fear that it will lead to difficulties in governance and community welfare in the village. The division of labour among castes has led to orderly growth and ease of governance. This was based on the natural capacities of the body, mind, intellect and ancestral traditions for the different castes. Should this age-old system be sacrificed for the freedom you speak of?"

Mohan replied, "It is true that the ancient Caste system was indeed based on sound principles. It had enabled peaceful and orderly growth of society. There was contentment as each of the Varnas or castes believed that it was their Dharma to follow the duties that tradition across generations had followed. No job was considered high or low; there was mutual respect for all. People saw life in villages as a synergy between different castes. Unfortunately, the purity of the Varna system has been corrupted due to the greed of people and the selfish interests of the priestly and rich class of people. The influence of western education has been, in some respects, a bad influence; we have become more greedy and intolerant. May I ask you father, isn't it true that not all in the village have had equal opportunities; how many of the lower caste children have gone to school?"

"True," replied the father, "There was no school in the village until recently when the government gave grants for opening of schools. Even so, our school is not really well equipped. We don't get good teachers. Trained teachers are not easy to find. The lower castes could not afford then, and even now cannot afford to send their children to schools outside the village. Importantly, attitudes of the lower castes have not changed. They still do not adequately value education for their children. Not every ill can or should be attributed to the upper castes."

"What work has the *Panchayat* done to improve the village school?" asked Mohan.

"Nothing substantial; they should be doing more."

"What about gender inequality and the abuse of women that we increasingly see? How can we condone the destruction of fetuses because it is that of a female child? Has this not led to so much gender disproportion in the population. In our own state of Haryana, young men do not find girls of marriageable age. Is it any wonder then that some of them resort to rapes and abuse of women?"

"It is a vicious circle. Attitudes have not changed; attitudes can change with the spread of education among the parents of children. It is still considered unnecessary that girls should also be educated. Girls start their family lives with a serious handicap."

"I see widespread discontent among the lower castes; their demands for increased reservations in jobs, seats in schools and colleges, and so on are symptoms of discontentment. Atrocities perpetrated in the name of caste are still rampant in many parts of the country. All this has led to disharmony in society further diluting the caste system."

The father did not reply.

Mohan said, "The *Panchayat* has forgotten that dissent is a legitimate form of expression; instead it has not only denied it, but stifled it. If we do not do the right thing for people now, we might face a violent reaction from the deprived."

"Son," said the mother, "Your words appeal to me; I don't want to come in the way of your future and your happiness. From the little we have seen of Pamela, I see she is a cultured, gentle person. She is also highly educated, like you. Irrespective of what might happen to us, I don't want to deny you your happiness. I can see that both of you are committed to each other."

"I agree with your mother," said Mohan's father. "Let me speak to the people in the *Panchayat*. Your mother and I would like your marriage to be held in the village."

"Father, I would like to come with you to the *Panchayat* meeting," said Mohan.

The meeting at Mohan's place was a satisfying one for all concerned. There was hope for the future of Mohan and Pamela.

The *Panchayat* was called specifically to discuss Mohan's proposed marriage. Some members reminded the meeting of the many times in the past when similar proposals had been disallowed, and of the punishment meted out to the erring young men and women who secretly did what was prohibited. The arguments that Mohan and his father put out were summarily disregarded; reason had no place in the discussion; only the dead past mattered, tempered with vindictiveness. It was decided that Mohan would be banished from the village if he disobeyed the rules. Before the meeting closed, Mohan spoke, "I am sorry that the *Panchayat* thinks that rules are more important than natural justice; that punishments should be meted out without regard to the nature of the alleged wrong; institutions are more important than welfare; freedom of choice for individuals in personal matters which do not affect others in the society is considered wrong. History has shown that people in society will tolerate injustice for some time; time will come when the forces of reason will overpower your limited thinking. The *Panchayat* will not allow me to marry a woman of my choice and has threatened to expel me from the village. I had made a promise to myself that I would build a hospital in the village and serve my people here. I am sad that this will now not be possible. I have given a detailed plan for a hospital. I hope the Sarpanch will take the plans forward. I shall not come to my village, I repeat—my village—which is as dear to me as to any of you. I and my future wife had dreams of being here and running the hospital, but the *Panchayat* will not allow this. By expelling me, the village would have lost two good doctors from your midst because you do not want to change."

Mohan returned to Delhi heavy of heart; he told Pamela of the meeting. Mohan's disappointment was as much for the intransigence of the *Panchayat* as for his inability to fulfill his dream of a hospital in the village. The disappointment was soon forgotten when they both immersed themselves in their work. Mohan's parents shifted from the village to Delhi, to live with Mohan and Pamela. A month later, Mohan and Pamela were married in Delhi at a simple function.

🍂　🍂　🍂

Mohan had performed several surgeries on children; none of these was thought of as extraordinary, until one day he got a call late at night that there was an emergency. The Minister's 10-day old granddaughter had collapsed. Mohan rushed to the hospital; his stethoscope heard the distinct murmur of a hole in the child's heart; she needed immediate surgery. The child was too young to bear the trauma of a defective heart. Mohan's intervention that night saved the child. This brought Mohan to the attention of the Minister. When the Minister visited the hospital next day to meet the doctor who performed the surgery, he found a young man in his late 30s and beside him a young lady, a foreigner. The Minister's visit brought in its wake obsequious media cameras and reporters hungry for news. The event received mention on TV channels; a reporter interviewed Mohan and wrote an extensive column for a regional language newspaper, and a highly pixilated picture of the doctor appeared alongside the article.

One day, a stranger walked into the hospital and asked for Mohan. "I don't think you remember me, Sir," he said. Mohan shook his head.

"I am Srikant; you and I were classmates in a nursery school before you went away; we were 5 years old at that time. I saw the newspaper report about how the timely surgery that saved the life of the Minister's grandchild. But for that report, I would not have known that you were in India."

Mohan smiled and said he was sorry that he did not recall the stranger.

The stranger said, "It does not matter. I came here to tell you that I heard from my father a few weeks ago about the *Panchayat* meeting. I was angry that the foolish elders have lost a good human being in you. When the newspaper article appeared, I made enquiries and connected with you."

Mohan asked, "Are you still connected with the village?"

"Yes, I am a small farmer. Thanks to my education—I have a Diploma in Agriculture—I have made some improvements in my farming methods and I advise the other farmers on these matters."

"I am so glad that to see you and hear of your ability to help. Tell me what I can do for you?" asked Mohan.

The stranger continued, "Many of us in the village are fed up of the politics in the village. I have talked to a number of the daily wage earners and other small farmers. These constitute the majority of the village. Our pre-occupation with earning our daily bread, and the fact that many depend solely on the rich for employment has blinded us. Our tolerance to autocratic ways has reached its limits. I am sorry to say that your father is as guilty as the rest. Tolerating injustice when you have a voice is as good as perpetrating it. The Sarpanch, who was like one of us until the other day, is now behaving like the rich and powerful. His corrupt ways have become obvious in the way he flaunts his ill-gotten wealth from the hospital project. We had only heard of such corruption in the outside world; now we see it on our doorstep. We will raise our voice, but we want a good leader."

Mohan saw the drift in the stranger's words. He said, "I am a doctor. I have no experience as a leader in such matters."

"On the other hand," said the stranger, "You are the right person. You are highly educated, you come from the rich with compassion for the less privileged; you have the welfare of the village in your mind; your dream of a hospital in the village will be possible only if you join the forces of good. This is your chance. We will be with you."

"The village has expelled me," said Mohan.

"I know," said the stranger, "You have nothing to fear. You will be well protected. Just commit yourself to a worthy cause; we will overthrow the *Panchayat* and change the rules. Your work will show who the true citizen of the village is. The forces of good will prevail only if good people join together. Please understand that the politics of the evil can only be defeated by the politics of the good."

A hole that was closed in one heart had opened the mind of Mohan. He saw new directions to his life; this was his opportunity to make a difference. He had to burn his boats as a doctor at least for some time, and take on the role of a leader, without forgetting that the ultimate objective was to change the mind sets of people in his village to a more humane one. He looked afresh at the fruition of his dream of a hospital in the village to serve surrounding ones as well.

His new calling had just begun.

The Wronged One

Suresh and Sudhir were fresher classmates in the Rajampur College of Engineering (RCE). Both boys were good looking and tall; Suresh, the tougher of the two, had a complexion which was like coffee with too much milk in it. Sudhir had more coffee in his looks. They were born within a few months of each other. Both came from middle class families of Rajampur, brought up in similar value systems. The parents had spared no efforts to bring up these boys so that they could become responsible adults. They were inseparable playmates in childhood; both went to the same school and now the bond, away from home, would no doubt become stronger in RCE.

Rajampur, once the capital of the erstwhile royal house, was known for its liberal culture and its commitment to the establishment of educational institutions. The University of Rajampur, founded more than a century ago, was highly respected, and RCE was considered one of the prestigious Colleges of Engineering, with a tradition of excellence built by pioneer teachers over many years. Its high standards were preserved in the face of IITs that came up in the country. It was co-educational and compulsorily residential for all students.

For young men and women who had come from small towns and single gender schools, such as Suresh and Sudhir, the experience of studying in a co-educational institution was new. Among the girls, some felt awkward, some felt threatened and so moved about in motley groups, and some of the more adventurous were keen to show themselves off. For young men, in the majority, the experience of having girls around was exciting; it was an opportunity to show off their masculinity. The competition to attract the attention of good looking young women would sometimes be a cause for unhealthy rivalry. Many students were in their final teenage years; this added to the confused minds. The management of RCE, experienced in handling such situations, had put in place checks and rules; these were established to be unobtrusive, but aberrations punished strictly. The students who joined RCE came by virtue of a tough entrance test, like that of the IITs; it was assumed that most would be studious, once the academic sessions began.

One grouping of fresher girls that emerged was a threesome: Prerana, Chitra, and Sudha. Chitra and Sudha were from southern India, Prerana from Chandigarh in the north. All of them had joined RCE by virtue of their ranks in the entrance test. Prerana apparently came from a well-to-do family, as seen in the expensive dresses she wore. Prerana had a hostel room to herself, while Sudha and Chitra shared a room. By chance, their rooms were next to each other. Sudha and Chitra were from the same region, and the affinity of a common language brought them close. In fact, that is how they opted to share a room. Like many intelligent girls of their age, they had common interests in music, movies, and food. They laughed and joked at things that the elders considered silly and childish. Prerana frequently heard giggles and laughter from the room next to hers. She decided to befriend them. She walked in one day and introduced herself. The other two girls took to Prerana instantaneously, who was tall and had a truly charming face, as well as all the tough graces associated with Punjabi girls. The three gelled easily and became the most notice worthy threesome of the College. They were a study in contrast: Prerana the tough, tall, chiseled beauty; the other two gentle, delicately made charmers.

The college as a rule held a one-week orientation programme for Freshers. The programme introduced students to the campus facilities; educational rigour at RCE; how students would be evaluated; the norms of behavior expected of students; the library-centric teaching; the opportunities for creative expression. Subject teachers spoke to student batches. Freshers were encouraged to ask questions in an interactive session. A welcome party was the finale of the Orientation. The programme succeeded in presenting the institution as a coherent whole, offering itself to the students as an opportunity for their growth. The uncertainty of a new environment for the students was considerably watered down. New associations between students developed.

The academic sessions soon began, and with it came a change of scene for students: from a relatively less challenging regimen at school to one that demanded more concentration and ability to cope with pressures of weekly, time-barred assignments and colloquia. Some students in the past could not withstand the pressure and had left their courses midway. The atmosphere became a charged one, punctuated by an occasional cinema or music performance on the campus. The library of the college became a heavily used facility; it was open for 14 hours every day.

Four months into the first semester, an incident took place that disturbed the otherwise studious environment. The threesome was returning to their hostel rooms from the library at 10:00 p.m. They were accosted by a man from out of the blue. Sudha was violently pushed; she fell down and raised an alarm. Chitra broke free and ran for help. Prerana seemed to be the target of the prowler. Suresh and Sudhir, who were not too far away, heard the alarm and rushed to the scene. Sudhir was felled with a violent blow on his chest. Suresh, the taller and stronger of the two and a Karate black belt, pounced on the prowler who was grappling with Prerana, who would not let the prowler get the better of her. The intervention of Suresh into the fray, added to Prerana's bold resistance, was too much for the prowler. In the meanwhile, a warden had also rushed to the scene; the prowler was overpowered and dragged into the closest hostel. It was discovered that the prowler was none other than a frustrated 2nd year student, who had got poor grades and was warned about it. He was an egoistic boor, given to having his way at all costs; he had few friends and his attendance had been erratic. He was not really interested in studies and had been warned for his misbehavior in and out of the classroom. His parents were summoned. Only his mother came. The student was suspended for a year. He was sent home with a stern warning that unless he mended his behavior in and out of the classroom, he would be debarred from the college. Prerana had suffered scratches on her face and hands and was bleeding from one of them. The two boys took her to the campus dispensary where she was treated. The girls were escorted back to their hostel.

When Prerana was questioned by the college authority as to why she was the target of the foolish student, she revealed that the student had made several advances to her during the last few months; on one occasion, she had even slapped him and warned him that if he continued to harass her, she would make a written complaint.

The news of the incident went around the campus. The Principal and hostel wardens felicitated Suresh, Sudhir, and Prerana for their bold action. The three of them now enjoyed celebrity status in the campus. As a side effect, the three girls struck a bond with the two boys; they got together frequently in the campus canteen and in laboratory assignments. Suresh, who was good at Math, was consulted in problems. Sudhir, who was a wizard in structural analysis and machine design, became the group's mentor in this subject. Chitra was good at Data Structures and Algorithms. In short, they became a fivesome group, much sought after and even envied by the other students. Surprisingly, their friendships were devoid of any emotional overtones or attachments between the boys and any of the girls. The fact that the fivesome group complemented each other with their knowledge and that it had benefitted the group was seen in the excellent performances of the five. Each of them had well-defined goals: Prerana wanted go back to Chandigarh and play an important role in her father's bicycle factory; Sudha had plans of going to the US for higher studies; Chitra had decided that she would remain in the country and take care of her aging parents. The two boys had similar dreams. All of them were quite focused on their dreams. Like many youngsters of the day, love affairs and marriage were not their priorities; the priority was doing well at studies, getting good jobs, going abroad, and having fun, by which they meant enjoyment of many kinds without any personal attachments thrown in.

The relationship of the three girls with the two boys was indeed unique. One might even say, unnatural. One would have imagined that the relationship of a young man and young woman in the prime of their youth who enjoyed each other's company, day after day, would mature into a desire for long-term attachment between any two of them, something that nature wholeheartedly sanctions. Instead, what was seen was more like filial attachment. Once, Suresh fell ill after a violent bout of vomits due to food poisoning. He had to be kept under nursing care in the five-bed clinic of the College. The concern that the three girls showed for him and the time that they spent with him pandering to his needs was nothing less than how sisters would have cared for their brother. Similarly, during brief festival vacations that the College had, Sudhir or Suresh, by turns, hosted the three girls in their homes, drawing the affection of their parents to the girls. How these relationships would change over time did not concern any of them at the moment. They believed in living in the here and now.

During the third year of their studies, a tragedy occurred that would leave an indelible mark in their lives. Sudhir and Suresh always went together for dinner to the hostel's dining room. As usual, one day, Sudhir walked to Suresh's room and knocked the door. He waited for some time and then, finding no response, pushed open the door. Suresh was lying on the floor and bleeding. Alarmed at what he saw, Sudhir first thought that Suresh was unconscious because of a wound he had sustained; Sudhir shook him, shouted his name and threw water on his face. When there was no response, he raised an alarm. The hostel warden and some other students rushed to the scene. The three girls also heard the commotion and came on the scene. The doctor was called. He arrived and pronounced Suresh dead. This was truly a tragedy because Suresh was a fine young man, popular, always smiling and willing to help. The police were called amidst the anguished cries of Sudhir and the girls. Photographs were taken; fingerprints collected; the room searched for clues; there were no signs of a break-in. The culprit had walked in and out of the room's door. The body was then shifted to the mortuary. The room was sealed, pending enquiries. Suresh's parents were informed. They arrived the next day, unbelieving and shocked. This was now a police case. The body would be handed over to the parents only after the enquiries into the incident and postmortem reports. The college received unwanted publicity in the newspapers and electronic media.

Sudhir went into shock at the sudden turn of events. He was shifted to hospital that night. His parents were called. He was not allowed to leave the city before enquiries were completed. The three girls cried their hearts out; even Prerana the tough one could not contain herself. When the parents of Chitra and Sudha came to know of the tragedy from the newspapers and TV and saw that their daughters' name was somehow linked to the tragedy, they rushed to the college; permission was sought and both the girls went home with their parents. Prerana sought permission and flew back to Chandigarh. The girls were given four weeks to recover from the event and return.

Police enquiries began the next day. The first person to be interrogated was the Warden of the hostel. He vouched for the close friendship between Suresh and Sudhir. When asked about the company that the two boys had kept, the names of the 3 girls and a few others were mentioned. The Principal and subject teachers also vouched for Sudhir. The Police had to wait for Sudhir to recover from the shock; they were told that the three girls were not available for enquiries until their return. The post-mortem report revealed that Suresh had died at about 8:00 p.m., an hour before he was discovered by Sudhir. It also showed that he had bled to death with a stab wound in his stomach. There were two clear sets of fingerprints, that of Sudhir and Suresh. Sudhir's fingerprints were found to match those found on Suresh. The stab weapon was nowhere in the room where Suresh died; Sudhir's room was searched. A blood-stained large kitchen knife, wrapped in a towel belonging to Sudhir, was found under the bathroom sink, hidden carefully away in the garbage bin. Apparently, the knife was stolen from the hostel's kitchen. This piece of evidence pointed to Sudhir as the suspect. After he was discharged from hospital and questioned, he was taken into police custody, pending a hearing by the magistrate. The news of Sudhir's arrest and the evidence found was received with mixed emotions. Those who knew Sudhir and Suresh wowed that Sudhir could never have done such an act. Some doubts were fuelled by rumors that both of them might have fallen in love with Prerana and that she had shown a preference to Suresh, which could have been the cause for jealousy leading to the crime.

When the three girls returned to RCE, they were shocked to learn of Sudhir's police custody, and the evidence that had been found. They were questioned by the police. All of them categorically vouched for the impeccable behavior of Sudhir and their confirmed belief that he could not have committed the crime. The jealousy angle was probed into as the motive for murder. The girls were not allowed to leave the city until the case was heard in the Magistrate's court.

The police submitted a report on the case with the data collected. The prosecution presented its case as one of murder. The witnesses for the prosecution were mainly the policemen who went to the scene, the postmortem report, and the doctors who did the post mortem. The witnesses on behalf of the suspect were the students, teachers, kitchen staff, and the warden of the hostel where the two boys resided. All of them vouched under oath that Sudhir was incapable of such a crime. The prosecution concluded that the crime was an inside job. Nobody, including Sudhir, could explain how the hostel's kitchen knife wrapped in his towel was found in his room. The Magistrate sentenced Sudhir to seven years in prison on the basis of circumstantial evidence.

The life of an intelligent young man had been turned upside down in the matter of a few weeks. The tragedy left an indelible mark in the minds of the three girls. They had lost two of their precious friends, in a sense their male anchors: Suresh forever; Sudhir to prison. Their studies seemed irrelevant in the face of the tragedy into which they had been unwittingly dragged. Time as the healer did its job. Other priorities would take over. Even so, the three never failed to pay visits to the parents of Suresh and Sudhir as frequently as possible.

Misfortune decided to visit Sudhir with a vengeance. His father was preparing the ground to appeal to the High Court; the strain on his already weak body took its toll. He passed away, probably to appeal to the highest court. The mother, devastated, passed away a few months later. Sudhir had received a triple blow. He now had no one to come back to after his sentence.

Sudhir in prison dreamt of his parents and their sacrifices, their love and care. He silently cried that fate had denied him the opportunity to give back his care and love to them in the evening of their lives. He often thought of his dear friend Suresh and the manner his life was snuffed out like the flame of a candle. Sudhir did not have any guilt feelings, but during nights when sleep was elusive, he imagined that Suresh visited him, he knew not from where. He imagined that both of them laughed at the silly things they did as children; he also thought of their friends, life at RCE, the attack on the girls, and their giggles. He imagined Suresh, in a serious moment, telling him that he would soon be vindicated of his crime.

Two academic years went by. Final exams were completed. All students were getting ready to leave the campus. Last minute clearances were needed. Prerana collected the books that she had borrowed from the library to be returned. Her eyes fell on a book titled 'Advanced Engineering Mathematics' by Kreyszig. "My god," she recalled, "I had asked Sudhir to borrow that title for me on the fateful day of Suresh's murder." She had asked Sudhir to come to her hostel that day to teach her something in Finite Element Theory that she could not fully understand. Sudhir had come to the girl's hostel that evening. RCE had strict rules for boys or other visitors wanting to meet girls in their hostel. They had to sign their names in a register with the time of the day when they entered the hostel, the student they wanted to meet, the time they left and the purpose. Boys were strictly prohibited entry into girl's rooms. All meetings were held in the hostel's common area. Prerana then recalled that on that day, Sudhir had come to her hostel at about 6:30 p.m. and left after a little before 9:00 p.m., the time that Sudhir and Suresh went together for dinner. She wondered if this was not clinching evidence that Sudhir could not have committed the murder. She immediately went to the library to get evidence of when, how many times and by whom, the title was borrowed. Thanks to an automated system, the library could quickly list the borrowers of the title in question and when one or more of the copies of the title were returned. The system could also retrieve the dates and times when a title was borrowed and returned. The listing confirmed her surmise; a copy of the title was indeed borrowed by Sudhir at 6:17 p.m. on that fateful day. The listing also showed that the copy was returned much after Sudhir's imprisonment.

Excited at her finding, she rushed back to the hostel to look up the Register of Visitors, and requested the Warden to pull out the register that contained details of Sudhir's visit that day. When she explained why she needed it, the Warden retrieved the register and gave it to her. She saw the entry in Sudhir's handwriting, the times of entry and departure, the purpose of his visit and her name in the register on that day. She made a photocopy of the page and showed it to the Warden. The two pieces of evidence now in her hands were enough for the case against Sudhir to be re-opened. She sought an appointment with the Director. Impressed with the two findings, he asked the Registrar to begin the process for re-opening the case. This would obviously take time, but Prerana was promised that it would be done. A day later, all students left the campus.

Only those incidents that affect us directly are remembered either fondly or in pain. Sudhir's classmates soon forgot him; at best he was a roving blip in the radars of their memories. With time, their memories, like twilight that merges into darkness, would fade into the dim corridors of their minds. All of them had to move on; that was the law of life. Sudha prepared herself to go abroad for more studies; Chitra was selected in a campus interview for employment in an IT firm. Prerana went back to Chandigarh. She secured admission for an MBA degree.

There was a nagging thought in her mind: had she seen the book by Kreyszig earlier and the entry in the Hostel's Visitor's Register, Sudhir might have been cleared of the murder charge that resulted in his incarceration. The fact that she went away to Chandigarh immediately after the tragedy had perhaps hidden these facts from her mind. "I wonder if the case has been re-opened," she thought.

Thanks to her initiative and the new data that she had collected, three months later, RCE petitioned the High Court. The case was reopened. A well-known criminal lawyer was appointed to plead against Sudhir's murder charge. The college bore all expenses. Sudhir was absolved of the crime. He was compensated financially for the wrong done to him. The college welcomed him back and allowed him to complete his education free of charge. Sudhir, scarred by the unfortunate charge of murder, his prison term and loss of his parents, was patiently counseled to look ahead and make his life an example of courage and fortitude in the face of unfortunate circumstances. The enlightened management received praise in the press for their noble gesture in rehabilitating Sudhir.

Fresh inquiries into the murder of Suresh revealed that it was the work of a contract killer, who was nabbed in another murder case. On intense questioning, he confessed that he was hired by the very same 2nd year student who, jilted by Prerana upon his advances, decided to take the extreme measure. It transpired that the student was the son of a politician, with known criminal records. It was not surprising that the son, brought up in a vicious family environment should have also imbibed the arrogance and criminal tendencies of his father. He was besotted by Prerana; his desire for her bordered on insanity. He had undeservingly entered RCE under the management quota because of the influence of his politician father. His angst against Suresh for exposing his attempt at molesting Prerana which had resulted in his suspension from the college was the reason for his urge to get Suresh murdered. As a former student of RCE, he used his ID card to enter the campus. The contract killer slipped into the campus during the night before the day of the murder. A knife exactly like the ones available in hostel kitchens was given to the killer by his employer. The knife, after its use, was slipped into Sudhir's room when he was away. These facts came to light when the contract killer was nabbed in another murder. The student accomplice was also nabbed and was sentenced for planning and abetting the murder. When it became known that the knife was not stolen from the hostel, an inventory of the hostel's kitchen revealed that all knives in the hostels stock register were intact. This and the other two pieces of evidence that Prerana had provided confirmed the correctness of the verdict to absolve Sudhir of Suresh's murder.

When Chitra and Prerana heard about Sudhir's release and re-entry to RCE, they went to see him. Old memories were revived. When they saw Sudhir's face, wasted by the years in prison, their emotions, as a pregnant silence, more poignant than tears, inevitably, silently bubbled up. Prerana, unknown to the other two, had arranged with her father that Sudhir would be employed in her father's industry after he completed his course.

There was apparently something more than compassion for Sudhir in her heart. Before parting that day, Prerana had told him, "Sudhir, never think you are alone."

Two years later, Chitra received an invitation for Prerana's wedding with Sudhir.

Marriages are made in Heaven

That marriages are made in heaven is a saying we have often heard. This presumably means that man and woman come together in matrimony because of a benevolent hidden hand. Sudhir, the younger of two brothers, had dismissed this statement as poetic nonsense, much as he did the other concept, 'Love at first sight,'. He reasoned with cold logic that if indeed marriages are made in heaven, then divorces must be made in hell because you can't have heaven without hell.

Sudhir's elder brother, Satish, six years his senior, was a fine person; intelligent, well qualified and a warm human being. He was not one of those go-getters. He allowed things to happen; he didn't think he should make them happen. The Internet and social networking sites had not made the slightest dent in his life. He did not think the company of young women of his age worth cultivating. He was, in this sense, an antithesis of a young man of the 21st century. He was born two years after his mother had suffered the trauma of a miscarriage, so she had lavished her attention to her first born child as a precious belonging and thus spoiled him. Satish depended on his mother for the simplest of decisions. This caused his father no end of despair. "You have spoiled him by overindulging him," he often chided his wife. It had no effect on the mother. She just smiled benignly and let her husband's remark bounce off her like water bounced off a duck's back. This only added to the father's despair. Over the years, he had resigned himself to the knowledge that nothing would change simply because he thought it was right.

Sudhir found this drama involving his brother and parents most amusing. He was quite different. He believed in taking his own decisions, consistent with the values that his parents had brought him up with. He chose to do the so-called new things, but with deliberate thought behind them.

Satish had resisted his mother's wish that he should get married until he was 32, but one day something changed. He told his mother that he was ready. Predictably, he then depended on his mother for the selection of his bride. The news that Satish was ready for marriage was spread among the mother's large circle of relatives and friends. Proposals from far and near, and from known and unknown families, came in as quickly as the news percolated.

The chief instrument in Sudhir's mother's social network was the old-fashioned landline telephone. She did not believe in cell phones. Ever since Satish's decision to tie the knot, the telephone was constantly in use. Her calls to and from relatives and friends, or relatives, relatives kept the phone abuzz. Gossip about a family that had sent a proposal was the topic, or a call from one or other of the lady's whose daughter or niece or granddaughter was the proposed made the air waves. The unique ability to remember small details of what was exchanged about people, their family backgrounds and antecedents, number of children, their social standing, *et al*, consigned to the mother's safe memory became the database on which decisions would be made. A potential bride's horoscope needed to be matched with Satish's and so visits to the family astrologer became necessary. Satish and his father were often the last to be consulted when all other things, according to the mother, were equal. Satish was shown photographs of short-listed potential brides. He did not have strong views and left things conveniently to his mother; after all she had always had his best interests in mind. Her husband did not have much to say except that the family and background was important. Her decision on those proposals that would be considered, and those that had to be either shelved or given lower priority became final. Polite letters to the effect that horoscopes did not match or that the age difference was too much, or too little, became the reason for not proceeding any further with some proposals.

Soon, the day of the first interview for a bride was upon the family. Satish was as nervous as a new-born chick. He fidgeted with his hair, dabbed himself with a little cologne, racked his mind if the blue shirt on a steel gray pair of trousers or a cream coloured shirt on brown trousers was better. Not able to take a decision, he ran to his mother for help. Her advice was that he should not wear a steel gray one; it was almost black, and black is an inauspicious colour for an auspicious occasion. The father, standing close by, heard the advice. He smiled to himself at the confused state of mind of his son. Within hearing distance of his wife, he said, "Don't worry son, you will be in a perpetual state of confusion after you get married." Son and father both laughed, while mother ignored them, saying nothing in response. Satish, true to his submissive nature, in spite of his predilection for steel gray—he had three pairs of trousers in that colour—went with his mother's advice.

The prospective bride's party was due at 6.00 p.m. How many of them would comprise the party was not known. The mother's guess was that there would be at least 6 people in the party. This was based on hearsay and some prior knowledge of the bride's immediate family. A light snack and a sweetmeat brought from the local vendor of sweets were ready. The living room, usually a mess with newspapers and magazines lying around on the sofas, was made to appear neat and tidy. The groom's party of four was aleady all dressed up. The mother was in a pink saree, with a perfectly matching blouse. She had spent a few minutes in prayer before the altar at home. Her face glowed in her excitement. For her, this was a new experience that had probably played onher mind for many days, ever since Satish's decision to agree to tie the knot. The father, dressed elegantly in a white dhoti and a sparkling white shirt, looked his usual cool, collected self.

The bride's party arrived sharply at 6.00 p.m. There were six people in the party: the prospective bride's parents, two young women and two other elders – presumably an uncle and aunt of the prospective bride. Sudhir immediately recognized the older of the two young women. She was Lata, who worked in the same company as him, but in a different project. He smiled at her and she smiled back. "What," he thought, "Is Lata the prospective bride? What's her big hurry?" He kept his thoughts to himself. He did not know Lata well enough, as they saw each other only at meetings.

She was a self-assured and confident young woman; she had created a niche for herself as an innovative young woman; her ideas were frequently sought. There was no doubt that she was a bright spark. Sudhir had talked to her on a few occasions, mostly on professional matters.

The event began with the initial awkwardness of people who were meeting for the first time. Eyes moved hesitantly, awkwardly from one to another across the room. It was not difficult for them to make out who the prospective groom was since Sudhir looked younger than his brother and Satish was better dressed. Satish's family, on the other hand, thought that Lata was the prospective bride; she was older, well dressed and certainly looked ready for marriage. There was no need for any formal introductions; the who's who on both sides seemed quite clear.

Sudhir's mother set the conversational ball rolling. She began with her family's credentials, Satish's qualifications and his brilliant academic career. The other side nodded their heads in appreciation, while Satish held his nerve and looked as if he deserved all the praise. The two young women looked quite animated.

The prospective bride's mother joined in and began to talk rather hesitantly. There seemed a reluctance to talk in the first place. The father, in the meanwhile, had welcomed the party in his usual effusive style. His enthusiasm did not seem to infect the guests; they seemed excessively restrained. He started his own conversational thread with the two elder men. The topic was about corruption in the country and how it had eaten into the vitals of our society—the one topic on which it is easy to talk for hours. Satish, meanwhile, sat sphinx-like, absorbing the happenings with occasional furtive glances at the two young women. Sudhir was the amused observer of the goings on, silently hoping that when his time came, he would not need to go through this painful rigmarole.

On a cue from his mother, Sudhir went into the kitchen and brought the tray of eatables. Lata rose and took the tray in her hands.

"May I do the serving?" she asked.

Sudhir looked at her and whispered: "Are you the prospective bride?"

She just smiled in reply. She went about handing the eats to people with a warm smile. This little gesture on Lata's part warmed Sudhir's mother's heart. She looked approvingly and asked Lata to sit next to her.

When people had finished the small talk over the eats, Lata turned to Sudhir'smother and spoke:

"Aunty, can I have a word alone with Sudhir, please?"

The mother, surprised that she knew Sudhir by name, said, "Sure, but I think you should be talking to Satish, my elder son. He is the one who is to be married."

"I know," replied Lata "but I want to talk to Sudhir please."

Lata spoke with so much self-assurance that Sudhir's father took the lead,

"Go ahead my child," he said, "You can talk to Satish later, if that's how you would like to do it."

Lata's parents sat with concerned looks on their faces. It was clear that something was amiss. There was a hushed silence as Lata and Sudhir walked out of the room.

"Sudhir," she said, "what I am going to tell you might come as a rude surprise. I thought it best that you should know it first, so that you can talk to your parents about what I am about to tell you." The mystery that Lata thus wove heightened Sudhir's curiosity. His looks urged Lata to continue.

"You know," she continued, "my elder sister, Chitra, could not come with us today. Just 20 minutes before we were all to come to your place, my sister got a call from the CEO of her company in the US, asking that she should stand by for a conference call with an MNC client. The company was to finalize a multimillion dollar contract, of which my sister would be the project leader. She was left with no choice. My parents were nonplussed. If we cancelled or postponed our visit to your place at the last minute, your family would have valid grounds for misunderstanding and think that the last minute conference call was just an excuse and that we were not really interested in the proposal. I took charge and insisted that the visit to your place would take place and that I would handle the situation."

Sudhir was impressed because he could see that Lata was not telling a lie. He saw that she wanted her openness to be her ally in defusing what might otherwise have caused a huge misunderstanding between the two families.

Lata continued, "I know now that coming here today was the right decision, because we now know your family better. I hope all of you too have had a chance to us know better than if we had just called you and told you that we could not come. My sister wanted me to apologize on her behalf to all of you and does indeed want to come to your place and meet your family, whenever you say. When I saw you, I heaved a big sigh of relief. I found a known face to confide the predicament we were all in. I hope you can help us."

"I will do my best," said Sudhir.

The two returned to the living room, where the others were waiting, no doubt, with bated breath to know what had transpired between Lata and Sudhir.

Sudhir smiled and spoke aloud. "Mother, Lata's family has had a minor crisis and that's why her sister Chitra, the prospective bride, could not come with the family." He then went on to relate what had happened and how Lata had insisted that they should not cancel the planned visit to avoid misunderstanding. There was a noticeable relief in the eyes of Lata's parents. Lata went up to Sudhir's mother and asked for her understanding in the matter. Lata's mother apologized and asked for forgiveness that they were not able to bring their daughter along. Lata's father addressed Sudhir's father and Satish and asked for forgiveness for not being able to bring along his daughter. The sincerity that was shown by all won the day for Lata's family.

Sudhir's father took the lead. He said, "I was afraid that something serious had happened and that your daughter had run away with someone." The laughter that followed defused the charged atmosphere. Satish joined in the laughter. It was decided that Lata's family would revisit a few days later.

"I am glad all of you came, instead of telling us on the phone of your predicament," added Sudhir's father. The meeting ended that day on a note of cordiality. Lata had saved the day for her family. She had earned the respect of Sudhir's mother and the admiration of his father for her poise and quiet confidence.

After they left, Sudhir's father said, "I am so glad that Lata's family had shown that they valued good education for girls without compromising traditional values." He went to his wife and said, "I congratulate you on giving priority to this family among so many proposals that came." She just smiled a knowing smile, as if to say, "You will never understand a woman's intuition."

As it turned out, Lata's family returned to visit after a suitable date was fixed. Satish and Chitra agreed to the marriage and a date for the event was fixed.

The visit of Lata's family and the arranged match for Satish was a cause for a charged, happy environment at Sudhir's home. Satish was teased about his secret meetings with his fiancée. His own reticent nature changed; he became more talkative. His dependence on his mother for simple decisions changed, presumably because his future wife had already assumed the role of advisor and problem-solver.

Satish and Chitra, brought up in traditional south Indian values, did not even consider going out on dates. It was more fun to meet briefly in restaurants after their work. That this was happening more and more frequently became evident as Satish returned home from office later and later every day. When he returned late, the mother looked at his glowing face and understood what was going on in his mind. She smiled to herself.

There were many goings and comings between the mothers of the two familes. They became the chief actors and decision makers in the preparations for the forthcoming wedding. The fathers on both sides became glorified chauffers. Satish and Sudhir became little more than errand boys to fetch things from jewelers, gold merchants, sari shops, gift shops and so on. Chitra was taken to sari shops with her mother to select her wedding trousseau. Satish was taken by Chitra's family, accompanied by his mother, for him to select a wedding suit. Unhesitatingly, he opted to get a steel-gray coloured suit tailored. At dinner time one day, his mother asked Satish: "Why did you select steel-gray for your suit? Don't you already have enough steel-gray trousers?"

In a rare moment of uninhibited frankness, Satish said with a sly smile and a wink, "My fiancée told me that I looked dapper in steel-gray."

"Wow," said Sudhir.

"The chick has at last decided to fly," said the father. The mother joined the hearty laughter that followed.

Sudhir, not wanting to be left out in pulling Satish's leg, said: "Now *Anna* (elder brother), you can graduate into becoming, dash, dash pecked dash."

Like in most south Indian families, pre-wedding days were more exciting than the actual wedding ceremonies.

Lata and Sudhir met more frequently at work. They exchanged notes and e-mails; had extended coffee and lunch breaks. Sudhir seemed unusually impatient for the arrival of break times.

Sudhir's neighbour in the office, a young woman, Sudha, noted how he frequently looked at his watch close to breaks, made fun of him, "Hm Sudhir, whats going on, man?" Sudhir just smiled and tried unsuccessfully to appear nonchalant.

Sudhir soon found that Lata, like a virus, had silently infected his thoughts. He replayed her face, her laughter and her words in his mind frequently each day, sometimes laughing to himself at their jokes.

"My God, what's happening to me?" one day, he asked himself. "Why am I thinking so much about her?" But the thoughts returned, more and more insistently day after day. "I have had enough of this; it's eating into my other interests, my job as well," he told himself.

He made bold one day and went to his mother. "Mother, I want to marry Lata; I am always thinking of her."

The mother laughed aloud. "You know what," she said." Ten minutes ago, Lata's mother called and proposed her as a match for you. What do you say, you rascal. I suppose you arranged all this." Sudhir protested that this was not so; his mother refused to believe him.

The marriages of the two brothers were celebrated on the same day six months later.

"Was there indeed a benevolent hidden hand in all this?" Sudhir wondered, as he held his wife in a tight embrace.

The Guest

Most of us have a love-hate relationship with our mobile phones. We love the convenience of being in touch, with a mere touch, with friends and relatives; no more need to open the mail client on the desktop, now relegated to a corner of our lives. But we do find that these gadgets are pests because we are never left alone; each notification sound demands attention; we are woken up at odd hours, including the precious afternoon siesta, and so on.

One evening, at 23:20, when sleep was about to mollify the tired body and even more tired mind, I was woken up by my phone's ringtone, a well known Bollywood tune, '*Kisi ki dard ho sake to le udhar; kisi ki vasathe ho tere dil me pyar; jeena isiska naam hai*'[79] which my mischievous grandson had slipped into my phone. Being technology challenged, I could do nothing about it. Be that as it may, I picked up the phone. The voice on the other side said:

"Beta, I am Professor Kambhoj speaking from Jaipur. I am your Mama's colleague in the university here."

The words Mama and Jaipur perked me up. I wanted to get up from the bed and mentally touch his feet. He was our venerable Mama, my mother's elder brother, a Sanskrit scholar and teacher of Vedanta and Ancient Indian History in Jaipur.

---

79   *If you can take on someone's pain; if there is love in your heart for someone; that is the meaning of life.*

The voice continued, "Your Mama gave me your number and asked me to ask you if I could stay with you for 3 days. I have been invited to lecture at your university. I have a sensitive stomach and eating in guest houses and restaurants is bad for my health. Please let me know if it is all right for me to come and enjoy your hospitality."

It would have been more appropriate, I thought, if he had said 'your wife's hospitality' because she was already stressed with the cook on leave and a guest would be the last straw. These thoughts were racing through my mind, but I had to say something on the phone. It was one of the unfortunate occasions in the life of a married man when he has to take a decision without his wife's consent, and suffer the consequences thereafter, especially when the decision should really have been hers. I couldn't wake her up at that hour.

"Sure Sir," I said, "please come and stay with us. How are you coming?"

"I am coming tomorrow afternoon by air. Just give me your address and I will get to your place." I gave him our address and went to bed, rehearsing how I would break the news to the lady of the house the next morning.

I was wary next morning. I waited for a suitable moment to break the news of the guest to come and 'enjoy her hospitality.' I found it when she was listening to Pankaj Mallick, on the kitchen radio, mooning over '*piya milana ko jana*.'[80] The wife was engrossed in the song, eyes blissfully closed. "Poor thing," I thought to myself. "I wonder if she is thinking of the 'Piya' of her youth." I tentatively poured out the news, conveying by the apologetic tone of my voice the helplessness I felt in inviting Prof. Kambhoj to be our guest. My face must have looked as if it was ready to shed tears. I was waiting for an outburst. Instead, she said "Oh, if he is Mamaji's friend, you did right by asking him to come over." My God, I thought to myself. The Bard should have said, "Unpredictability, thy name is Woman."

"Crisis over," I told myself, and went on to attack my breakfast with gusto.

When I returned from work that evening, I found our guest lounging on the sofa, with his spectacles precariously perched on the edge of his

---

80   *Oh, how longing I am to meet my lover*

nose, looking much like R K Laxman's common man but without the dirty Nehru jacket. I greeted him, touched his feet, and asked how his journey was. The wife walked in and handed over a cup of '*Adhrak chai*[81]' to him. There was a distinct zip in her manner as she handed the tea to him. I could make out that the gentleman had already carved a niche in the wife's heart. I felt jealous. The saving grace was that I too received a cup of *Adhrak chai* that evening.

"You know, Mamaji is so knowledgeable," my wife said, "He has given me so many tips about healthy food and so many recipes." I then realized that she had adopted their guest, Mamaji's friend, as another Mamaji. So far so good, I thought. I then asked Mamaji what his area of specialization was. When he said it was Ayurveda, my heart missed many beats and my head figuratively reeled many times. No wonder he has my wife's admiration, I thought. Consternation about the new recipes that may take concrete shape on our menu raced through my mind. My wife was a fiend at collecting recipes and an avid watcher of the many programs that aired on TV showing sage women about how to cook those mouth-watering dishes, none of which, fortunately or unfortunately, actually saw the light of day in our house. I was hoping that the future of my meals at home would not be filled with herbs and roots of the most exotic variety, leaving my tongue the hapless victim.

"Life is so unfair," I thought. "You do a good deed by offering hospitality in your home and you find that your wife is influenced into getting '*Ghas phus*[82]' cooked for you."

I consoled myself that I would have to put up with the new Mamaji only for two days and then he'll be gone, returning us to *status-quo-ante*, which seemed less painful than the herbs I was already eating, courtesy Mamaji's recipes, under his able supervision. I found my wife pandering to Mamaji's every wish, like she was a genie that the redoubtable Mamaji had invoked. I had never known jealously like I felt during those two days. My wife, I thought, was giving more attention to him in two days than she had given me in 25 years. I was fervently praying that this Guru of spices and

---

81 *Ginger tea*
82 *Bland, un-spicy dishes mainly with green leafy vegetables*

herbs should leave me in peace. I told myself that, when the time came, I should make sure that my driver was available to see that he was taken to the airport.

Luckily, the date for his departure did come. I wished him goodbye before leaving for work. Hypocrite that I am, I even touched his feet, more out of gratitude that he was leaving than any reverence I felt for him

I returned that evening feeling much relieved. My wife must have missed her new Mamaji. She was avidly pouring over his erudite book on Ayurveda, which he had kindly gifted her. I was disappointed though that there was no 'Adhrak chai' for me that day, but the usual Brooke Bond Red Label tea.

About 20 minutes later, my brother walked in.

"I was on my way back from the police station and thought of dropping by," he said, almost casually, as if he was returning from his morning walk.

"Why, what's happened? Did your cook run away with the maid," I asked.

"No such luck," he replied. I knew he did not like his arrogant cook, who was constantly threatening to leave and constantly pampered by the wife so he would not leave. He tolerated this cook because between his wife's cooking and the cook's arrogance, the latter seemed better, as he once confided in me. In a fit of remorse, he had also added:

"You know the wife, poor thing, has forgotten the culinary art, not having practiced it for years." All these things were told to me in confidence, of course. My brother and I had the same genes; irreverence was our creed.

I tried again to pick up the lost thread. "Why did you go to the police station?" I asked.

"Well, I didn't go," he said, "I was summoned."

This was more serious than I thought.

"Well, you remember our Jaipur Mamaji?" he asked.

"Of course," I replied.

"He called me this afternoon and told me that his friend, Prof. Kambhoj's wife had called him to express her anxiety about her husband's whereabouts since he left Jaipur to deliver lectures here."

I opened my mouth to say something, but before I could do so, my brother continued.

"Mamaji apparently had told the Professor's wife that he had asked Prof. Kambhoj to stay at my place. It seems the wife called our house a few times and asked for her husband. Each time, she was told that no one by that name had made his presence at our home. The Professor's wife then became worried and lodged a police complaint. The Jaipur police called our police station here. I had to go the police station to confirm that Prof. Kambhoj never came to our place. The police now have a case of a Missing Person on their hand."

I laughed loudly and said, "My God, what a comedy of errors. Why, he came and he has left."

"What are you talking about?" my brother asked.

"Mamaji gave Prof. Kambhoj your name and my phone number. He then gave the wife your phone number. Oh, these scholars," I said rather cryptically. My brother looked at me, nonplussed, as if I had lost my bearings. I then told him the story of our guest's visit.

"Let's go back to the police station first," I said, "and then we will call Mamaji and tell him the full story," I said.

My wife, who never missed the opportunity to have the last word, especially if it concerned the behaviour of my family, said, "I knew that there was something seriously wrong with your family. It must be in the weird genes that all of you inherited."

"Will the real Sheela come to the witness box?"

My aunt heard the court's Crier, "Will the real Sheela come to the witness box?" There was no response. The Crier repeated himself, this time more loudly than before. My aunt's maid, alarmed, woke up my aunt. "What happened," she said, "Why did you shout?" My aunt opened her eyes for a few seconds and, in a stupor, went back to her afternoon's siesta.

My aunt and her husband lived in a large house in Bangalore. The two of them and a housemaid and companion for my aunt made up the household. The house was built when their only son and his family lived with them. The son had just gone away, in search of greener pastures. My aunt's husband was a champion contract bridge enthusiast and the secretary of a local club. He spent the best part of the mornings and evenings at the club. The couple decided that one room would be offered at a nominal rent to a deserving single woman. That way, my aunt would have educated company when the husband was away. They hung a 'Room to let' board on their gate.

One afternoon, my aunt heard the clang of the gate. She looked out and saw a good-looking woman, dressed in a simple sari, probably in her late 30s. She went up to the gate and asked if the visitor was interested to rent the room on offer. "Yes Madam," the woman replied, "but only if the rent is not too high." My aunt, impressed with the woman's manners, asked her inside, and so began a friendship between the two.

The lady introduced herself as Sheela. She said she was a teacher in a nearby school, but lived 10 km away, commuting by two buses to and fro. Her husband had passed away two years ago, she confided, and she lived with her only daughter in a single-room tenement, given to her on compassionate grounds. Her daughter, 15, was a student in a high school close to their home. After her husband's death, Sheela had taken up a teacher's job. She was a graduate in chemistry and could find a job as a teacher quite easily. Her husband's pension and her teacher's salary were their only means of survival. Sheela seemed to be a self-assured woman, facing boldly up to life's ups and downs. My aunt concluded that the visitor was indeed a worthy and needy woman to rent the room. She offered it for Rs. 150 per month. Sheela bent down to touch the feet of my aunt with tears, and said she would consult her daughter before she accepted the kind offer.

A week passed by without any news from Sheela. My aunt, in fact, was so taken up by Sheela that she eagerly waited for her. One afternoon, Sheela showed up, looking tired. "Madam," she said, "I am sorry, I did not respond to your offer of the room till today. I was called away to Channapatna, where my elderly sister-in-law fell ill. I returned today. My daughter is not keen on shifting here because of the distance from her school. She is now in the 9th class and has to attend special classes in the evenings. She is afraid to travel alone in the evenings. I am sorry that we cannot come and live with a wonderful person like you."

My aunt was disappointed. "I can understand," she said," The safety of your daughter is important. Let's have coffee. You look tired."

My aunt's disappointment was also because she had looked forward to Sheela's company. In the brief meeting that the two had had, my aunt was impressed with Sheela's keen intelligence and her interests.

Compassion for a woman who was struggling to make both ends meet, and her concern for her teenage daughter, melted my aunt's heart. She spontaneously offered financial help to Sheela and asked her not to hesitate in seeking any help. Sheela demurred and said:

"Madam, when my husband was alive, I had no cares in my life. His passing away has indeed put us into difficulties, but I am grateful to Lord Srinivasa; I know He will never let me down. You are so kind. If I need help, I will certainly approach you. Just being with you and talking to you is so comforting."

Sheela became a regular visitor to my aunt's place. The bond between the two soon became as one between two sisters. Sheela began to address my aunt as *Akka* (elder sister). Their common interests aided their mutual attraction. They exchanged books and notes on the writings of great Kannada authors. The two went shopping, to temples, and occasionally to the movies. There was genuine affection between them, one that goes beyond friendship. They looked eagerly forward to each other's company. My aunt sensed an undercurrent of insecurity in Sheela, because she would lapse into inexplicable silences at times. The vulnerability that my aunt sensed in Sheela awakened her protective instincts, much as an elder sister would feel for her younger sibling. My aunt went out of the way to make Sheela feel loved and wanted. She showered her with small gifts from time to time and on festival days, to show how much she liked Sheela. She also introduced Sheela to her friends and relatives who lived close by. My aunt's social group welcomed the newcomer with open arms. Sheela basked in the affection she got from my aunt and others.

One day, Sheela's face was animated and excited when she arrived at my aunt's house. She said, "*Akka*, I want to show you something." She opened her shoulder bag and pulled out a jewel case, which contained a pair of exquisite bangles. My aunt took the bangles in her hand.

"Whose are these, Sheela?" she asked.

"*Akka*, I have taken up an agency with a jeweler who was my husband's class fellow. When he came to know that my husband had passed away, he offered me the possibility to earn a commission if I could take his ware to people and sell them to known persons. I thought that this would give me a chance to earn a few Rupees to meet my growing expenses. Today is my first day of this experiment."

My aunt in the meanwhile was admiring the sparkling bangles. She said, "Sheela, the bangles are beautiful. I really don't need these, but I will see if oneof my neighbours would like to buy them."

"I'll leave them with you, Akka. Please see if you can help in selling these. The pair costs Rs. 36000. Your neighbors are free to take it to any jeweler and make sure that these are made of 22 carat gold. If I sell these,

I'll get a commission. I will also try and see if I can get a reduction in its price."

My aunt, keen to help Sheela, managed to convince her neighbor, who was building up a collection of jewelry and ornaments for her daughter's wedding, planned a year away. Sheela had made her first sale. The news of the bangles bought by my aunt's neighbour spread among the close community where my aunt lived. This led to other sales. Sheela, in a year or so, made good money in the business she had taken up. She confided in my aunt that she was seriously thinking of giving up her teacher's job to work full time on the business. Word of Sheela as my aunt's friend went around. Sheela's circle of potential buyers for her goods expanded beyond my aunt's reach.

Some months later, Sheela came to my aunt looking very bright, her improved financial condition showing clearly on her face and in the saree she was wearing. My aunt, genuinely happy, spent a few joyful hours that day with Sheela.

Sheela had created much goodwill and trust with her customers. The jeweler, encouraged by the business that Sheela had generated, decided to go a step further. He told her that she could now offer to take orders for re-modeling old ornaments in new designs. Sheela was trained in assessing the quality of gold in an ornament, the extent of wastage if an old ornament was melted down, and the making charges. She was given an electronic weighing machine. These, together with a colourful catalogue of new designs, became the tools that Sheela began to use. By then, Sheela had learned the ropes of the gold ornament business. The fact that she was articulate and convincing without sounding overenthusiastic made her an excellent saleswoman.

The new tools that Sheela now carried on her visits to clients, combined with her persuasiveness, paved the way for a successful re-modeling business. Customers willingly parted with their ornaments. Sheela became so fully involved in the business that she did not have time to make social visits to my aunt, who had by then resigned herself to seeing Sheela as one of those pleasant, but alas transient, experiences that life throws at you from time to time.

A year later, a friend came hurriedly to my aunt's place. "Malathi, did you see this news item?" she asked, showing her a report of a woman who had conned many women of their gold. There was a hazy picture of the woman culprit. "Does this picture not remind you of your friend Sheela?" she asked.

My aunt saw the picture. The face looked very much like that of Sheela. My aunt could not believe that Sheela would carry out the fraud that the report spoke of. She made up her mind to visit the lock up where the lady mentioned in the report was lodged. She called up her uncle, a retired police officer, and asked him to find out the police station where the lady in the report was lodged.

The next day she visited the police lockup, hoping against hope that the culprit would not be Sheela. My aunt's face turned ashen and her eyes filled with tears when the lady in the lockup was Sheela.

"Why, Sheela, why did you have to resort to all this?" my aunt asked. Sheela looked down in shame and turned her face away. My aunt, not able to bear the agony, left wiping her tears. The inspector offered her a chair. She sat down and collected herself.

The Inspector asked, "Madam is she your sister?" "No. She was a good friend of mine. I never expected that she would cheat people." The Inspector then showed a history sheet of the culprit. Her real name was Rajamma. This was not her first conviction. She came from a broken home; her father left her when she was a teenager, soon after the mother died. She worked as a domestic servant for some time. She had passed her 9th class quite creditably, was articulate and presentable, so she managed to get odd jobs as a sales girl in shops for some time. She never stayed in one place for more than a few years at a time. My aunt saw that she was not married, so she had no daughter; she was never a teacher. The police psychologist had observed that the Sheela that my aunt knew had deep-seated and conflicting impulses and lived in many worlds of her own making. She survived by creating a web of lies about herself, but performed her roles with the consummate artistry of a veteran actor. She was many people rolled into one physical body. She needed therapy. She was sent to women's homes, but apparently never stayed long enough in any one place.

In response to the Court Crier's loud shout in her mind's ear, "Will the real Sheela come to the witness box?" My aunt wanted to shout equally loudly, "There is no real Sheela, how can she come to the witness box."

Faces, Names and Memories

Some people have a natural ability to remember the names and faces of people and to make quick connections about whose brother or sister or brother-in-law the face just seen is or was. I do not have this ability. My brain's neural network is not wired to remember names and to make connections with other names or faces. I have got into some hilarious and embarrassing situations because of this.

I was buying groceries in the local supermarket the other day when someone gently tapped my shoulder. I turned around and saw someone who I thought was my college classmate, someone I had not met or heard from for several years. The face seemed vaguely familiar from the dim past. I smiled warmly and greeted him, "How are you? It's so nice to see you after so many years." I did not address him by name because I didn't remember it. Apparently, he remembered my name; he even recalled my shortened first name.

He said, "Hey Jai, my God, it must be years." I nodded my head and mouthed one those inanities: "True, the world is a small place; meeting after 30 years or so, isn't it?"

So far, so good, I thought. I wanted the conversation to remain in the neutral zone of pleasantries. Not wanting to rake up past memories with someone I remembered so little of, I was about to tell him that I was in a hurry and that we could meet leisurely when we were both free, etc., etc. I thought that it was best to exchange telephone numbers, which I would then promptly forget. But before I could do that, he held me by the hand

and said that this chance meeting after so many years called for a minor celebration in the coffee house next door. So there I was, faced with the prospect of being closeted for a while with this classmate, whose name I did not remember, nor did I recall anything of our association. But I did not want to be rude, so I went along.

Let me go with the flow, I thought; who knows something good may come up, I argued to myself. I racked my brain in vain to recall his name and see if I could peg the face with an event worth remembering. My memory simply failed me. In such situations in the past, my mind has feverishly looked at various alternatives. I have resorted to being a passive listener while I searched my unbending memory for clues. This classmate of mine was full of himself; I did not have to make any effort or say much to him, for he jabbered along like an old chugging steam engine. For some time, he spoke of his achievements, while I listened with a forced smile on my face and an occasional "I see" interspersed at appropriate times. Having exhausted the descriptions of his own great deeds, he turned his attention to my life and its events.

A sly smile lighted up his face, "What happened to the girl that you were passionately in love with, but never managed to talk to?" he asked.

"My God," I told myself. "I am now in a deep rut." True, I was a shy young man; I did not remember any girl from college that I was in love with, but I had to go with the flow. Sure, there were many girls that I wanted to befriend, but just didn't have the gumption to do so. "Never say die," I said to myself.

"You mean, Meena, our classmate?" I asked, picking at random the name of a girl, and hoping that the name would not ring a bell in his brain.

"No man," he said, "Meena is my sister; she was never our classmate; she was 10 years junior to us."

"Don't tell me you don't remember Suchitra, that beautiful but haughty girl?"

I was looking for an escape route out of the rut that fate had gotten me into. In a brief moment of humour, I told myself, "If indeed there was a beautiful Suchitra in my life, how Vichitra[83] that my memory had

---

83   *Vichitra: Hindi or Sanskrit for Strange*

not registered even a trace of this legendary beauty that my anonymous classmate remembered so vividly. But, "keep the flow open," I told myself.

"Oh, she," I said. "Well, I grew out of the teenage crush," I said, choosing to remain in neutral territory.

That was not to be, however. He persisted. "Well, after college, I went away to Bombay for a business management degree and another of our classmates, Raghu also joined me."

"My God," I told myself. "This irrepressible man is a fiend for names."

"He told me a few years after you and I parted that you had an arranged marriage. I felt sorry for you that you had missed the bus."

He had pricked my Ego, and now I had to retort in equal measure.

I said, "On the contrary," I said, "I got married to a beautiful girl. But thanks for your sympathies. I am quite happy that that is so."

The garrulous classmate was getting to be a bore and I wanted to be rid of his company as soon as possible. So I made bold, choosing a name at random, to ask, "You are Rahul Vaidya, right?"

"My God, he said, "You have confused me for that bore, Rahul he exclaimed," as if he was a great conversationalist. "I am Sumit Pande, the guy who was always making fun of girls and teachers." That jogged my memory. I now remembered the guy. He was a last bencher, and true to his native intelligence, a big bully. I too had been at the receiving end of this bore.

Now was my chance to get my pound of flesh. I said, "I don't think you remember me at all. Let me see if you remember my name?"

He retorted in a second. "You are Jayaram Haravu, right." That indeed was right.

"My God," I said. "What a comedy of errors. I am Jaisimha Naidu. No wonder I don't remember you or the beauty, Suchitra. I must leave now. Thanks for the coffee."

ॐ ॐ ॐ

One of the most painful things that can happen to anyone is to find oneself as an invitee at an event where one doesn't know anyone and vice versa. You go along to oblige someone. This happened to me six months back.

My wife and I were visiting with my son and his family in San Diego, California. While we were there, they were invited to a function; my wife and I became add-on invitees. I had no notion of the inviting family, but like obedient parents we followed my son and his family to the function. The alternative for me—my wife was keen to go—was not to go to the function and forego lunch, because I was forewarned that no lunch would be prepared at home.

On the previous day, my venerable cousin, Raghu from Mysore—a jolly, gregarious, fun-loving man with a great sense of humour, and great company to have—telephoned me. I told him that we would be going to the function the next day and gave the name of the family that had invited us. He was happy to hear this. He knew that family well. He also told me that he was a contemporary of the father figure, patriarch of the family, a gentleman called Sitaram. I was strictly instructed by Raghu to greet Mr. Sitaram and give him an important message. Raghu reminded me that he and his daughter, Shanti had come to Mysore. In fact, Raghu and I had lunch with them in a fancy restaurant. I remembered him well. He was a long-nosed, stockily built person, mostly bald. He had a boil on his face to boot. The boil, once seen, was not easily forgotten. I told Raghu that I would convey his greetings and pass on the message to Mr. Sitaram. This I took as a sacred duty because if I did not meet Sitaram and convey Raghu's greetings, I would be pilloried for the next five years about my well-known absent-minded incompetence to do something so simple.

We reached the house where the event was held. The main function was being held in a room, 12 feet by 18 feet, with about 40 people jostling each other, while the priest was reciting mantras that no one probably understood. I couldn't enter the room, nor did I have any inclination to do so.

My mission was twofold: (1) Locate Sitaram and convey Raghu's greetings and message, and (2) Have lunch that would be served after the ceremonies were over. I used my common sense to infer that as the father figure, Mr Sitaram would be in the thick of the celebrations in the 12 x 18. I stealthily peeped into the room. He was there but I couldn't catch his eyes. I stepped back and bided my time in the area outside, which was filled mostly with aging dowagers, with sunken or swollen faces, wrinkles galore.

They stared at my wrinkles; I at theirs. This was a most depressing situation. All the good looking women were in the 12 x 18. I told myself that I should find entry to the room, so I could get away from the facial depressions I saw everywhere. That way, I could rest my eyes on the good lookers inside. As luck would have it, Mr Sitaram briefly stepped out of the 12 x 18. I saw him and hastened to greet him with a wave of my hand before he vanished back into the 12 x 18. He smiled, came and sat next to me.

"How are you Sir?" I asked. He looked perplexed.

"Don't you remember me? We met you and your daughter Shanti at Raghu's place last year in Mysore." The stimulus was ineffective.

"Remember we all had lunch together." This too did not apparently strike a chord in his memory. The name Shanti had triggered something quite contrary to what I had expected. He looked at me like I had lost my bearings.

"Shanti?" he said.

I persisted. "I am Raghu's cousin in Mysore," I said, hoping it would jog his memory. No such luck. I had reached a dead end.

I made bold and asked in desperation, "Are you not Sitaram?"

He said, "Yes, I am Sitaram."

I concluded that his aging brain had forgotten to retain the memory of his trip to Mysore and the costly lunch we had, which I had ruefully ended up paying for, because my cousin always forgot to bring his wallet. I gave up. Mr Sitaram too must have thought I was some weirdo chap, trying to pull a fast one. I was quite saddened that he did not remember that he had a daughter, Shanti.

Another elderly gentleman walked over to where we were sitting. He did not know me. He knew Sitaram. He asked Sitaram who I was. Sitaram made it clear with a gesture that he did not know me from Adam. The gentleman turned to me. I tried my best to connect myself with Raghu who was very well known in the community to which we both belonged. I failed miserably. This was one case where the redoubtable Raghu had failed to make an impact.

Sitaram, in the meanwhile had slipped back into the 12 x 18. I went back to looking at more wrinkles. My worry was how I would convey the rather depressing news to Raghu that in spite of my best efforts, I could only meet Sitaram but could not pass on the message of Raghu to him and that the poor man had a memory problem; he did not remember Raghu and his trip to Mysore at all.

I was ruing the fact that Mission number 1 had failed. I was eagerly waiting for lunch to be called. Some people came out of the 12 x 18: one of them was my niece, Sandhya, Raghu's daughter. She saw me and came over to where I was sitting. I then remembered that Sandhya and Sitaram's daughter Shanti were great friends, thick as thieves.

I asked Sandhya, "Where is Shanti, Sitarams daughter. Is she still busy in the function?"

"She is in New Jersey attending another family function?" said Sandhya.

I said, "Oh, but I saw Sitaram here. Has he not gone with Shanti?"

"He is very much in New Jersey with her. How could you have seen Sitaram here?' she quizzed me.

Embarrassed, I pretended I had not heard her. Lunch was called. Now I had a good excuse that I could not meet Sitaram to give him Raghu's greetings and message. I then remembered the Sitaram who came to Mysore had a boil on the left side of his face, the one I mistook for the Mysore Sitaram in the function had a boil on the right side of his face. Was I the only one to come a cropper, I thought, but no. Raghu had come a cropper as well. The Sitaram who came to Mysore was not the Sitaram, the patriarch of the family that had invited us. I had buttonholed the wrong Sitaram. The position of the boil on the faces of the two Sitaram's, long noses and similarity of builds had led me to the merry go round of faces and names.

I consoled myself with the thought, "even the redoubtable Raghu, who is a walking encyclopedia of names and faces and relationships, can make a *faux pas*."

Poking Fun stories of a husband-wife pair

No Reference, No Context

"My wife has this odd—shall I say quaint—habit of speaking to me in half sentences, sentences with no subject or object, no reference to past, present or people and often no context on which to peg its meaning. I get into trouble because of this." This was my elder sister's husband telling me about his wife.

I loved this couple. My sister, 10 years my senior to me, had practically brought me up. My mother had given up on me because I was too unruly to handle. My sister took me on and moulded me with her unique mixture of love and discipline. She seemed to have an intuitive sense of when and how to stop me in the tracks in my wayward ways as a child. I hated her, but still went back to cry on her loving shoulders. Then she spoiled me, kissed me, and we became best of friends again. I was the one who cried when she got married and went away. But, soon, I became a great admirer of my brother-in-law. The man was a bundle of fun; he looked at all things and happenings as something to be cherished and enjoyed. He had the unique ability to laugh at himself.

Not yet experienced in the institution called 'Marriage,' I absorbed all the wisdom that others like my brother-in-law had to offer. I asked him to tell me more about my sister's odd or quaint trait.

"Take today for instance," he said. "She told me that she had switched on the hot water geyser because she had to have an oil bath, and that I should switch it off after 20 minutes. I nodded my head and went back to answering my mails. After 45 minutes, she returned from the morning's temple pilgrimage."

"Did you switch it off," she asked.

"I woke up from my work and rushed to the bathroom where she has her bath. I found that that the geyser switch was not on."

"Perplexed, I said to your sister triumphantly, you did not switch it on. How am I supposed to switch it off?"

"I thought I had scored some brownie points in the battle of the spouses when she was silent for a moment. But she looked at me and released one of her patent missiles:"

"You are hopeless. You never listen to what I say. Did I say that I had switched on the geyser in my bathroom?"

"I must have looked sheepish because what she said was true: I hear her but often don't listen to her, so I told her, I presumed that you wanted to have an oil bath in your bathroom, so that geyser would have been on. Not at all impressed, she sneered at me and left me to my confused state and switched off the geyser in my bathroom."

"Now go and finish your bath before the water gets cold."

"On another occasion, I saw her holding what was obviously one of those garish invitation cards."

"She exclaimed, Wonderful. At last she is getting married."

"Who is getting married?" I asked.

"Vidya, Who else?" She said.

"My brain's neural network is not wired for remembering names and faces. Who is Vidya? I asked. This put her in an adversarial mood."

"How many Vidyas do you know? Will I be talking about all and sundry Vidyas? I am talking about my younger sister's daughter, Vidya."

"The light of knowledge dawned on me. My wife had often talked of how her sister was concerned that her 32-year old daughter was still a spinster and not willing to tie the knot with 'any and everyone,' as she put it."

"So, she has found her prince charming, I suppose," I said.

"No," she said, "it's my brother-in-law Seshu's wife, Padma's cousin, Ramu's uncle, Vasu's sister's son."

"Apparently, my wife did not think of the boy in question as 'prince charming' suitable for her niece. This tangle of relationships reeled out to me with such rapidity left me reeling. I wanted to escape into the blissful air of ignorance. Wow, I said, and made a move to retreat to my castle."

"Where are you going? Pick up the phone and congratulate them," she said. Again I fell for the context-less bait."

"Well, whom shall I congratulate?" I asked. "You can now reconstruct for yourself, what followed in the wake of these interactions," said my brother-in-law with a knowing smile on his face.

Both of us laughed heartily. My brother-in-law was obviously enjoying himself in talking about his wife. I knew he loved her well in spite of her oddities. He needed no encouragement to continue.

"More recently, one morning, even before the morning's coffee had had its salient effects, she asked me, Did you call?"

"As usual, there was no mention of whom I was supposed to call. I scratched my head. While the scratching may have hastened the balding of my head, it did little good to my memory. Sheepishly, I asked, Who am I supposed to call? She laughed derisively."

"I don't know what's happened to you? You forget the simplest things. Remember, we had a discussion about plugging the leak in the bathroom last night. You were supposed to call our plumber."

"My face must have brightened. Oh, that, I said. In fact, I called last night and he said he would come this morning. I smiled benignly, as if to tell your sister that my dementia was some years away."

"I thought the crisis was resolved to her satisfaction. I repeat her satisfaction; my satisfaction is a thing of the past. I have long detached myself from such mundane expectations."

My brother-in-law's face brightened mischievously, at his smart remark about his expectations.

He continued, "My relief was short lived. At 11:00, our electrician announced his arrival. My wife welcomed him cordially and asked if he and his family were fine. He smiled and said they were fine and proceeded to ask why he was asked to make his presence felt that morning as requested by the Sir? My wife laughed loudly, waking me up from my morning chores. Her quick intelligence registered the fact that the electrician and plumber both have the same first name, 'Ravi,' and that, in my characteristic carelessness, I had called Ravi the electrician instead of the plumber—one of the disadvantages of using contact names on the mobile phone to make calls. She gave the electrician what would have been my second cup of coffee and sent him away, while I waited with calm resolve to see what fate had in store for me that morning. The rest I leave to your imagination."

$$ \mathcal{B} \quad \mathcal{B} \quad \mathcal{B} $$

I laughed again at the hapless man's absent-mindedness and my sister's freewheeling manner of speaking, often without reference or context, which had so often got him into trouble. I wondered if this manner of speaking was exclusive to her husband or if was it an inalienable part of her odd or quaint nature. Before I could ask him, he continued.

"Well," he said, "Three weeks ago, your sister told me that her brother and sister-in-law, settled in the USA, had planned to visit us; she also told me that they had not given a firm time or date when their visit would take place. They had not visited us for over 15 years, so my wife was quite thrilled. This news registered in my brain and vanished from it for good reasons. I was not a great fan of her brother. I remembered him as a bore; his conversations were only about the great country of USA, his business interests and the wealth he had amassed. I had wider interests, so I had switched off during his earlier visit, when he had chugged along like an old steam engine about his adopted country of golden opportunities, ad nauseam. But, my wife's sister-in-law was a fine lady. She was not only a fashion-model, slim and good looking, but also had a great sense of humour. So, when I heard that she was coming, happy memories came to me, since we had got along so well with each other."

"Three days ago, after one of her long conversations on the phone, your sister told me, I just heard: they are coming the Wednesday or Thursday next. There was no mention of who the 'they' were."

"Oh," I said.

"I did not want to fall into another context-less trap that usually resulted in my being called a moron. I pretended that I knew who was coming. I also hoped that the wife would give me a clue that I could connect to the mystery of the visitor to come."

I told myself, "Well if it's somebody I know, I would make out, so there is no need to fall for another of the wife's context-less baits and its aftermath."

"A few days later, the door bell rang. I thought it was the wife after her visit to a sick friend in the neighbourhood. I opened the door. Instead, I saw a fat lady with bulging cheeks, arms and belly. Had she worn a sari, her obesity would have been hidden, at least partly, but she was wearing a *salwar kameez*, cut perfectly for her size. I just couldn't place her. She hailed me heartily. Apparently, she knew me quite well; I did not know her from Adam or Eve as the case may be. She made a move to embrace me in her substantial warmth. Not wanting to be crushed, I deftly avoided it. Instead I reciprocated her warmth with a warm smile; I held her by the arm and seated her with a flourish that would have put to shame any Shakespearean actor ushering in the queen of England. I told her that the wife was away and would return soon. She looked at me curiously; I made small conversations in neutral territory, but the curious look persisted. I was getting more and more embarrassed whenever she looked at me."

"Your sister returned. When she saw the fat lady, she rushed to hug her."

"Samatha," she cried. "How wonderful to see you, but where is Ramu, why hasn't he come?"

"It was then that I realized that the visitor was none other than the wife's sister-in-law. I couldn't believe that time had metamorphosed the pretty lady that I had so admired so recently in my memory, into this giant of a roly-poly human soft toy. Now I understood why she had looked at me curiously."

"After the small talk between my wife and Samatha, she looked at me and said, "What's the matter with you Jai? You didn't recognize me at all; in fact, you acted as if you had never seen me before. You even refused to embrace me; you and I were such good friends."

"My wife glared at me. Her look was more potent than the words she intended, conveying to me the usual sense: 'what a moron you are'. I knew more was coming, but before damage could be done, I apologized to Samatha. But I made the cardinal mistake of telling her that she had changed so much that I couldn't place her after the many years since our last meeting. I had embarrassed her, by indirectly referring to her obesity. I also added that I would have recognized her easily if her husband had also come. My wife was obviously more embarrassed than her sister-in-law. She glared at me to tell me that I was in for another of her tirades."

"It transpired that her brother was delayed for a few days because of his business interests, but Samatha came in advance."

"I then decided that falling for reference-less and context-less baits was a safer alternative with my wife than trying to work around it," concluded my brother-in-law.

I laughed out so loud that peace was disturbed in the household. My brother-in-law and I were now at the receiving end of a scolding from my sister.

She turned to her husband, "You are spoiling my brother", she said, "and you," pointing to me: "beware of all the lies he utters."

The Wife and the Word 'Sorry'

"Have you ever heard your wife say sorry to you?" asked my irrepressible brother-in-law. He quickly corrected himself. "How would you know? You have not yet entered the blessed institution called Marriage."

"Thank god," I said and laughed. "But do I see frustration in your otherwise merry self?" I asked.

"On the contrary," he said, "I see humour."

I knew that his fertile brain would come up with some gems from his experience.

"I am convinced," he said, "that one of the unwritten or unspoken marriage wows exclusively for women in all religions is, I shall never say 'Sorry' to my spouse."

I waited for him to explain.

"I must have said sorry a million times to my wife in the 30 years of our marriage, but I cannot remember one instance of her saying sorry to me. Mind you, I am not complaining; I am just stating a matter of fact. I have made discreet inquiries in this matter with my friends, and I believe I have evidence that this is a fairly universal experience. Why this is so can be a path-breaking area of research for social psychologists. In fact, I mentioned this to a professor in our university, and you know what he said?"

The brother-in-law's question was rhetorical; he didn't expect an answer. Instead, I met his eyes with renewed interest, so he would go on with his thesis.

"You are a genius, the professor told him, he said. "I wonder why I hadn't thought of this when my own experience tallies with your insightful finding."

This must have been a blatant fib, but I allowed the brother-in-law some leeway as he spun his tales.

"I was, of course, thrilled to hear that," continued the brother-in-law. "A few seconds later, the professor added, I must be careful though; I should never suggest this as a topic to a lady researcher because it would not meet the objectivity required of quality research."

I was getting a little tired of this theoretical exposition of the so-called trait of wives that he was harping on. I was more interested in the practical evidence; that would be the fun part.

I asked him, "All that is fine, but I am looking for experience that validates your hypothesis."

"I am coming to that," he said. "If someone devises a popularity scale of 1 to 10; one being totally unpopular, or better still an absent minded creation of god, and 10 being the very acme of popularity, I will fall at 1, the nadir of popularity; my wife close to 9. Her friends and relatives congregate at our home at all hours of the day and she entertains them like she is royalty, on a huge dole by the Govt. I have never objected to her hospitality and the holes it has made in my pocket."

"A few days ago, I told my wife that I was going out to meet a long lost, dear classmate of mine, and I would bring him home for lunch. She nodded her head; her penchant for entertaining guests was my insurance that my friend would be well fed."

The brother-in-law fell silent for a few seconds and his face looked clouded. I guessed that the experience was not a pleasant one.

"Well, after a few drinks at the club, and exchange of memories of the college days, the families that we had acquired along our life's journeys, and career, etc., etc., I brought him home to find my front door locked. I checked with the neighbour lady; she did not know the whereabouts of my wife. I called my wife's cell phone: four times with intervals of 3 to 5 minutes. Each time I was told that the number is busy, and that I should hold or call back after some time. I guessed that she was on one of her interminable conversations with one or other of her many cousins, friends, aunts, nieces, cronies *et al.* I knew that when such conversations take place, time just stops; they could go on and on, and even branch into multifarious sub-topics. I felt frustrated. I left an SMS hoping she would see it. We went back to the club for more drinks and a bite. I apologized profusely to the classmate who was the only soul to sympathize with me in college; the other classmates knew me as a shy young man, afraid even to look at girls, much less talk to them or befriend them. I was quite good looking and some of the girls, I believe, were keen to befriend me, but my shyness prevented any such thing. In fact, the time came when girls giggled as I passed them, with my head hung on my shoulders. They had probably not seen a bigger nincompoop."

"I was born to a family of gentle folk; I was not taught to be assertive in the face of incorrect behaviour, so I was the butt of fun and ridicule of my class fellows. The classmate whom I had invited for lunch always took my side and shielded me from the boors in the class. Later in life, I did acquire the skill to be assertive when needed. I could be firm and yet polite."

"I was very unhappy because my classmate was denied my wife's cooking, which has always been of a high quality. I winced that I had even proudly praised my wife's culinary skills. My unhappiness—nay fear—was also because the impression my friend would have carried that I continued to be a spineless character even after so many years—someone whose wife just vanished after agreeing to feed her husband's friend. I was in no position to influence the outcome of what had happened, so I mooned over it in the club with a few more shots of good whisky after my friend left me. Sometime later, my cell phone rang; my wife was on the line."

"What is the matter with you?" She said, "You told me that you are bringing your friend home for lunch. I have been waiting since an hour. Disgusting. Why didn't you call me and tell me if you were not coming to lunch?"

"That she was angry would be an understatement. I should have been the one to get angry. I did not want her to get the upper hand, so I said, you don't know the whole story, so don't shout at me; you should be the one to say 'sorry' to me. When you calm down, I'll tell you what happened and explain everything after I return home. She called off the conversation in a huff."

"She was obviously not satisfied with my response. I knew her well enough. Her anger is like a vessel of boiling water that had just been taken off the stove. It would simmer for some time before one could touch it. A phone call from one of her mates has often been the best way to cool her anger. I knew that sooner or later such a call would come through, which would take forever to finish. So I thought, Let her cool down, then I'll go home. I indulged myself with one more leisurely shot of good whisky."

He smiled as he said that. It was then that I reflected that, true to his character, he never allowed difficult situations to get the better of him. This was one facet of his character that had often caused my sister frustration. She felt that on certain occasions, more manly assertion from him was called for.

I couldn't help laughing at the predicament he had fallen into and the simple causes that had often triggered small problems in their married life. Perhaps, these are the spice of married life, I wondered.

The brother-in-law went on, "Well, I returned home, hoping that her anger would have cooled and that I would explain everything to her satisfaction. She opened the door for me and looked at me for an angry second. Apparently, there was more whisky in my breath than carbon-dioxide. That was it. She slammed the front door. Fortunately, I was inside the house."

His face wore a look, which I thought was an amateurish effort to look pained, so I laughed. He looked angrily at me for not being sympathetic to the situation in which he had found himself. He recovered and continued,

"It was total incommunicado between us for the next two days. I knew that revisiting the events as they actually happened would be futile; it would be construed as one more of the justifications, this time drunken, according to her, of the foolish things I am capable of. As a wise man once said, 'A woman has the last word in any argument. Anything a man says after that is the beginning of a new argument.' I let things be; this too shall pass, I philosophized; the flood had to take its course and life would return to status quo ante. It did."

"Two days later, my wife and the neighbour lady met in the lift. I learned later about this. Apparently, after the usual pleasantries, the lady asked my wife— I have imagined their dialogue. I wish, though, I was around to see my wife's reaction to the piece of news she had heard; I would have given a million Rupees."

$$\mathcal{D} \quad \mathcal{D} \quad \mathcal{D}$$

Neighbour: "Where were you a few days ago at lunch time? Your husband came with another gentleman; they asked if I knew where you had gone. Your husband, poor man, and his friend waited for you and then left."

The wife: "My God, I never knew that. I thought in his characteristic carelessness, he forgot that he had invited his friend to lunch. I wonder why he didn't call me."

Neighbour: "He did call you, he said so. Your phone must have been busy."

$$\mathcal{D} \quad \mathcal{D} \quad \mathcal{D}$$

"That evening after my return from work, the wife's attitude seemed to have softened. Her face was made up. She was dressed in party-ready fashion. I surmised correctly that she was expecting a few of her regular mates. On seeing my serious face, she laughed her head off. I thought, foolishly of course, that she had gone off her rocker because I had not talked to her for 3 days."

"After the bout of laughter died," she asked, "Why didn't you tell me that your friend and you came home and waited for me the day before? Mala called me for urgent shopping help that she needed. I had stepped out for an hour. You must have come when I was out."

"She was practically accusing me of not having enough clairvoyance to know that she was out shopping. There was absolutely no remorse about what happened that day and the following two days."

"When did you give me a chance to tell you?" I asked.

"She went into another bout of laughter. After this had subsided, I ventured to ask: did you not see the SMS I sent you? She looked surprised, obviously because she had not seen it. A third bout of laughter followed. I resigned myself to the unpredictability of the wife; what makes her angry and what makes her laugh will forever remain a mystery."

"A few minutes later, she brought me a plate of freshly made, hand-crafted sweet dish beautifully presented, *Ras Malai* – my favourite sweet—with freshly brewed steaming coffee. She offered these to me with a smile to which I had long ago succumbed. I suppose that was her way of saying 'Sorry' without saying it."

Generosity to Small Faults

My sister walked in, my brother-in-law in faithful tow. I loved this couple; the man was irrepressible; he had a long streak of humour in the gold mine of his experience. My sister, of course, was the lovable but dominant, more serious character in the pair. They loved each other, probably because they had diametrically opposing qualities, like the South Pole of a magnet attracts a North Pole.

The man was a bundle of fun; he looked at all things and happenings as something to be enjoyed. He had the unique ability to laugh at himself. For a living, he worked as a senior executive in a finance company, who gave investment advice which, as he confided in me, he himself never followed. In addition, he wrote humorous Middles regularly for the newspaper, *Express Times*. My sister was the sedate one. She was singularly focused on what she wanted to do. She had her relaxation and fun moments too, when she and her husband discussed books they loved to read. They were both voracious readers, golfers, and to boot, great fans of P G Wodehouse. Both laughed together at the fun-loving, if somewhat dumb, Bertie Wooster and the idiosyncratic Lord Emsworth. In fact, in private, she often compared her husband's fun-loving character to the carefree nature of Bertie, not that she approved of the similarity, though. Attending and hosting kitty parties was another fun activity that my sister was happy with, leaving her husband alone for more serious work. My brother-in-law, on the other hand, saw his wife as the sedate and sage Jeeves, the faithful valet of Bertie, often getting into the hair of Bertie, but with noble intentions; not that he approved of the similarity. I had often thanked the Almighty, whoever HE—more probably SHE – was to have joined this pair in matrimony. They complemented each other well, even if they occasionally got into each other's nerves.

Like most middle class couples in urban India, their marriage had gone from the heady days of their youth through the steady days in the mid 40's and now in their mid 50's, to a tolerant intolerance, but never into the bitter or sour zone of relationships.

His face, usually smiling, looked cloudy that day.

I ventured to ask in Hindi for effect, "*Bhai mere, aap ka chehra kyun uthra huva hai?*" [84] Do I see the ugly storms of life threatening your sunny day?"

He turned to me and said quite emphatically, "*Nahin, Aisa kuch nahin.*"[85]

"Then why do you wear a glum face?"

"Well, I was deep in contemplation."

I smiled to myself. I knew that his contemplations could only be about the funny side of life. From past experience, I guessed it must be about his wife.

"Pray tell me more about the subject of your introspections."

"Well," he began, "It's about how women cannot be generous to small faults, particularly that of their spouses."

"Oh, oh," I said, "Do I see some marital distress that clouds your face today?"

"On the contrary, my friend, I always see the funny side of life, as I shall soon be revealing to you. I am planning to write a Middle about this."

I intervened, more to provoke him than in any serious quest for his 'profound' knowledge, "Are you speaking only about my sister, or does your thesis apply to the female gender in general vis-à-vis their spouses?"

He saw through my cunning.

"Well, I am fortunately married to only one spouse. Truthfully, I can speak only of my experience with her. However, it seems like a good idea to test my hypothesis with men in the Arab world who have more than one spouse. It might result in an Einsteinan discovery, which we might

---

84 *My brother, why is your face clouded?*
85 *No, it is nothing like that*

call the *'General Theory of Women's incapacity to forgive, with special reference to the small faults of spouses.'*

I laughed heartily, while he gloated on the idea he had hit upon of a new revolutionary theory.

"Let me give you an example," he said. "Today, after my shower, I found that I had forgotten to bring a fresh towel and underclothing. I was shivering in my pristine birthday suit, so I shouted out to my wife to bring me the needed coverings. I had to shout more than once. She had not heard my first shivered shout. The reason: she was busy with guests in the living room. The second louder shout was heard by her and the three guests. The shout probably sounded like an anguished appeal for deliverance from freezing into ice. The guests broke into hearty laughter that reverberated all over the house. My wife could have joined in their laughter, but no. She felt embarrassed. After all, mine was a small fault and could have been generously put to rest. The guests had no business to laugh, though. When they left, I got a mouthful. Instead of pitying my state of body and mind, she told me that next time such a thing happened, she would not be responsible for the consequences. That was an empty threat; I brushed it aside nonchalantly. In fact, I thought I should deliberately make the same mistake again to test my wife's seriousness."

I laughed my head off, while the brother-in-law waited patiently. My laughter obviously jogged his recent memory about the next small fault that was not forgiven.

"Last week," he said, "My wife was out of the house with a few friends. I was glued to the TV because India was playing South Africa in the second semi-final of the World T-20 championship. Dale Steyn was bowling thunderbolts; just his Steyn looks are enough to frighten lesser mortals, but not so our Kohli and Raina, who were at the crease. I was sitting on the edge of my seat. India needed 72 runs in 47 balls to win. Raina missed a delivery by a hair's breadth and Quentin de Cock, the keeper, caught the ball and appealed for a catch; high fives were making the rounds in their team. My heart was in my mouth. The umpire stood statue like. Raina was not out. Just at that moment, the calling bell rang and I got up, cursing the pestilence who came to interrupt my enjoyment of the match. I opened the door. A middle-aged lady was the visitor."

"Apparently, she knew me, but I did not know her. I smiled. She smiled and asked if the wife was home. Just then, I heard Harsha Bhogle's excited voice. My eyes went to the TV; I watched Raina's lofted shot land safely in the hands of ABD in the deep, just inside the boundary rope. India then needed 68 runs in 40 balls. I told the lady that the wife was not at home. The lady, obviously a sensitive one, apologized for interrupting our enjoyment, and told me to inform the wife that 'she' had come and she would call the next day. I nodded my head. Yuvraj had just come in. To cut a long story short Yuvi and Virat took India to the brink of victory. Virat holed out. Dhoni came in and the two secured victory with 5 balls to spare. India had reached the finals."

"It was almost 10 in the night; I lay on my bed to continue reading a novel that I had picked up from my collection. Sleep overpowered me and I was completely unaware that the wife had returned to bed. Next morning, even before the first cup of coffee had warmed my being, the previous day's visitor called the wife to tell her that she had come and left a message for her. That I had not told my wife about the visit was an unborn fault, because I did not have even half-a-chance to tell her, but she didn't think so. I got a lecture on how uncivil I was with such a venerable lady, an MP, who was leading a famous movement against child labour, etc., etc. I swallowed her lecture and gulped my coffee."

"In fact, I was about to ask her, "From when have you developed this noble interest in the welfare of children, changing from a woman who believed passionately in Kitty Parties?" but, good sense, born of years of experience prevailed and I kept quiet."

I laughed at my brother-in-law's predicament. My laughter was still making waves, when in walked my second cousin Rupesh and his wife, hand in hand. Their marriage was not quite 8 months old yet, so they could legitimately be called lovers, not man and wife. The fires of a recent relationship between man and woman were obviously still alight. I concluded this from the glow on their faces. Rupesh's wife sensed a men's party that was ongoing, so she slipped out of her husband's hand and went inside.

Rupesh asked, "What's going on that I see you people so merry."

"Before I tell you, let me ask what your experience has been vis-à-vis your small faults with your wife? Has she been generous and forgotten then easily?" He got the drift of my question.

He smiled and said, "Why would you think I am an exception? Even in the few months we've been married, I have been at the receiving end for small faults or imagined and magnified small faults."

"Shall I tell you what happened early in our marriage," he asked quite eagerly.

We were all ears.

"Well," he began. "We were on our honeymoon in Goa." He stopped for a few seconds, his face glowing. He looked at both of us. The word honeymoon, I believe, must have brought back to his mind the blissful days and nights of those unforgettable days in a man's life.

"We were staying in this fabulous sea-side resort, having a great time, thanks to my father-in-law's generosity. Both of us went for breakfast one morning. As luck, or bad luck, would have it, whom do I see at the breakfast area?" This was a rhetorical question that was best left unanswered.

He resumed where he had left off: "My recently married classmate, Radhika, and her husband. When she saw me, she jumped from her chair; I jumped out of my skin. We were a famous pair in the college. We were partners in all mixed doubles events: table tennis, badminton and tennis. We had won a few prizes too. I had not seen her since our paths had diverged after college. The sudden meeting must have caused a rush of blood to us both. There was a spontaneous embrace, followed by a few minutes of recalled memories of a shared past. Her husband came up and reminded Radhika that they had to catch a flight, so Radhika collected herself, waved to my wife; her husband gave me the thumbs up, and I went back to my wife. All this took place in about 3 minutes. I must have been still smiling from ear to ear about this chance meeting with a good friend."

"I went back to the table where my wife was seated. She looked at me but didn't say a thing. Breakfast was eaten in stony silence. One didn't need much intelligence to make out what had got my wife into a sullen mood. I opened my mouth to say something. She stopped me short. Back in the room, she pilloried me for not telling her about my former girl friends and how she felt sooooo terrible that she had to sit alone when I was talking away with Radhika and that I didn't have the courtesy to introduce my friend to her. I tried to tell her that I just did not have time for such niceties, etc., etc., but my wife would not relent. My fault was small and eminently excusable, given the suddenness of happenings, but that wasn't how my wife felt. One whole day of our honeymoon was wasted."

The brother-in-law looked at me and said, "Did I not tell you that my experience is not unique."

He turned to Rupesh and said, "You are still in the early days of married bliss, Rupesh. Let me recite an Urdu couplet of the great Mirza Ghalib for you."

Ibtedayi Ishq hai rota hai kya;
Aage Aage dekh, hota, hai kya.

Early days in your love affair;
Already distressed you are;
Wait and see what the future has in store for you.

The Seventh Sense

My brother-in-law looked at the book on lies that I was reading. "Interesting, but I have my own theory of lies," he said, with a smile that portended the flowering of his unique, even weird sense of humour. Those who know him, feel compelled to listen to him, quite sure that there would be hilarious stories, some made up, no doubt, but others drawn from his rich experiences. He needed no encouragement to expound his theory of lies.

"I am sure you have heard Benjamin Disraeli's statement on lies. He said there are three types of lies: 'Lies, Damn Lies and Statistics.' There are other theories of lies as well, but let me not digress. My theory also says that there are three kinds of lies: *white lies, true lies* and *damned lies.* Damned Lies are not interesting; we hear these lies every day. They are the grist of despots and politicians. These lies have caused no end of harm to the world. True Lies are spread by religious dogmatists and evangelists; they truly, fervently believe in the many lies they teach and spread as the truth, vouchsafed to them, they say, by a higher power. The vicious lies and hatred that they spread, especially among the young and impressionable, makes today's suicide bombers and Jehadis. Western nations are no better; there are strong evangelical trends that result in hordes of blind, unthinking men in their cities and bastions of science. Leo Tolstoy described religious institutions as 'the product of deception and lies for a good purpose' but I think the 'good purpose' is being diluted by dogma and hatred."

"White Lies are the most interesting for ordinary people like you and me," he continued with a wry smile. I knew that juicy bits would soon be forthcoming from the fertile streak of humour that was hidden in the gold mine of his experience. I perked up, and my face must have showed animated surrender to him.

"The definition of white lies is that these are diplomatic, mostly harmless lies; lies that get you out of a tight corner. That's probably how the phrase, 'diplomats mostly lie abroad' came about. White lies are also spoken by most husbands; poor fellows can't help it. Marriage rewires their brains; they are compelled to utter these white lies every now and then in the interest of their fragile domestic harmony. Mind you, I am not speaking about husbands in general, but specifically of those husbands in a good marriage, like mine for instance."

My brother-in-law suddenly made a mental U-turn.

He asked me, "Have you read Oscar Wilde?"

"Yes, but long back. Why this tangent in your narrative about white lies," I asked rather testily.

"Well, he said, Oscar Wilde made an insightful statement in his novel, 'Picture of Dorian Gray' and I quote:"

> *'One of the charms of marriage is that it makes a life of deception absolutely necessary for both parties.'*

I interrupted my brother-in-law. "I don't want to listen to your diatribe on lies. I have read about these, so please spare me this lecture."

"Alright, alright. Be patient," he said "What Oscar Wilde had said applies perfectly to me, and I am sure to many other husbands as well. He had said that wives never get confused about dates and events while husbands are just the opposite. Also wives know how to lie and get away with it."

He paused for a second. "The good chaps don't know that women in general and wives in particular have a 7th sense, a most effective marital lie detector."

I interrupted him. "You mean 6th sense."

He looked at me sternly, and said, "I said 7th and I mean 7th," chiding me for doubting his words. "Women already have a sixth sense; marriage endows them with the seventh. Let me give you an example."

"Suppose your wife cooks something for lunch. She places the dish on the dining table and waits to know how you liked it. You don't say anything; like most good husbands, you are non-committal." Then she asks, "Did you like it?"

"You taste the dish and find it awful, but you utter a white lie, 'Oh, It's good' or some such thing. The wife's 7th sense kicks in. She sees through your white lie in the subtle nuances of your voice, its intonation, the twitch of your eyes and the twirl of your lips. She knows that you are telling a white lie. Come dinner time, she piles the stuff on your plate, much to your consternation, as a reward for your lunch-time white lie, while she enjoys your discomfiture. You simply curse your luck and eat the stuff."

I laughed at his explanation.

He continued, "Suppose you tell the truth that the stuff was not good, she will catch you."

"But you said you liked this dish at the Olive Garden last month, didn't you?" she might ask.

"You don't remember what you ate yesterday; how can you remember what you ate last month?" my brother-in-law continued. "You don't even remember whether the last time you said you liked it was a white lie. As a result, your white lies, over time become a welter of contradictions. You don't remember these, but the wife has special memory cells that, like Google, catalogue and store these automatically, ever ready for recall."

My irrepressible brother-in-law was obviously enjoying himself in talking about his theory of lies. I had a hunch that he made up all the stories on the fly, but I dared not tell him so. He was not done with his thesis.

"I must tell you also that an important precursor to the white lies of husbands is their lack of attention to the words of their wives. The man hears the wife, but doesn't listen to her. The words spoken by wives seem to vanish into the thin air inside and outside the heads of their husbands. Let me give you an example. Yesterday, it was almost 10:00 in the night. I told your sister that I would step out of the house and get a prescription drug that I needed before bed from the still-open friendly neighbourhood pharmacy. She immediately asked that I should get a bottle of one of her medications, as well. She showed it to me. I nodded my head faithfully, wondering why she took the potion that looked like it came out of a witches cauldron brewed with dead lizards and rotten lime juice. Once in the pharmacy, I completely forgot the name of the blessed drug. I tried my best to remember it. I could have called the wife and asked her to tell me the name of the blessed drug again, but I would be exposing myself to the stark truth that I only heard what she told me without really paying attention. I described the bottle and the colour of the liquid as vividly as possible to the pharmacist, but to no avail. Soon I was being stared at by curious eyes, no doubt of other harried husbands in the shop. They must have thought I had left my bearings at home, so I left sheepishly. Back home, the very question I dreaded confronted me. "Did you get it?" she asked.

"I was prepared: I could tell the truth and get bitten by her anger — worse still her derision, which does hurt a good and loving husband like me, or tell a white lie and hope for the best. I chose the latter."

"I said, "They had run out of stock; they should be getting new stock tomorrow." I took care not to look directly at her, lest my white lie became transparent. For once, I thought I was safe. I decided that I would make it up to her as soon as possible the next day even without her reminding me, I told myself."

"Oh no, I need this first thing in the morning," she said, and picked up her cell phone and called the pharmacy. "Yes madam, we have it. I shall send it over immediately." "My wife glared at me. I thought of running for cover under the dragon fire I imagined was raging within her. Obviously, after a hard days toil, she did not have too much fire left in her."

"Finally," said the brother-in-law, "another characteristic of a husband's white lies is that they are like germs; they propagate rapidly in the brain until you become a nincompoop like me."

I burst out in uncontrollable laughter at his frank confession, wondering if he was telling another white lie. Just then, my sister walked in and saw me laughing, while her husband wore a patented sage look. She looked at her husband.

"What lies are you discussing?" She demanded. I was stunned. How did she know that the subject of our profound conversations was lies? I wondered. I asked her.

"Come on Akka, be fair. You were inside, how do you know what we were discussing?"

"Well," she said, "I saw the title of the book you were reading as I came in. I know my husband well enough. I knew he would be talking of lies. He is incorrigible; he just does not know how to lie, white or otherwise."

She left me, wondering if the 7th sense theory was indeed true.

Poems of the Head and Heart

Life and Living
Divinity and the Divine
Guru's Wisdom
Meditation
The Mind

Life and Living

Life's Daily Cycles

Life's daily cycles:
Mind thinks, feels, dreams.
Intellect reasons;
Heart craves.
The "I" deluded: it thinks it acts;
It endures, suffers, enjoys.

Body's cycles: waking, dreaming, sleep.
Each in cycle its own, lost in revelry.
In the dim background;
The silent ever wakeful awareness,
To cycles, unending, is witness.

Mind, heart, intellect unsated;
Dreams return, ad nauseam;
Answers not found;
To fresh cravings awakened, turns;
The "I" in endless cycle.

Witness ignored;
The cycles, relentless, churn and turn;
Until one day,
No more dreams, the reasons, the cravings;
And no more 'I';
Only the Witness remains.

Glass Bottles

Egos, like glass bottles, always on edge,
Placed on precarious ledge;
Into thousand pieces break when touched;
Pieces prick and poke the puerile mind;
Until time puts the Bottle together, it;
Goes back to the edge.

Foolish man, slave of identity: glass bottle;
Unlearning, his bottle always on edge;
Anger, self pity, suffering
In mind experienced.

The bottle like all experience, is
Product of reflected Consciousness;
Like all, but a passing mind experience;
Know this, of the bottle, the Truth;
Then bottle none can touch, none reach;
Peace, harmony reap.

The Plight of Man

Man, most difficult, being alone with himself, he finds;
The morn with it brings sounds, sights external;
Senses drawn to world phenomenal;
Deafens, deadens, Being's call.

Morning, noon, eventide, in doing, doing engaged;
Life roles and duty calls engrossed;
In all and sundry thoughts;
Mind ever occupied;
Night befalls, passions aroused;
In flesh's call, satisfactions sought.

Night's blessed sleep bringeth daily death;
Dreams create, fancy worlds surreal;
Awakened into morn, the cycle returns;
In cycle after daily cycle, Being forgotten;
Man has no time into his Being to awaken.

The Ego

Beware your Ego, formidable foe;
Insatiable demon within;
The more you feed it;
The fatter it grows.

The fatter it grows;
The more it veils,
The Real within;
Beware your Ego, formidable foe.

In your mind;
Too much of I and my;
In word and thought; me and mine
Fictions of greatness;
Actions to self, you falsely attribute?
The demon is having its sway;
Feed not the demon;
Your Ego, formidable foe.

Mind engrossed with thoughts of others?
In sadness, rage or anger;
Imagined hurts to you;
The demon is having its sway;
Feed not the demon;
Your Ego, formidable foe.

Dwell do you on imperfections of others?
Their behaviours;
Hold unto yourself, a mirror;
Before you speak ill of another;
The demon is having its sway;
Feed not the demon;
Your Ego, formidable foe.

Bloated with pride are you?
Knowledge, power; wealth or body you possess;
Delude not yourself;
You're the one possessed;
The demon is having its sway;
Feed not the demon;
Your Ego, formidable foe.

Are you like a balloon?
A small pin can prick, loud noise to make;
The demon is having its sway;
Feed not the demon;
Your Ego, formidable foe.

Make no mistake;
It's a masquerading fake;
Born of nature;
Make it not your master;
Enslave it instead;
Gently deny its sway.

Watch, listen to your mind;
As habit, day after day;
By Guru's wisdom unveiled:
Ego like all experience;
Is reflected consciousness?
Deny the Demon's domain within;
Your Ego, formidable foe.

Is it not meet that we ask?

Is it not meet that we ask?
Where's the being lost in restless doings?
Where's the substance lost in immaterial material?
Where's the garden of love lost in attachments forests?
Where's the destination lost in life's journey fruitless?
Where's the silence of soul lost in din of daily noises?
Where's the end lost in thoughts endless?
Where is fulfillment lost in binding desires?
Where is mind of man in his mindlessness?
Where is the human lost in animal acts?

Is it not meet that we ask?
Where is the Only God?
Lost in Gods of religions;
In futile debates;
Controversies;
Your God, my God?

Is it not meet that we ask?
What avail religion?
That makes Man unthinking;
Blind dogma believing;
Divinity denying;
Man enemy of fellowman;

Is it not meet that we ask?
What avail knowledge?
Man taken away from his true nature;
Slave of material immaterial;
Instrument of destruction?

Is it not meet that we ask?
Why we don't abide?
By the wisdom of the ages,
Ancient Seers and Sages.
Enough say the Sages;
Arise, awake, reclaim;
True destiny seek;
Godhead within.

Gods chosen species;
To that haven arise;
Freedom of body;
Mind, senses, intellect;
Everlasting happiness.

Subject and Object

You have a choice;
The sages say;
Live as object;
Time-space limited.

As body object,
With senses, mind, intellect;
Thoughts fleeting, transient;
Sensations, feelings, emotions,
Criss-crossing your mind,
Suffer joys and sorrows,
Pains and pangs;
Like waves that rise and fall.

As object, surrounded by other objects;
Around that abound;
Take pride in those;
Wealth you posses;
By burning desire, posses you so.

Be greedy, jealous,
Obsess, you don't possess,
What others possess.
Suffer dismay;
Worry each day,
Your objects will go away,
Lost, stolen, by decay.

As object, surrounded by people;
As objects that abound;
Foolishly think you love;
Selfishly from whom;
Your expectations; theirs;
Belied time and again;
Suffer again.

As object, you're born;
You grow;
You're sustained;
You change;
You decay;
You die one day.

Is this the life you want?
Ask the sages;
Or, can you be? they ask;
The unchanging, Blissful Subject behind;
All the objects in and out of the mind?

Happiness

Fragrance of a flower;
Beauty of a rose;
Touch of a beloved;
Melody of a song?

Why do these simple things;
Make me happy, but fleetingly so?
Why do I soon return?
To poverty of mind before?

Is there a source unknown?
That makes happiness;
Is the source so poor?
It makes, once a while;
Fleeting happiness in measures so small?

Of a sage, I ask these questions;
He says:
Fragrance wanes;
Beauty fades;
Touch pales;
Tastes change.

Anything that changes;
Unreal it is;
Cannot sustain;
To poverty of mind, you soon return.

Close your eyes;
Look within;
By practice daily;
Witness the mind.

Neither examine nor define;
Ask nor doubt;
Dissect nor analyze;
Praise nor criticize.

Empty your mind.
Immerse yourself in the ocean of your soul;
There the unchanging, inexhaustible source;
Of happiness within.

Go within, though surrounded by worlds without;
Be in touch always;
The beauty and charm;
Joy and melody;
These your path will ever cross;
You'll live in paradise.

Connection

I looked at you;
You looked at me;
No words spoken;
Smiles exchanged;
Conscious connection felt.

Connected we all are, are we not?
By a common connection;
Ageless connection;
Timeless connection;
Causeless connection;
Boundless connection;
By the Universal Consciousness,
Unbroken thread through all creation.

That connection I felt;
When I looked at you;
You looked at me;
Like in a mirror;
Where left is right;
And right is left.

Inspiration

Inspiration, like intuition;
Strange phenomenon;
Root of creativity;
Like shoot it sprouts;
From the ground;
Of fertile minds;
Sprouts when ripe;
Compelled to rise;
Magically to surprise;
The very ground;
From which it rises.

Inspirations roots sown;
In tender hearts;
Fertile minds;
In past unknown;
Imagination born;
Devotion dipped;
Reflection nourished;
Contemplation nurtured;
Arises when the divine desires.

The immortal works of;
Newton and Einstein;
Kalidasa and Shakespeare;
Tyagaraja and Mozart;
Sages of yore;
Wonders Inspiration gave rise.

The One Divine in the many;
Manifested as brilliance;
Sanctions inspiration;
Pearls of wisdom;
Gems of insight;
Jewels of the heart;
Hidden in the bosom of the Divine.

The Path

Divinity within me;
By body, mind, intellect;
Seemingly enveloped;
Ego's cravings, hopes, frustrations enslaved;
Each day, take me from You, away.

Till, I realize;
T'is Thee alone that illumine;
Body, Mind, Intellect;
T'is Thee unheard, unseen;
Subtly sanction all my actions.

To Thee these now I surrender;
At thy feet I offer.
Each moment that I think of Thee;
Not 'I', not 'Me', not 'Mine', but Thee, only Thee;
A small candle lights up to Thee, my path;
One day, brilliantly lit my path;
Surely will lead me true;
To my abode in Thee.

Lonely Travelers

Like lonely travelers;
Thirsty for water;
We seek on desert sands;
Oases of happiness;
All we find;
Mirages of capricious mind.

Each day for new oases, we seek;
Oases of fleeting kind we find;
Waters of which soon dry.

Back again, we seek;
Mirages more capricious mind to find;
Unlearning: again, again;
Until one day;
Swallowed we are by desert sands.

Awake instead, says the Sage;
Into the one true Oasis;
One beyond the mind;
Waters of which never dry.

Today's Opiates

Modern day opiates;
Soap operas;
Daily television shows;
Must have my morning dose;
As well evening dose;
I await seven o'clock show;
Eight and nine shows;
With bated breath I wait;
What's happened to the hapless hero?
Whose wife left him in the lurch?
Or one who plots?
Downfall of the spouse.

Sadists we are;
What excitement we feel;
What entertainment we think;
Other's plight to enjoy.
Are we safe within the pale;
Of ills daily shown?

These shows;
The saving grace;
Lovely faces;
Eyes on which to rest;
Painted, well endowed;
Like kings and queens dressed;
With hearts of stone;
And minds of clod.

I know this;
Because I gaze and gaze;
Hypocrite I am;
Like addicts around;
Drink daily these opiates;
Who is greater fool?
In front or behind the screen?

Indian Scam a day

Scam a day;
Electronic media well-fed each day;
More scams the merrier they say;
More ads they reap that way;
Merrily shown between scams they air;
More ads than news they air;
Inconclusive garrulous talk shows they air.

Hungry public laps up news: fresh scam each day;
Yesterdays scam lost to memory today;
CBI most active body today;
Scam after scam their grist;
Retired judges plum jobs to get;
New enquiry commissions to head each day;
Millions to commissions lost each day;
Tax payer's money lost day after day;
Fund commissions of the day;
Prices of commodities, up, up they go by the day.

Scams of rich, scams of barons;
Scams of the elected, scams of bureaucrats, scams of sportsmen;
Indefensible scams of the Defence;
Offence after offence.
Government denuded;
Hands honest bureaucrats bound;
Administration paralyzed;
Governance dead.

Parliament, legislatures;
More undisciplined each day;
Discuss scams than welfare each day;
Throw mikes at each other every day.
Reports of Commissions;
More heat than light they shed;
More futile discussions aired to feed.

None knows where lies the truth;
Between the lies;
Or between the lines?
In reports no one reads;
Finally buried one day.

Dhoni and his men merrily play on each day;
Match after match they play;
Public loves the games they play;
Better than the scam games they say;
Seems the most sensible thing;
In the world of scams we live in today.

What have you given today?

What have you given today?
My Guru, asked me;
I shook my head;
Sheepish, I must have looked.

Pity, he said, when we think of giving,
We think only of the immaterial material.
What of the oft forgotten, more enduring, life enhancing;
That daily ought to be given.

The least you can give is gratitude,
For the Life that flows in you.
To the Force that powers your being;
The ever wakeful Consciousness in all experience;
The one behind heart beats, and,
Blood that flows through veins.
And to the Fullness within.

Have you silently thought in gratitude of your parents, elders?
Your mother who demonstrated what selfless love truly is,
The father who disciplined, but taught you do what is right,
Their sacrifices paved the way for you,
Opportunities that made what you're today.

Your teachers?
Remember do you their dedication?
Often not well paid, still straining, inspiring,
Gave you foundations of your learning?

You're the product of an ageless culture,
Its deep rooted values, its teachings,
Legends and heroes that inspired you,
Moral and spiritual bases of a purposeful life,
Give back to that culture, by example, commitment,
That the best gratitude you can show.

You stand on the shoulders of the many,
You're products of the past, of many who selflessly gave,
As producer of the future, search your heart;
Ask what you can give back.

Truly said it is, no greater Joy than Giving;
Truly said it is, giver is Blessed Receiver;
His harvest, joyous heart; his bounty, peace of the infinite.
His attitude: You not I.

Like the blessed rain-bearing cloud;
Gives itself away along the life enhancing rain;
Ask, what you can give back today.

Divinity and the Divine

Divine Love

Today I felt Divine Love;
Love indescribable;
Love ineffable;
Love so encompassing;
Love so Flooding;
No seeking, nor asking;
Just flowing.

Flow so complete: no me, only You;
Only totality;
In the flow;
White light of bliss.

I am sure now;
No barriers to Divine love;
There, there;
Ask or not there;
We allow it not to flow;
Our doors we close.

Nothing the divine lacks;
Not your offerings;
Nor empty prayers.
Seeking mundane favours;
Or things, as if shopping.

Love from the heart love just offer;
That the Divine yearns;
That unconditionally give,
Divine love to eternally enjoy.

Transcendent Prankster

Transcendent Prankster;
Beyond perishable and imperishable;
Awesome game you play.

I know not if You Create,
Project or Manifest;
This tangled web called Life;
Then unconcerned thou liest;
On ocean's bed of Time;
Watching unfold the game of life;
Human dramas: Joys, sorrows;
Pain, gain, good, evil, devil;
Unrequited love;
Death after life, Life after death;
In endless cycle.

Transcendent Prankster;
Awesome game you play.
You take shape as a tiny trickster;
Sometimes, a mighty monster.

Everything You paint;
With the brush of Maya;
Our roles we act in the Drama;
That you say is our Dharma;
For all woes, You we blame;
Not knowing, we play out our Karma.

Your game the Yogi knows;
Lovingly to you he surrenders;
In meditation, song and prayer;
What choice then do You have?
But to take the him under;
Your care forever.

Here, There, Everywhere

You are here, there, everywhere;
In, out, about, up, above, below;
Like space everywhere;
Imperceptibly, all You envelope;
Yet ignorant we are.
The Life Principle;
One Unchanging substratum;
Behind all changing phenomena;
The Divinity within all creation;
That singularity beyond all duality;
One ever existing beyond time-space.

Like the One Sun illumines the world;
You illumine all mind events;
Thoughts, feelings, sensations;
Joys, hurts, bodily pains;
Anger, desires;
Yet ignorant we are.
The Life Principle;
One Unchanging substratum;
Behind all changing phenomena;
The Divinity within all creation;
That singularity beyond all duality;
One ever existing beyond time-space.

You empower my intellect;
Logic I use, abundant ignorance;
My limited knowledge material world;
Essence behind all substance;
Sentience behind insentience;
Yet ignorant we are?

The Life Principle;
One Unchanging substratum;
Behind all changing phenomena;
The Divinity within all creation;
That singularity beyond all duality;
One ever existing beyond time-space.

When I die;
My gross body, of Life Principle devoid;
Will be taken away;
Returned to its elements;
Where go my beings' subtle elements?
Thoughts, experiences, impressions;
Unfulfilled desires, dispositions;
Accumulated inclinations?

The sages who know say;
These too carried subtly away;
Like the wind carries fragrances of flowers away;
Remain unmanifested;
Until another day;
Even aeons away;
In another to Manifest;
Life Principle afresh;
Unfulfilled desires to fulfill;
Tasks to finish;
Destiny to seek;
And so on and on, the sages say.

This the theory of Karma;
Endless Cycle of birth, death, rebirth;
Until we merge with That Singularity;
Then no more the Cycle's force;
The bubble to sea returns;
Never to become bubble again.

Parcel of Love

To You, Within, Without;
From my heart;
In faith, dipped,
In gratitude enveloped,
With sincerity sealed,
Parcel of love I offer.

I know neither sacred Sastras;
Nor soulful Slokas;
Rituals, nor mantras;
Not temple prayers;
From my heart;
Parcel of love I offer.

Gold, silver, money?
What use to You?
My love you want;
From my heart;
Parcel of love I offer.

Nothing I need from You;
All is from You;
Gratitude alone I have for You;
From my heart;
A parcel of love I offer.

In toils daily;
Mind may not always pray;
In my heart, believe me;
A parcel of love, there's always one for You.

Divinity

Tell me about Divinity, my Guru I asked;
Divinity is State of Perfection, he replied;
State of Freedom, of Unconditional, Eternal Bliss;
Bliss beyond Man's limited experience;
Bliss no words can describe or minds conceive.

This Bliss is beyond;
Pale of Time, Pale of Space;
Beyond Man's ordinary consciousness, because;
Man himself, a prisoner of Time and Space.

Know that the Bliss I speak of,
Beyond Causation;
This Bliss neither Cause nor Effect;
Man conceives not such Bliss;
Product that he is of Cause and Effect.

Beyond Time, Space, Causation, This Freedom;
Neither beginning; nor end, no birth, nor death;
This the Eternal State of Perfect Equanimity;
None, no condition can shake.

Know this Divinity beyond Time, Space, Causation;
Can only be ONE, the Singular, the Infinite;
Tell me how can there be another Infinite beyond this ONE?
This the Vedantist calls Bramhan;
The Single Reality behind all Duality;
All else Unreal; all else Binding, all else Delusion; all else Illusion.

Know that the Causeless Infinite;
Pervades All, particles, the atoms, the cosmos;
I speak not of Imagination, Story or Myth, the Vedantist avers;
Be not waylaid; seek within; Know the Truth;
You are Divine; Divinity the Unlimited SELF of limited self.

You cannot attain what's not already Yours;
Struggle not; Divinity is your Birthright;
Awake, arise. Constantly to Yourself proclaim;
That You Are; You are That;
Om Tat Sat; Om Tat Sat

My Divinity?

You tell me that all creation is potentially divine;
Where is my divinity, my Guru, I asked;
Ask yourself, he said, what about you has never changed?
Body, mind, thoughts, emotions, intellect?
Are these not ever changing; ever vibrating to different tunes?
Think how often these have brought you peace.

Ask how you're aware of thoughts in your mind;
Has this awareness ever changed?
Does it with every experience change?
Reveal did it not joys, sorrows too?
Reveal did it not, your pains, sensations?
Ask who knows your dreams in sleep?
Is not this awareness a dispassionate witness?
To everything that passes your mind?

Ask, where does this awareness abide?
Is it outside of you? If not, is it not reasonable to say?
This unchanging awareness abides within you and All;
This the One Common Subject, all other Objects.

Concentrate. Put your mind on That Subject within;
Shut out thoughts all else;
Unfailingly you'll find it brings you peace;
Peace that transcends your Mind, your Intellect;
Longer your mind dwells on That your Awareness,
Longer you're connected to That Awareness,
Longer you'll remain in joy;
That Joy transcends all known changing joys, you ever had.
Know that this Awareness is your Divinity within;
The State of Perfection, of ever new Bliss, your True Nature;
The True Self of all selves.

Change and Beyond

Streams of water time immemorial,
Into rivers, oceans have flown.
Streams of water,
Out have endlessly flown,
Change happens unchangingly,
We call it yet the river, ocean same.

Violent quakes time immemorial,
Have shaken Mother Earth;
Continents have come; continents gone; Atlantis no more;
Islands many, invading waters have swallowed,
Change happens unchangingly,
We call it yet the Earth same,
Our forefathers inherited.

Billions of stars, planets emerge; millions become black holes,
The incomprehensible cosmos, they say,
Relentlessly expands, we know not where.
Change happens unchangingly,
We call yet it the Cosmos same,
Time immemorial inherited.

The breath in Man, from
Life to death, flows in and out.
Thoughts like waters of the river;
From Minds of men in and out they flow;
Moment to moment, in and out, all men change;
We call him yet the same;
We think we know.

All change within pale of changing space, changing time;
Wonder of wonders, Incomprehensible;
How little do we tarry and think,
To wonder, to pray, to dream of the Unchanging One,
Beyond the changing Minds, Rivers, Earth,
Beyond the Stars, the Planets and all;
Beyond Space and Time.

The Path

Divinity within me;
Seemingly enveloped,
By body, mind, intellect;
Ego's cravings, hopes, frustrations enslaved;
Each day, from You, take me away.

Till I realize:
T'is Thee alone illumine;
Body, Mind, Intellect;
Thee unheard, unseen;
Subtly sanction all my actions.

To Thee these now I surrender;
At thy feet I offer.
Each moment that I think of Thee;
Not 'I', not 'Me', not 'Mine', but Thee, only Thee;
A small candle lights up to Thee, my path;
One day, brilliantly lit my path;
Surely will lead me true;
To my abode with Thee.

Temple in the Heart

There's a temple in all hearts;
Where silently resides the formless Divine;
There fathomless abode of peace;
There nectar of bliss everlasting;
There ocean of love infinite;
There, Divine waits to be invoked.
With your mind open temple's doors;
With thoughts of love, light temple's lamps;
Shower the Divine with Roses of the Heart;
Petals of love let fall,
Like oil that sustains the lamps;
That's all the Divine within needs;
That alone the Divine within seeks.

Lovingly offer all acts outward;
To the Divine inward;
Think, often in gratitude;
For opportunity to pray, to act;
For the loves in your life;
The graces that graced your life.

Your roses, petals, love;
The Divine returns manifold;
Poem to the Divine, your life transformed;
Why tarry?
When Divine glory;
So simply, waits to be tapped.

Take me into that Temple

Take me, my Transcendent Lord,
Into Your Temple within,
Where desires sully not my thoughts;
Thoughts lead not to actions, tainted;
Actions tainted unleash not causes;
Causes give not rise to effects;
In endless cycle, birth and death.

Take me my Transcendent Lord,
Into Your Temple within,
Where the heart feels only love,
Love that flows unhindered,
Only to you attached;
Where Intellect un-deluded,
Firmly established;
Knows but one Truth;
There is none else but You within;
The All of All, the One of All.

Take me, my Transcendent Lord,
Into Your Temple within,
Where lamp of pure Consciousness burns bright;
Shining with eternal Light, the Light of all lights;
Beyond All darkness and Light;
Bathed in eternal peace;
Beyond time and space;
Where only love is allowed to flow.

Guru's Wisdom

Margins and the Core

My face clouded like monsoon sky;
To the compassionate Guru I went;
From him solace I sought;
Solutions to my problems.

Neither pity, nor sympathy he offered.
Problems he said:
Life mired in your margins
Body, Mind, Senses, Intellect;
Deluding ever changing, perishable nature of creation;
Ignorance of your Godhead, Your unchanging Core;

Majority men, indolent, care not to know;
They want short cuts to paradise;
Some hear this Truth but go not beyond;
Some vaguely understand but do not experience.

Bereft of knowledge, understanding, experience;
Man like rudderless boat in life's stormy seas;
Anchored to ever changing margins;
Battered by relentless waves that rise and fall.

Few who desire to know;
Beyond unverified belief they don't go;
Their faith: external anchors;
Religion, postulates, teachers;
Superstitions, rituals;
They care not to make Truth their own;
In life, living, their own.

Not knowing this or that the truth;
Though striving;
Faithless, confused;
Plunged they remain in darkness.

Very few who truly the Truth pursue;
Path to the knowledge of Core;
Possess intense desire to know;
Listen, question sages who know;
Read words of sages who lived the truth;
Devoted in chant and prayer;
Reflect daily Truth of the Core;
Contemplate on thoughts heard and read;
Long, lonely, daily, faithful, silent enquiry in the mind;
See daily the truth learned in life and living.

From known experience to Unknown Core;
From faith unverified to living faith experienced;
This the scientific Vedantic way;
Knowledge, understanding and experience to gain;
Become beacons of living truth;
They touch and thrill in the Core.

There firmly established, nourished by the Core;
Equanimity of Mind reaped;
Mind cleansed of dross; illumined in peace;
Intellect driven by wisdom to act;
Empowered, their actions unattached;
Nothing in the margins shakes their peace;
Total is their identity with their Core.

The path is long;
The path is lonely;
Your faith and you walk alone;
Along the path the Core becomes your ally;
First like a humble candle;
Then a bright lamp;
Then like the Sun;
Slowly but surely dispels darkness of ignorance;
Faith you'll know you're in Truth, the Core.

This only way, the Guru concluded;
I offer no magic, nor miracle;
Go home: practice living in your Core;
By and By your margins will trouble you no more.

Life Lesson

Give me a practical lesson for life,
My compassionate Guru, I asked;
Into my eyes, he looked and replied.

As often as you can, examine;
The state of your mind;
Is it like a placid lake?
Sometimes rippled but never ruffled?
Is it like a gurgling river?
Fed by mountainous waterfall,
Running, flowing, dried up sometimes?
flooded sometimes?
Is it like an ocean of unruly waves?
Not knowing whence it comes; where it goes;
Battered from shore to shore?

Answers to these questions,
Tell you how proceeds your journey, your life.
Joyful is it, ever anchored in peace?
Tossed is it, against imagined problems?
Sinking is it, to the depths of depression?
Life's a journey, be not concerned with destination.

The Sage

In the phenomenal world,
Like you and me he lives;
Like you and me he sees, hears, speaks;
Touches, thinks, feels.

Unlike you and me,
He acts, but in truth acts not;
By the Eternal within propelled;
His acts, spontaneous, pure;
He knows neither fruit,
Nor fruit he seeks.

His mortal life he thus lives,
A trail to the Infinite, he leaves;
For infinitessimals -- you and me.

Drop of the River

A tiny drop of river water;
Once asked the might river;
Where, oh, where do you take me Master;
The rocks hurt me so;
The burning Sun dries me so;
Sands, my journey, they slow.

Little drop, little drop,
I love thee so, but see;
Where you go?
Into the margins, away you go;
There rocks will pierce thee;
The Sun into the clouds suck thee;
There sand slows thee so;
There the grass swallows thee.

Come back, your true home: my centre;
There neither rock pierces you;
Nor sands slow you;
Nor into the clouds, by the sun away you go.

Might I ask where the destination?
Of your Centre, oh mighty river;
Asked the innocent drop;
Glad you asked, said the river.

The tiniest drop in my centre;
To its source, Eternal goes;
Of peace, love, harmony Ocean beyond
There you and all the drops;
Merge Into the infinite ALL;

The rest of my drops;
Back to nature they go;
To become river again;
Long journey to begin again.

Tiny Drops, Momentary Sparks

Sages, time immemorial ask,
Think you are mortal? Then,
Like Waves on the ocean;
On the Wave, the Bubble,
On the Bubble, a tiny drop of Cosmic Ocean;
You evaporate soon; come back as drop again.

Like one-act play on worldly stage,
Passing shows in the Cosmic Drama,
Insignificant events in Space-Time Warp of Eternity,
Like spark of fire, into fire of time, soon extinguished.

Delude not that you're the wave or drop, bubble or spark;
All is Bramhan, One Eternal Bramhan,
Bramhan thou art;
In that consciousness, play your part;
From un-manifested Bramhan, manifested, you come;
Unto Bramhan you return.

Drop of the River

A tiny drop of river water;
Once asked the might river;
Where, oh, where do you take me Master;
The rocks hurt me so;
The burning Sun dries me so;
Sands my journey they slow.

Little drop, little drop,
I love thee so, but see;
Where you go?
Into the margins, away you go;
There rocks will pierce thee;
The Sun into the clouds suck thee;
There sand slows thee so;
There the grass swallows thee.

Come back, your true home: my centre;
There neither rock pierces you;
Nor Sands slow you;
Nor into the clouds, the Sun away you go.

Might I ask where the destination?
Of your Centre, Oh mighty river;
Asked the innocent drop;
Glad you asked, said the river.

Even the tiniest drop in my centre;
To its source, Eternal goes;
Of peace, love, harmony Ocean beyond
There you and all the drops;
Merge Into the infinite ALL;

The rest of my drops;
Back to nature they go;
To become river again;
Long journey to begin again.

The Ego Cage

Like trapped bird that sees not beyond its cage,
Knows not the freedom of the skies,
Wings it flaps in vain.
Like cocooned moth;
Knows not it's a butterfly;
Among flowers, free to flit and fly.

Man entrapped in Ego cage, Alas,
To his cage he surrenders;
Deluded in search of happiness that eludes;
His mind twists and turns in vain;
In the material immaterial, he seeks joys of shadows.

In relationships, foolishly attached, unfulfilled, he wallows;
In the wine and women of transient joys time he wastes;
Answers he seeks to life's meaning outside;
The day of reckoning dawns;
By then too late;
He perishes within his cage;
Not knowing the freedom of his Soul.

Sages for time immemorial have taught;
Man, beware of pitfalls, the Unreal in life;
Freedom your birthright;
Your Ego deludes, leads you astray;
Search for the Real within; claim it within;
Before 'Tis too late.

Meditation

The Seeking

Into the space between my thoughts;
My being dissolves;
I come back to the space of thoughts;
Where was I? I ask;
Everywhere and yet nowhere, a voice answers;
Is that my Truth, I ask;
I get no answer;
Into the space between thoughts,
I return to seek again.

Surrender

In meditation;
Unto thee I surrender;
Supreme Self of all Selves.
Bless me I may see;
Only thee in me;
Me in thee;
Your peace in me;
Your love in me.

Your promise to me fulfill;
Reveal to me you will;
Eternity, infinity,
You in me, me in You.

There's work to do;
Roles to play;
Duties, miles to go;
I promise;
I'll come back always;
Ever striving, always;
Until I become one with you;
Your promises to me fulfil.
Supreme Self of all Selves;
Your promise to me fulfil.

Pure Consciousness

Abiding in me,
In meditation I seek;
I concentrate within;
Thoughts intervene;
Flow broken.

Restless mind,
Born of Nature;
To interfere is your nature,
Your handpicked maidens,
Thought and memory;
Layers of ignorance they build,
Eternal Self to hide.

I have you my mind;
I am not you the Mind;
Transcendent Self I am;
Beyond nature;
Beyond duality;
Behind fringe of mind.

I daily persevere;
Ignorance Layers to pierce;
In moments absolution;
Pristine peace;
Enough these moments enough;
Back once more, Truth to pursue;
Until I merge into that Oneness.

How can you hide?
In that singularity;
You and I become one.

Unquiet Mind

Unquiet mind;
Thought after thought;
Like wave after wave;
Lashing shores of my mind.

So what, so what?
I witnessed, I watched;
Clouds of thoughts remained;
But between clouds;
Beyond the fringe of mind;
Vastness of space;
Silence of peace;
Beyond description, bliss of joy.

Nothing more I need;
Nothing more I ask;
That the gateway to my Godhead;
Beyond description, Bliss of Joy.

Watch. Observe. Witness

Let thoughts come and go;
Let feelings rise and fall;
Let emotions emerge and wither;
Watch. Observe. Witness.

You are not the mind;
The mind is not You;
You have a mind;
The mind, you're not.

Ever wakeful consciousness you are;
That alone eternally abides;
Behind the fringe of the mind;
Beyond the mind;
Its thoughts, feelings, emotions.
The One, only One in all.

Thou art That. Thou are That.
Watch. Observe. Witness;
Thou art That. Thou art That.

My True Self

I sit daily to meditate;
I wait, lovingly await;
Those moments of peace within;
Unfailing come into the mind;
Sometimes like a gentle breeze;
Sometimes like a flood that engulfs.

Day after day, I am surprised;
Unfailing these moments come within;
Day after day as fresh flowers;
As pristine and ever new as morning's dew;
Peace, call it bliss or call it love within;
Day after day, ever new, unfailing to thrill.

Come it must from an endless source.
No beginning, no end, unborn, undying.
The state of peace, from Source within;
Lovingly to worldly calls responds.

During day's travails;
My mind I often lift within;
Recall the peace, the thrills;
My life, my thoughts, actions;
Magically empowered;
Each day I feel blessed.

Pranayama

The Prana I inhale is You;
The Prana I exhale is You;
The Prana that fills my lungs is You;
My act of inhalation is in and through You;
My act of exhalation is in and through You;
Thoughts as I breathe in and out are in and through You;
The peace I feel as I breathe in and out is You;
If Prana is You, the Act is in You, the thought is in You, the Peace is You;
Then where is the I?
There's only You, only You.

Meditation

Why should I meditate?
What for should I meditate?
My Guru I asked.

Meditation is acknowledgement:
Of the Spark of the Divine within,
Of the Sublime within,
Of the Immaculate within.

Meditation is Surrender:
Of the Outer to the Inner
Of the peaceless to the peace within
Of the Deluded to the All Knowing within.

Meditation is Gratitude:
To the Subtle One within,
The One that enlivens the Gross,
The One that empowers all actions.

Meditation is the unfolding:
Of the ordinary into the sublime
Like the morning's young bud
Unfolds into the beautiful rose

Meditation is the Expansion;
Evolution of the limited to the unlimited;
Of the infinitessimal to the Infinite.

The Bee, Rose and the Soul

Early morning's bud,
By Sun warmed;
Bees and butterflies nourished,
Bud no more;
Into blessed rose, blossoms transformed.

One-pointed Meditation on the Eternal,
By Souls' honey nourished,
Ego consciousness vanquished,
Sorrows all destroyed.

Busy Bee's soon depart;
Soon all Roses drop;
Back to nature they pass, but before;
The many in brief existence they nourished,
Live on in the other buds, bees, roses.

Nature's impeccable cycle tells us,
Beings perish and pass, eternal beauty remains eternally.
The Rose and the Bee,
God's renunciants,
Selfless, unattached,
Come to manifest the beauty of Nature.

The Sages who know tell us:
Drink deeply now of the Honey of your Soul; one day;
You too into eternity will perish and pass, but before;
Manifest within the imperishable Blissful Soul.

The Mind

The Mind

Primate mind;
Branch to branch it jumps;
In thoughts' tangled tree;
Conspires craftily;
Leads itself astray;
In wilderness of;
Forest called life.

What avail this life,
Restlessness always?
A sage, I asked

Quiet corner choose, he says;
Close your eyes;
Quieten the mind;
Thoughts witness;
Let them emerge;
Silently, dispassionately;
Don't participate;
By faithful practice daily;
As habit daily;
Moments of tranquility;
Glimpses of peace;
Longer and longer each day;
From the unreal carry you away.

This the best way;
To unshackle the mind;
From restless ways.

Easier said than done I say;
So the primate;
Goes on its wayward ways.

The Mind's colourful glasses

The mind has many beautiful looking glasses;
Pity we store them on forgotten shelves;
Pity we mostly wear Ego's dark glasses;

When you're sad;
Your sadness see with gratitude's glasses;
The wonderful Joy's you've so far enjoyed;
Hidden they are in your memories past;
Your sadness like all else too will soon pass.

When failure brings you despair;
Things not going your way;
Pull out the bright glasses of perseverance tucked away;
See new doors that show you the way;
Courage, faith, two companions lift you anon from despair;

When you're depressed;
Your depression, see through tinted glasses of rainbows in life so far;
Tucked they are in memory's recesses;
Recall the many colourful joys of the past;
Your Depression like all else too will soon pass;

When you're seething with anger about another;
Take out your soothing green glasses of tolerance;
Hidden they are in your heart;
Cool, they will, your anger to a thing of the past;
Build you'll bridges that last.

When you're hurt by another's shafts of words;
See reflection of words through inner glasses of understanding;
You'll see the other needs your balm;
He knows not what he says; burdened he is, in his own heart.